Death of the Drunkard

Anne Louise Bannon

HH

Healcroft House, Publishers
Altadena, California

ISBN: 978-1-948616-34-8

Library of Congress Control Number: 2023918238

CONTENTS

ACKNOWLEDGEMENTS

I have to start with thanks to Jared Lo Nigro of the Los Angeles Railroad Heritage Foundation, for the loan of books and helping me scan a truly awesome map of Los Angeles in the 1870s. He truly shed light on the contemporary reports of what I was reading.

Then there was the lovely gentleman at the Seeley Stable Museum in the Old Town San Diego park, who happily showed me their mud wagon, freight trucks, and stagecoach (and maybe even demonstrated something he shouldn't have). He didn't have a card and didn't give me his name, drat him, but he was very kind. The blacksmith I spoke with almost a year later didn't give me his name, either, but was very helpful.

As always, thanks to go the usual crowd of suspects. My wonderful editor and good friend, Carol Louise Wilde. My family, Michael Holland and Corrie Klarner. And the Sisters in Crime Los Angeles, who are always an inspiration.

Thanks to you all.

Content Warning

As noted in Death of the Chinese Field Hands, one of the difficulties in writing a story set in the Nineteenth Century is that attitudes were very different, especially those of White people toward those who were not White.

Also, it was considered humane to euthanize animals that were injured or ill, often very quickly. Which is why a horse is shot in this story.

I have made every effort to present the reality without condoning it. It is important to see where we have come from if we are ever to get past the ills of racism, misogyny, and animal cruelty.

Dramatis Personae

Some of the characters in this story have the real names of people who were living in Los Angeles in 1872. However, since this is a work of fiction, they are technically fictional characters who may, in varying degrees, bear some resemblance to the real people they are named after. Those with real names I have noted. As for anyone else, the reader may assume that he or she is fully the product of my fevered imagination.

RANCHO DE LAS FLORES
Maddie Wilcox, owner, winemaker, physician
Sebastiano Ortiz, winery manager, husband of Olivia, brother to Enrique
Olivia Ortiz, cook, and wife of Sebastiano
Elena Ortiz, assistant to Maddie, daughter to Sebastiano and Olivia
Ramon Ortiz, son to Sebastiano and Olivia
Enrique Ortiz, vineyard manager, husband of Magdalena, brother to Sebastiano
Magdalena Ortiz, housekeeper, and wife of Enrique
Jaime Ortiz, son to Enrique and Magdalena
Hernan Mendoza, field hand, husband of Maria
Maria Mendoza, maid, wife of Hernan

Rodolfo Sanchez, field hand, husband of Anita
Anita Sanchez, nanny, wife of Rodolfo
Marisol Velasquez, personal maid to Maddie

MADDIE'S FRIENDS
Angelina Sutton, undertaker's wife who prepares the bodies for burial
Walter Lomax, a deputy on the city police force
Mrs. Ruth Lomax, wife to Walter Lomax
Ernesto Navarro, a deputy on the city police force
Regina Medina, madam, sister to Thomas Mahoney
Thomas Mahoney, saloon owner

LADIES OF LOS ANGELES SOCIETY (and their husbands)
Mrs. Carson, she and her husband Mr. Carson are presumed to have existed. Mr. Carson owns a stationery store
Mrs. Glassell, she is presumed to have existed, as her husband, Andrew Glassell, was a prominent attorney in town at the time, he also founded the Glassell Park neighborhood and helped found the City of Orange, California
Mrs. Hewitt and her husband Mr. Hewitt may have existed. They own and run the buggy manufactory
Mrs. Downey and her husband Governor John G. Downey did exist and were active in Los Angeles society at the time
Mrs. Judson and Mr. Judson, a banker in the pueblo

OTHER ANGELENOS
Mr. Wiley, agent for Maddie
Mr. Lyons, manufacturers agent
Mr. McKinley, a land broker

Mr. Wills, a notary

Mr. Meyers, an attorney

Mr. Melvin, another attorney

Mr. Jessup, owns a shipping company

Mr. Brownlow, a title attorney

Mr. Handley, an insurance agent

Mr. Gluck, a local laborer and servant to the Glassells

Edgar Sutton, the undertaker and Angelina's husband

Mrs. Dunbar, mother of Shirley

Shirley Dunbar, an orphan

Mr. Lowman, owner of the livery stable

Mr. Medrano, owner of a second buggy manufactory

Mr. Ledbetter, foreman for the Hewitt buggy manufactory

To Michael and Corrie – Christmas is always nicer with
you

Chapter One

No crime is more heinous than murder. That is without question. Nonetheless, what particularly grieved me about the murder of Mr. Thomas Hewitt was that it was utterly needless. The state of Mr. Hewitt's dissipation was such that, with some patience, the malefactor's ends would have been achieved in but a month or two and no one else would have died.

I stood with Mrs. Hewitt on the street that night outside of the new social hall here in Los Angeles, in close conference regarding her husband. In fact, it was very early in the morning of December 1, in the year of Our Lord, 1872, the clock having struck midnight some minutes before. We had been at a fete being held by Mrs. Glassell in the hall. Mr. Hewitt had disgraced himself by getting very sick all over the ballroom floor. Mr. Judson and Mr. Jessup had been kind enough to help Mr. Hewitt from the room to his buggy, hitched in front of the hall, and both had returned to the party.

I pulled Mrs. Hewitt several paces away so that Mr. Hewitt would not hear us as we waited for her foreman, Mr. Ledbetter, to come drive the two of them home.

"Your husband should not have come," I said softly.

I am a medical doctor and had been tending to Mr. Hewitt, who was in the final weeks of liver disease.

"I know, but he insisted," she said, weeping freely. "My poor daughters. I don't know how they will be able to show their faces at school after tonight. And with their exams so close."

I glanced back at the hall. Social ostracization was a very real possibility after such a humiliating event. As terribly difficult as it would be for Mrs. Hewitt's daughters, such shame could also spread to the buggy-building business the family had, with disastrous consequences.

"Pray forgive my unseemly display."

"There, there," I said, patting her arm. "As tried as you have been, especially this evening, I don't doubt that you are strained to your very limit."

"I'm afraid it's not only that." She applied the handkerchief to her eyes. "Yes, Mr. Hewitt has been a considerable trial to me, and especially after tonight's utter mortification. But now that his demise seems imminent, I find that I have a far greater affection for him than I would have thought."

We both wore solid capes over our party finery, I, in my yellow silk polonaise gown with flowered trims, she wearing a neat shade of blue. She was a tiny woman who could be quite fierce when angered. Indeed, I had been surprised that she had contained herself after Mr. Hewitt's gross indiscretion, but then I remembered that she kept her temper in check when among the pueblo's society.

I could barely see her in the darkness, as the street lamp outside the hall was not lit, although it should have been. The night air was crisp and cold. We'd had hints of rain coming, but none had actually fallen. I patted her arm again as she dabbed at her eyes.

The report of gunfire very close by startled both of us into screaming, although our cries were drowned out by panicked neighing from several nearby horses. The dark figure on the other side of the Hewitt's buggy fired several times. Alas, I was so startled that I failed to count how many. The figure hurried away into the darkness, a cloak or coat flapping in the light breeze.

"Thomas!" Mrs. Hewitt screamed, this time even more loudly.

The buggy's horse neighed again and reared in terror, snapping the rein that had held it to the hitching rail. Fortunately, the horse did not bolt and run. I had to hold Mrs. Hewitt back as she tried to run toward the buggy.

Mr. Judson appeared from the hall's front lobby. He leaped toward the horse, which continued to stamp and neigh. It took a moment to calm the beast, but Mr. Judson managed it, then retied it with the other rein. The Glassell's buggy nearby rattled as its horse continued to neigh loudly.

"I heard gunfire and screaming," Mr. Judson gasped as he approached me and Mrs. Hewitt.

"I'm afraid so," I said.

Mrs. Hewitt wrested herself from my arms and ran to where her husband's corpse lay on the floor of the buggy, having been jostled there when the horse reared.

There was no moon that night, but in the faint glint of starlight, I could see that the bullets had landed in Mr. Hewitt's chest. Mrs. Hewitt howled in misery. Other party-goers emerged from the hall, and confusion reigned until Mr. Lomax, one of our policemen, appeared from the police station with Mr. Resendez, another policeman, close behind. Mr. Lomax, tall and square-jawed, took over getting the crowd settled, whilst I pulled Mrs. Hewitt away from the buggy. Mr. Resendez, of average height, with black hair and an unruly beard, found a serving boy to alert Mr. Sutton, the undertaker.

Several of the women who had been at the party surrounded Mrs. Hewitt and started walking with her toward the house next to the buggy manufactory that Mr. Hewitt owned. I suppose I should say that Mrs. Hewitt owned it as well, as she had the primary responsibility of running the place. Regrettably, Mr. Hewitt was seldom sober enough, although that had been a closely guarded secret. Mrs. Hewitt was inconsolable. As I watched the women walk away, I briefly considered sending for my medical bag and giving Mrs. Hewitt a dose of laudanum, but decided against going to her house. Instead, I followed Mr. Lomax and Mr. Resendez as they walked the horse and buggy to the Suttons' home and funeral parlor.

My dear friend, Angelina Sutton, stood in the doorway to the back room, where she prepared the bodies for burial, wearing a blue chambray day dress buttoned askew, her dark hair in its night braid hanging down her back. Mr. Sutton, a somber fellow barely taller than his petite wife, stood behind her with a glowing lamp. He gave it to Angelina, then went to help the policemen with the body.

"Another murder," Angelina sighed.

We did not see, as one wag put it, a murder a day in the pueblo. But we saw it often enough. Los Angeles, at the time, was still very rough and there was a great deal of violence among the many saloons and in the streets.

"I'm afraid so," I said. "Mr. Hewitt, no less."

Angelina gasped. "Oh, dear! What happened?"

"He was shot," I said, swallowing. "I didn't see by whom. It was too dark."

"Poor Mrs. Hewitt." Angelina stepped back from the door as the men brought the body inside.

"Indeed," I grumbled. "Well, I won't keep you from your rest." Both of us were accustomed to being roused from our beds at all hours of the night, but that is not to say that we enjoyed it. "Besides, as I saw the deed being done, I suspect there will not be much to learn from the body itself."

Angelina's eyebrows rose, but then she yawned. "Excuse me. Well, we shall see."

"I will try to come by after services," I said.

Angelina nodded, and I left to find that Ramon Ortiz was waiting for me in the alley with my buggy and my roan mare, Daisy. Ramon was the oldest son of Sebastiano Ortiz. Sebastiano and his brother Enrique were my partners in the winery and vineyard that I owned. Ramon, who was in his early twenties at that time, worked at the Pico House Hotel during the days and some evenings. However, that evening he had chosen to be my driver for the party at the social hall.

There was a faint whiff of pomade about Ramon as he helped me into the buggy. I guessed that there was some lass to whom the young man was paying his attentions, and my being occupied with the party had given him a chance to offer a buggy ride to her and, quite probably, some other friends. I didn't mind as long as I was fetched in a timely manner. He got onto the buggy's box, then clucked the reins.

"Who died?" Ramon asked over his shoulder as the buggy began to move.

"They didn't tell you at the hall?"

"No. Mr. Medrano simply said that he saw you heading to the funeral parlor with Mr. Lomax and Mr. Resendez."

"Mr. Medrano?" I frowned. "He wasn't at the party."

Ramon shrugged. "He was on the street, looking at the crowd near the social hall."

"That is very interesting." I mused, wondering if Mr. Medrano could have been the figure I'd seen or if he'd seen something.

"Why?" Ramon asked.

"Mr. Hewitt was shot and killed, I'm afraid." I said.

"The buggy maker? Why would anybody kill him?"

"I can't imagine why," I replied. "I hope I will not be expected to find out."

Ramon laughed. "I'm sure you will. There is nobody else in the pueblo who is as good at that sort of thing as you are."

I couldn't help letting out a very unladylike snort. Alas, he was right in that I had found out more than one killer. Even more aggravating was that I was already wondering who might have some sort of grudge or complaint against Mr. Hewitt, who, in spite of being a drunkard, was largely inoffensive otherwise. Mr. Medrano was another buggy maker in the pueblo, but I couldn't see how killing Mr. Hewitt would benefit him, as it was clear that there was more than enough work for both manufactories, and that Mr. Hewitt's manufactory managed quite well without his active oversight.

On Sunday mornings, my habit was to sleep quite late. Given my medical practice and the fact that Saturday nights were generally the longest, I frequently saw the dawn break before going to sleep. That Sunday, I had gotten to bed in comparatively good time, and so, rose at an earlier hour than usual for a Sunday. My maid, Marisol Velasquez, got me dressed in my ochre visiting dress for services at the Congregational church, but well ahead of when I needed to be there. I found the pan dulces that Olivia, my cook and Sebastiano's wife, had left out for me. The rest of my extended household, which included both of the Ortiz brothers and their wives, their children, and several ranch hands, some of whom also had wives and children on the rancho, were all Catholic, and as such, did not break their nightly fast until after services at their church. I hesitated, but then ate and headed out to the pueblo and the social hall with my spirits in considerable turmoil.

There not having been any rain in quite some time, the earth around the hitching rail outside the front of the hall was packed quite solidly. There was some dust, but that was filled with the prints of all manner of boots, ladies' slippers, and hoofs. Sighing, I looked toward the back of the hall, then headed that way, my eyes on the ground in front of me. So engrossed was I that I nearly stumbled into Mr. Lomax.

"Good Heavens!" I gasped.

He smiled. "I see you're looking for the same thing I am."

"I dare say I am." I looked at him fondly. He was a good friend. "And what, if anything, have you found?"

"Nothing." He shook his head, then yawned. "Pray forgive me, Mrs. Wilcox. Had jail duty last night."

Which meant he had been up all night, as Mr. Lomax was far too principled to sleep on duty.

"Oh, my goodness. Why, in Heaven's name, are you not headed to hearth and home at this very instant?"

"I am," he replied, laconic, as always. "Just thought I'd stop here first and see if there was anything to find."

"Alas, I have found nothing here," I said. "Have you learned anything else?"

He shook his head.

"Oh. I have found out that Mr. Medrano was on the street outside the hall just after the shots were fired," I said.

"I saw him." Mr. Lomax nodded. "And that big German fellow. Gluck?"

"I should hate to think he had anything to do with this." I frowned. "He's a laborer, is he not? Do you know for whom he's working?"

Mr. Lomax shook his head again.

"Well, I suppose I shall have to find out," I said. I smiled at Mr. Lomax. "And how is Mrs. Lomax doing?"

His eyes lit up and he smiled broadly. "Quite well."

"And the children?"

"Growing like weeds. Hannah has a cold, though."

"All too common this time of year." I reached for my leather satchel that I carried with me everywhere. "I do believe I have some lozenges in here that should help with the cough. And they taste quite pleasant, too."

"No spirits?" Mr. Lomax chuckled at the memory of my first meeting with his daughter.

"None whatsoever."

I handed him the small tin and sent him to his home while I went to services. For a change, Reverend Elmwood did not fulminate on the various evils in the pueblo, but instead chose to preach on Jesus meek and mild. I was relieved, but still paid little attention. Actually, it is perhaps a sad commentary on the good reverend's abilities that I actually paid more attention to him when he was fulminating that I might eventually point out the errors in his text.

That Sunday morning, however, I could think of little but the murder of Mr. Hewitt. I had no reason to consider it, no personal involvement in the act beyond that I had been a witness to the foul deed. Mrs. Hewitt and I were friends, but without any particular intimacy. As for justice, Mr. Hewitt was not some forgotten and forlorn soul without anyone to see to it that justice was done on his behalf. Indeed, many in the pueblo would be clamoring for it.

I tried to convince myself that I had a duty to see to it that the killer was caught before he (or she) killed someone else. I had certainly seen enough of that happen. In addition, I was horrified by how callous the act had seemed. However, as much as I wanted to excise that bit of civic cancer, I felt a deep reluctance to engage in the pursuit.

I did not get much of an opportunity to consider that particular bit of thinking. Immediately after services, a young woman hurried up to me.

"Mrs. Wilcox?" Maria Carranza was a timid thing, slight, with glossy, black hair and russet skin. "Mr. Brownlow asked me to fetch you. The girls are sick again."

Mr. Brownlow was a title attorney who had arrived in the pueblo the previous summer with his three little daughters and Miss Ritter, their nursemaid. His wife had died the year before. Miss Carranza was the housemaid, errand girl, and general lackey, although I had no reason to believe that she was treated harshly in any way. From what I had seen, Mr. Brownlow was a kind master, and his housekeeper and cook, Miss Roberts, no less so.

After gleaning from the maid that the girls had no fever, nor any symptoms that would require my immediate presence, I sent Miss Carranza back to her household with the reassurance that I would be there as soon as I could. Sick children do tend to overflow with all manner of noxious things, and I did not want to soil my good visiting dress unless I had no choice. Marisol, and her immediate predecessor, Juanita Navarro, had been grieved many, many times by the many odorous stains and spots that often decorated even my best dresses.

I dined with my household. We had dinner early on Sundays thanks to the before mass fast. Then Rodolfo Sanchez, one of the hands on Rancho de Las Flores, the proper name of the vineyard I owned, saddled Daisy, my roan mare. Rodolfo was a very large man with a back that was bent over, black hair, and a drooping mustache and whiskers.

I should, perhaps mention, that we commonly used our Christian names among ourselves on the rancho. My late and greatly lamented mother had always treated our family servants with great respect and love. I had endeavored to do the same after my late and unlamented husband dragged me out to Los Angeles in 1860, bought the rancho, then promptly died. But the practice of using our Christian names began when I would call for one of the Ortiz brothers and without fail, the brother I did not require was the one who responded. Because most of the ranch hands were related in one way or another, many had the same last name, and so the practice continued.

When I arrived at the Brownlow house, Mr. Brownlow did not wait for Miss Roberts to open the door, but opened it himself. He was of medium height, and somewhat portly, though not excessively so. He ran his hand through his light brown hair, and the matching beard quivered with his anxiety.

"Miss Carranza said you did not think it was serious," he said.

"It very probably isn't." I followed him to the stairs of the wood-framed house. "Still, you were right to send for me."

"You are kindness, itself, Mrs. Wilcox."

I left him in the hallway of the house. The poor man was prone to fretting over every sneeze or sniffle from his daughters. Given that the illness that had killed his wife had started with very mild symptoms, his concern was not entirely unwarranted.

The girls, Pearl, Carrie, and Ada, were quite charming and very polite. And they were feeling rather poorly, indeed. All three had nasty coughs and sore throats, but there was no fever, and the youngest, Ada, who was four years old, was still playing with her dolls. She, like her middle sister, Carrie, who was six, had perfectly golden curls. Pearl, who was seven, had her father's light brown hair and a grave mien.

The room was whitewashed and very clean, with a cheerful patchwork quilt on the large featherbed that the girls shared. Mrs. Ritter, a large, brown-haired German woman, smiled when she saw me, as did all three of the girls.

I examined them and determined that while it was possible that their colds could develop into something worse, it seemed unlikely. I told Mrs. Ritter to rinse their noses out with warm salt water, to apply a mustard plaster, and to call me if any one of them began to become feverish. There was little else to be done.

"Mrs. Wilcox, will you come again?" Pearl asked me as I readied my bag.

"Any time you need me, dearest." Smiling, I touched her cheek.

"I'm glad," she said.

"Good-bye?" Ada looked up, tears welling up in her eyes.

"It's all right, Miss Ada," I told her, stroking her fine, golden hair. "I will be back. You just be a good little girl, and do as your nurse tells you, so that you get well."

Ada sniffled and coughed, but fortunately, did not burst into tears. I made my way downstairs, where Mr. Brownlow paced.

"Well?" he asked, his eyebrows rising in fear.

I smiled. "It is naught but a catarrh."

"But…"

"Yes, it is possible that the congestion could develop into something grave. But catarrh doesn't usually, and Mrs. Ritter knows to summon me at the first fever."

"Mrs. Wilcox, I cannot thank you enough," he sighed.

He most certainly could have, and I cleared my throat with a tight smile to remind him of that.

"Oh!" he gasped, digging into his pocket. "Pray forgive me. Here is your fee."

He produced a dollar and two quarters.

"Thank you." I smiled.

I will admit, I was prone to extending my services as charity to those who would find it difficult to pay, such as the Lomax family or other impoverished families in the pueblo. However, it was the fellows such as Mr. Brownlow, who could well afford even my increased fee, who inevitably forgot to offer it.

I went to check on my other ailing patients, including a case of pneumonia that had only worsened overnight. Mr. O'Hare, a ranch hand, coughed hard as his fellows looked on, and the fever raged. I listened to his lungs and shook my head.

"I'm afraid it won't be much longer now," I told the five men.

"There's no hope at all?" one of them asked.

"There is always hope, I suppose," I said. "However, if by some miracle he does survive this, his lungs will be forever scarred."

I looked down at the coughing man, my heart filling with sadness.

The men shuffled, but between them, collected sufficient coins for my usual fee. One followed me outside the hands' barracks and helped me onto Daisy.

I made my way from the ranch to the center of the pueblo and the Suttons' home and funeral parlor. Angelina was in the back room, and happy to see me. Indeed, her eyes glowed with mischief.

"I believe you said last night that there would not be much to be learned from the body," she told me.

"Well, given that I was right there when it happened, it certainly seemed unlikely." I smiled as I shook my head. "But based on your expression, you must have found something, after all."

She shrugged. "Well, it isn't much, but it is something. I counted six holes in his chest."

"As in, the killer fired all of the bullets he had."

"Exactly. And it looks as though it was from a fairly large six-shooter fired close by."

I closed my eyes, trying to envision the scene.

"It's hard to say how close the killer actually was," I said. "He was on the other side of the buggy."

"But one thing we can say," Angelina said. "Is that the killer was most probably very angry with Mr. Hewitt."

CHAPTER TWO

I made my way back to my rancho, thinking furiously about what Angelina had said. It was true that I had considered Mr. Hewitt to be largely inoffensive. I had found, however, to my sorrow, that just because I had found a man to be a congenial and capital fellow, that did not mean that he was such. Furthermore, in that earlier instance, had I'd paid more attention to the rumors I had so handily dismissed, I might have found out much sooner that the man in question was anything but capital.

I had since gotten much better about listening to rumors and not dismissing them out of hand. It was not an activity that I relished, but it had proved necessary. So, that afternoon, I cast my mind back to all that I had heard about Mr. Hewitt. Yet there was little that would account for any significant rancor. The only complaints or titters that I had heard referred to his dissipation. If anything, there was a grudging admiration that a fellow so frequently drunk could manage his business so well.

I knew that was because it was Mrs. Hewitt who managed the business, and not Mr. Hewitt. It was supposedly a closely guarded secret. But however closely guarded, secrets seldom remain so, and in the Pueblo's circle of businessmen and their families, there was plenty of room for gossip, accurate and otherwise, to flourish.

We had an early supper on the rancho that evening. After I'd eaten, Marisol helped me back into my visiting dress. Enrique drove me in the buggy to the Hewitt home for the viewing. The buggy's lantern lit up the rutted road, as the sun had already set, and the Clocktower Courthouse bell rang six of the evening.

It was dreary, at best. Mrs. Hewitt sat beside the casket, weeping copiously, her mother and three daughters at her side. Both older women wore fine black poplin, elegantly trimmed with lace and jet. I couldn't help but wonder how they'd managed to find such well-made mourning dresses to fit their small stature and trim figures from the stock at Strelitz's store. Because Mr. Strelitz was a Jew, the dresses could have been procured on a Sunday. It seemed more likely, though, that Mrs. Hewitt already had the dresses made in anticipation of the inescapable conclusion of Mr. Hewitt's illness. The girls were clad in simple white frocks with black velvet sashes as befitted their young age, including the oldest, who, at fifteen years old, was getting to the point of wearing more womanly clothes.

The crowd spilled from the nicely furnished living room across the hall to the dining room, where tea and biscuits of varying sorts had been set out. I paid my respects to Mrs. Hewitt, then made my way to the dining room, where Mrs. Carson was gossiping. I stirred a little sugar into my tea, profoundly grateful that Mrs. Carson had lowered her voice as she spread her spitefulness.

"It's a fine display of grief," Mrs. Carson said to Mrs. Glassell and Mrs. Fletcher.

All three women were very stout, although Mrs. Carson had lost some of her plumpness over the previous six months. Mrs. Fletcher had a chronic cough and her clothes reeked of tobacco smoke. She blamed it on her husband's habit of smoking, although I suspect Mrs. Glassell and Mrs. Carson were fully aware that Mrs. Fletcher also smoked cigarettes.

Mrs. Glassell had gray hair that had once been light brown, and a mildly bombastic mien. I had often thought that she was the twin of Mrs. Carson, even though the two were not related to my knowledge. However, besides Mrs. Carson's newly slimmer figure, that lady's hair had grown completely gray and her eyes had sunk and darkened.

Mrs. Carson had also become very bitter after the loss of her daughter the previous June. She and Mrs. Glassell had always been terrible gossips. But since her daughter's death, Mrs. Carson's comments and observations verged on the cruel rather than the usual mild maliciousness that she and Mrs. Glassell had spread before. Mrs. Carson still wore her black mourning suit, while Mrs. Glassell wore dark blue. Mrs. Fletcher had on a brown bombazine visiting dress.

"Well, we all know what a trial Mr. Hewitt was to her," Mrs. Fletcher said in her high-pitched and raspy voice. "Poor thing won't be able to show her face in the pueblo."

"A trial, indeed." Mrs. Glassell sniffed in high dudgeon. "Especially after last night. But even before that dreadful event, I thought I saw Mr. Jessup gazing at her. It was rather embarrassing."

"I saw that, too!" Mrs. Fletcher gasped. "And it almost seemed as though Mrs. Hewitt returned the attention."

"I would not be surprised." Mrs. Carson sniffed as well. "The other day, when I went with Mr. Carson to fetch our buggy from the manufactory. It was being repaired again. In any case, I saw Mrs. Hewitt looking at her foreman in the most unseemly way. If it hadn't been—" She cleared her throat. "Well, if it isn't Mrs. Wilcox."

"Good evening, Mrs. Carson," I said with a smile I did not feel in the least. "Mrs. Glassell. Mrs. Fletcher."

Mrs. Fletcher simpered. "I am glad to see that you've recovered quite well after last night's terrible event."

"It was a horrible thing to witness," I said. "For me and even more horrible for poor Mrs. Hewitt, who was right there, as well."

The three women looked at each other nervously.

"Well," said Mrs. Carson. "Perhaps the new Common Council will see to finally getting us more policemen and see to it that the lamps stay lit on the streets. It is a travesty that we have so few officers. Nor was the lamp outside the hall lit and there was no reason it shouldn't have been."

"Indeed," I said and moved away.

Mrs. Carson and Mrs. Glassell continued complaining about the Common Council not enforcing the street lamp ordinance and not acquiring more policemen for our tiny force. That the next day was the annual municipal election only seemed to egg the two on, with Mrs. Fletcher coughing and covering it with titters.

I barely stayed long enough to finish my tea. Again, I offered condolences to Mrs. Hewitt, who accepted them blankly. The poor thing was in a complete state of shock and seemed barely conscious of what was going on around her. I made my goodbyes, but Mrs. Hewitt's mother, Mrs. Perry, signaled me to join her at the door to the house.

"How is she?" I asked.

Mrs. Perry, who looked even more gray than usual, shook her head.

"It is the most terrible of events," she said with a sniff. "The poor girls. I know Mr. Hewitt was not long for this world, and they knew it, too. But the poor dears were not even able to say goodbye to their father."

"How horrible for them."

"My daughter is quite beside herself with grief." Mrs. Perry blinked back tears and dabbed at her eyes with a black-edged handkerchief.

"She certainly seems so." I looked back at the new widow. "Have you dosed her with anything? Some laudanum, perhaps?"

"No! Do you recommend it?"

"Absolutely not. I know that it is commonly given for the vapors, but it is the worst thing for the condition. And your daughter is suffering from grief, not the vapors. Laudanum will only make it worse."

"Oh, dear." Mrs. Perry sighed. "Then I don't know what to do."

"The only thing that can heal her pain is time." I smiled weakly at Mrs. Perry. "It will be difficult for all of you, but time does heal."

"He was not a bad man, you know." Mrs. Perry swallowed. "Yes, he was a drunkard, and that was terrible. But he was kind to all of us, even when he was in his cups."

"I most certainly saw that myself." I patted Mrs. Perry's hand. "I must leave, but please feel free to call upon me as needed."

"Thank you, Mrs. Wilcox. You are most kind."

I left feeling more than a little relieved that I hadn't been asked to hunt down Mr. Hewitt's killer, never mind that I'd already been looking for the malefactor. I was, in fact, in a significant quandary. My past investigations into crimes had not been without significant consequences, not just for myself, but for the people I professed to care about.

The night air was quite chilly and with the moon still being new, it was very dark. I was grateful for the lantern that Enrique had on the front of the buggy. Fortunately, we made it back to the rancho without mishap, but somewhat behind the arrival of my good friend Regina Medina.

Her beautifully appointed buggy, drawn by a glossy black horse, stood in the rancho yard, hitched to the post I had near the front of the barn. Regina was inside in the front parlor. Olivia, Sebastiano's wife and my cook, had put out ample biscuits and pan dulces, along with a full pitcher of the angelica wine that our region was renowned for, and that I made from my vineyards.

Regina, who was quite tall and emphasized it by piling her dark hair on top of her head, then wearing tall hats on top of that, stood as I entered the parlor, removing my gloves. Marisol appeared immediately and took the gloves and my leather satchel, then disappeared.

How to explain Regina? I have formed many an unexpected attachment over the course of my long life, but none stranger than that with Regina Medina. That she was the proprietor of the preferred house of ill-repute in the pueblo was strange enough, especially when one considers how much I despise her profession. However, Regina had an oddity that it escapes me how to describe it - and I tried to in a report for a medical journal some years ago.

She certainly thought of herself as a woman. In fact, when I questioned her about the ordinance in the pueblo that forbade residents from taking on disguises, she remarked that being a woman was less of a disguise than the identity that others would say was her true one. However, she deigned to assume that very identity, no matter how false she considered it, at least once a year so that she could do what she could not as a woman. That is, vote.

She also knew how bitter I felt about the fact that even into the eighth decade of the nineteenth century, after we had freed the slaves and given them the right to vote (not that they were actually allowed to), women's suffrage remained well out of reach. As it happened, both Angelina and I were decidedly bitter about not having the vote.

So, on the night before any election, Regina came to my adobe. Angelina would join us. And the three of us would plot out how best to mark the ballot that two of us were forbidden. Regina always said it was the very least she could do.

With the election that next day, Regina had come for our usual conference. Angelina arrived shortly after, bearing her little wooden travel desk and plenty of paper so that she could write down our decisions. The angelica made Regina's memory a touch tenuous. Or rather, the amount of angelica that eventually was consumed.

We set forth upon our task almost immediately and while there was some earnest discussion, we quickly made our choices among the candidates vying to represent Regina's ward, not to mention the mayor. To be honest, I did not make note of which were my choices, nor did I make note of who actually won, although why I didn't, I have no idea.

Fortunately, we had half of the pitcher of angelica left by the time Angelina finished writing up the list for Regina.

"And now," Regina announced, holding out her glass for me to fill. "We need another list, that of the suspects in the murder of Mr. Hewitt."

"Good Heavens," I exclaimed. However, I waved the pitcher instead of serving the wine therein. "Why would you assume that I am already on the hunt for the killer?"

Angelina giggled. "Aren't you?"

"Oh, dear. I suppose I have looked about a little." I sighed as Regina removed the pitcher from my hands and filled her glass. "But I have not been asked to do so and am not terribly sure I should. Fortunately, Mr. Hewitt has no lack of men to speak up for him. And no one appears to be the victim of grave injustice."

"Nonsense." Regina poured a glass of the wine for me. "You stand the best chance of finding our malefactor. Therefore, you have no reason to shirk your duty along those lines."

"Let us not be ridiculous," I said, then took a deep sip and sighed. "Whatever skill I have, I am sure I am not the sole possessor of it. Furthermore, both of you have suffered as a result of such hunts, not to mention others of my household. I would not want to expose any of us to that danger without a very good reason."

Angelina snorted. "I do not like the idea of getting shot again. On the other hand, it has gotten about that you are asking questions."

"It has?" I gasped. "But I haven't. All I did was look for footprints in front of the social hall, as did Mr. Lomax."

"Ah, my darling Maddie." Regina laughed. "Why, in Heaven's name, is it such a terribly bad assumption that you would want to find the killer? And you are remarkably good at such things."

"But at what cost?" I cried.

"Just because your, ahem, posterior got perforated the last time," Regina said, reaching again for the pitcher.

"As did yours," I pointed out.

"That was unpleasant." Regina shrugged. "But neither of us seems to be any the worse for it. And Angelina is quite correct that it has gotten about that you are searching for the killer. If this killer has reason to believe such, then we are not safe whether you actually are on the hunt or not."

"Oh, dear." I sighed deeply and profoundly. "Sadly, it does seem as though we might be useful in the inquiry. Angelina made an interesting observation this morning about the likelihood that the killer was somehow enraged by Mr. Hewitt."

Angelina repeated to Regina what she'd told me about the shooting.

"All six bullets?" Regina mused. "Could it be that the killer couldn't see his target well enough in the dark to be sure he'd hit his target?"

"That is possible," I said, musing myself.

"But the holes were spaced fairly close together," Angelina said. "All in the chest. If the killer couldn't see his target, why wouldn't the bullets have gone everywhere?"

My eyebrows knit together as I thought. "That is true. Also, the bullets tend to go all over if one shoots several times at once. It's the recoil of the gun that does it, if what Sebastiano tells me is correct. So, our killer must be an accomplished shooter. But it was also very dark out last night. No moon to speak of, and the lamp outside the hall was not lit."

"Besides that, the wounds themselves suggest that the man who shot Mr. Hewitt was very close to him," Angelina added, pulling out another sheet of paper.

"Wait a minute," said Regina. "Why are we assuming this killer is a man? There are any number of women in the pueblo who have considerable ability with a gun, myself included."

"I suppose it's possible." I shut my eyes and tried to remember what I'd seen. "I did see something flapping that looked like a cape of some sort, although it could have been a skirt." I gasped. "Mrs. Glassell. She was wearing black that night, and not only has she killed before, she has quite a large six-shooter."

"But why would she kill Mr. Hewitt?" Angelina asked, scribbling the name down, nonetheless.

"That is an excellent question," Regina said, reaching for the pitcher of angelica.

I frowned. "I did hear her earlier this evening, at the viewing, bemoaning that Mr. Hewitt had been such a trial to his poor wife. Even as egregious as Mr. Hewitt's behavior was that night, that hardly seems like much of a reason to murder somebody."

"We have seen lesser reasons in the pueblo." Angelina nibbled on a pan dulce. "But those are the situations that involve too much drink and angry men." She sighed. "And Mrs. Hewitt seems quite bereft."

"Not to mention the fact that she was standing next to me when it happened." I poured myself another glass of angelica.

"She could have paid someone to do the deed," Regina said, gazing at her half-filled glass.

"I suppose," I said. "But there was no reason to. He was clearly dying and not likely to last until the New Year. I had been quite frank with her on that point. She had but to wait. What benefit would there have been in risking getting caught doing such a foul thing?"

Angelina's eyes opened wide. "An insurance policy? What if it wouldn't pay if Mr. Hewitt died from a disease rather than being killed in an accident?"

"Do such things exist?" Regina asked. "It seems rather an odd way to conduct business."

"It's insurance," I grumbled. "I have been blessed in that Mr. Handley is comparatively honest. But I do know that he is unusual among his colleagues. And as I think about it, I do not know for certain that he has been that honest, in that he may have stretched a point when I made that claim two years ago."

I winced at the memory. It had been a nasty business in which my home had caught fire, and I had found that I had only insured my winery against such events. Mr. Handley had seen to including the damaged adobe as part of the winery, which had been largely untouched.

"How will we find out if there is any insurance?" Angelina asked. "It seems a rather personal thing to be asking."

I thought. "You might be able to, Angelina. You're helping with the funeral. Perhaps you could ask quietly as a way of helping the new widow deal with all the papers and such that always must be dealt with. You helped Mrs. Donatelli with that when her husband died. Mrs. Donatelli was immensely grateful."

"I don't know about life insurance, and Mrs. Donatelli and I are friends." Angelina frowned. "But I suppose I can ask. In many respects, it would be a kindness. There is so much to worry about."

"Indeed," said Regina. "So that's Mrs. Glassell, Mrs. Hewitt hiring an assassin. Who else?"

"It's hard to say." I thought again. "Mr. Judson was right there. He settled the Hewitt's horse as it reared."

"That dreary fellow?" Regina snorted.

I regret to write that the above statement is not accurately reported. Both Angelina and Regina could be very coarse in their speech, and while I, in my golden years, have perhaps loosened my tongue somewhat, that salty I cannot write.

I sighed. "Regina, such language."

It was true that Mr. Judson, a prominent banker in the pueblo, had made himself rather unpopular. It was not so much that he was rigorously honest and circumspect, but that he thought everyone else in the pueblo believed in and would adhere to his exacting standard of rectitude. That he was constantly disappointed did not seem to sway him.

"Nonetheless," Regina continued. "He hardly seems the type to kill someone."

"Perhaps in self defense," Angelina said.

"Which this, clearly, was not." My eyebrows knit together. "Mr. Jessup was there."

"The shipping man?" Regina reached for the pitcher and poured.

Mr. Jessup ran a very large freight company. I did not directly do business with him, but my manufacturer's agent, Mr. Wiley, who saw to selling my wines in San Francisco and elsewhere, often used Mr. Jessup's teamsters and wagons to ship not only my wines, but other goods that Mr. Wiley represented. Mr. Wiley thought quite highly of him.

I took the pitcher myself. "Mr. Jessup helped Mr. Judson carry Mr. Hewitt to the buggy after the incident in the social hall. I do not see how he could have done the deed, though. I know he'd followed Mr. Judson back into the social hall, although it was only Mr. Judson who came out when the shots caused the horse to rear. Perhaps I should speak to Mr. Judson and Mr. Jessup to see if either of them saw anyone leaving the hall at the time."

Angelina scribbled on her paper. "Who else was at the party?"

"Most of Society." I got up and paced around the parlor. "Mr. Brownlow was there. Mr. and Mrs. Carson. Mr. Wills, Mr. and Mrs. Meyers, Mr. and Mrs. Glassell, Governor and Mrs. Downey, Mr. Handley. Alas, none of those people appear to have any reason to harm Mr. Hewitt, let alone kill him."

"And there was no one outside the hall to see anything?" Regina poured herself yet another glass of angelica. "It was Saturday night, after all. Surely someone was on the street."

I blinked. "Well, Mr. Medrano was apparently there. I did not see him. Nor did I see Mr. Gluck. But Mr. Lomax told me this morning that both were there."

Angelina thought as she sipped from her glass. "Mr. Medrano. He owns the other buggy manufactory, doesn't he?" Her eyebrows raised. "Perhaps he didn't want to compete with Mr. Hewitt's manufactory."

"As I understand it, there's more than enough business here for both," I said.

"That is my understanding as well," Regina replied. "However, it does not account for greed. With no other buggy makers in the pueblo, Mr. Medrano can ask as much as he wants for conveyances or repairs, and the poor citizens will have no choice but to pay him."

I shuddered. "I suppose. Still, to murder someone simply for the chance to earn more money seems... I'm not sure what it seems like."

"It happens." Regina chuckled. "I'm sure it happens a great deal more often that we know."

"I do not question that in the least." I shook my head. "Especially if one used poison. That can be rather hard to detect unless one does an autopsy and sees the signs of it on the corpus. But in this case, the killer was brazen. Shooting on the street with nothing to hide himself. Admittedly, it was quite dark, but surely somebody could have seen something."

Regina picked up the pitcher and sighed. "I fear this is empty. Which I suppose means that our work is done for the evening. I have my path ahead of me in listening to my customers as they gossip. Angelina has her task." Her gaze fell on me with an evil grin. "And you have most of the pueblo's society to ask questions of."

Chapter Three

I cannot say that I was feeling my best the next morning, but that was frequently the consequence of a conference with Regina and Angelina together. Nonetheless, I rose at my usual hour, wondering how I could disabuse the pueblo, not to mention my two dearest friends, of the notion that I was needed to seek out this foul murderer.

I put on my ochre visiting dress right away, but after I had broken my fast, I spent some time conferring with Sebastiano and Enrique on matters related to the winery and vineyards.

I do not know anyone who particularly enjoys going to funerals. Nonetheless, they are a common enough occurrence that one does not usually find any great distress at the thought of attending one. Fine feelings and sympathy, to be sure, but not usually dread. Yet that is exactly what I felt as I made my way to the Hewitt's buggy manufactory that morning.

No matter how little I wanted to be involved with searching for the killer, Mr. Hewitt's death wore at me. I could find no reason for it. I could only surmise that the poor man had managed to grievously offend someone to the point of rage. After all, he had been shot multiple times and at close range. But it had been very dark that night, so it was possible that the killer had thought he (or she) was shooting someone else. I did not think that was entirely likely unless the killer had taken to randomly shooting people in buggies for no reason.

The main service was held on the floor of the manufactory, which had been cleared of all dirt and debris, to accommodate the large number of people who wished to attend. I couldn't help but see that as further evidence that there was no reason for Mr. Hewitt's death. But as I surveyed the faces of my fellow citizens, I did not doubt that there were those among them who did not see Mr. Hewitt as a friend and comrade. Nor were they likely to say so. Even the most villainous of us are seldom spoken of badly when laid out in the casket.

Alas, Reverend Elmwood's sermon did little to ease my disquiet, choosing to preach his usual text, "Well done, good and faithful servant." Not only was it the dullest of sermons ever pronounced, given that the Hewitts had been members of his congregation for as long as I'd been in the pueblo, I would have thought that he could have found something more personal to say. I have heard preachers express better knowledge of complete strangers than the reverend did toward someone he presumably knew fairly well.

I did try to be charitable. Perhaps Mrs. Hewitt had requested the text, and if she found comfort in it, then there was little I could say against it. Although, from the way her shoulders trembled under her widow's weeds, I formed the belief that there was little that would offer her comfort.

We followed the horse-drawn casket to the cemetery. Mr. Sutton led the horse. Both Mr. Jessup and Mr. Judson walked with Mrs. Hewitt, while Mrs. Perry walked with her granddaughters, with Angelina behind them, ready to help as needed. If, as I had heard the night before, Mr. Jessup had been gazing at Mrs. Hewitt in an unseemly manner the previous Saturday, his comportment that morning was perfectly circumspect.

As Reverend Elmwood began his final eulogy over the gravesite, I saw Mr. Ledbetter watching Mrs. Hewitt with tears in his eyes. Mr. Ledbetter was the manufactory foreman and fiercely loyal to Mr. and Mrs. Hewitt. I did not doubt that he felt quite grieved at the loss.

Fortunately, the good reverend kept his remarks brief. We said the Lord's Prayer, then the casket was lowered into the ground. Mrs. Hewitt, her face hidden by her heavy black veil, sobbed loudly, as did her youngest daughter. I was quite touched as Mrs. Hewitt reached over and took the babe into her arms, and the two wept together. Mrs. Carson, who stood nearby, sniffed, and there was no question that she disapproved of the scene. It was, perhaps, a bit more demonstrative than one usually saw, but it was hardly unheard of, and the feelings were certainly heartfelt. I would have thought that Mrs. Carson would have found some greater charity for the family, given her own relatively recent bereavement. Indeed, she'd barely come out of deep mourning after the passing of her daughter six months before.

As I made myself ready to leave the cemetery, Mr. Jessup and Mr. Judson approached.

"Good day, Mrs. Wilcox," Mr. Judson said, his smile appropriately somber. "It's a sad day, isn't it?"

"Very sad," I replied.

Mr. Judson smoothed his full gray beard. He had the girth of the prosperous and a full head of hair equally as gray as his beard.

"Indeed," Mr. Judson said. "Very sad." He cleared his throat. "Such a devastating and terrible crime to have occurred."

"Murder is the most grievous of all crimes," I said, wondering what the two men wanted.

Mr. Judson barely acknowledged my existence unless I happened to be in his bank to transact business. I barely knew Mr. Jessup beyond his name and that he had a freight company. He was a tall man, with a slender build, brown hair and a neatly trimmed beard. That either should want to speak to me at all was grossly out of the ordinary.

"Yes, very grievous," said Mr. Jessup.

Mr. Judson cleared his throat. "I am sure it would be a comfort to our fair citizens if they heard that you are looking into the matter."

It took a significant effort, but I somehow managed to restrain the deep sigh that I felt. It had never been my intent to create such notoriety, and it was a source of deep embarrassment that my reputation in that respect seemed to hover over me, not to mention my own reluctance to take up the chase.

"I am doing no more than any good citizen who has witnessed a crime should do," I replied, once again feeling the turmoil that had assailed me the day before. "And I am confident that you gentlemen are doing just the same."

"Nonetheless." Mr. Judson shifted. "It is possible that we do not possess the same perspicacity that you seem to have. Nor does anyone else in the pueblo."

I had a great deal of trouble preventing my jaw from dropping to the ground in shock, but somehow I managed it. Mr. Judson was not the sort of fellow who readily admitted that anyone, let alone a lowly woman, knew more than he did. That he was crediting me with an ability that he lacked, well, that was the very definition of amazing.

"I, eh, am quite gratified that you think so highly of me," I managed to say after several moments.

He shuffled uncomfortably, which, in turn, helped me to see what had occurred behind closed doors. Mrs. Judson, his wife, was also a rather formidable presence, and I did not doubt that pressure had been brought to bear upon her husband. Even as we women were (and to a certain degree still are) treated as little better than children, many of the more clever of us had found ways to influence the men in our lives to our betterment.

I smiled at him and made my way toward Angelina, who hovered near Mrs. Hewitt and her family, deftly turning away all but the closest of friends. However, before I could reach the family, a relatively small man who looked as if I should recognize him stumbled across my path.

"F-forgive me," he said, his speech more than a little slurred.

It took but a whiff to tell his sad tale. He positively reeked of whiskey.

"It's quite all right," I said, even though it wasn't. "I don't believe we've been introduced?"

"I am Charles Hewitt," he said, over deliberate in his pronunciation. "I have lost my younger brother."

"I'm so terribly sorry," I said.

He stumbled away. I turned toward Mrs. Hewitt and noticed a brief shudder of rage as her head turned toward the man I had to believe was her brother-in-law. Mrs. Hewitt had quite the temper, and already being in the throes of considerable emotion, I was not surprised that ill feelings had surfaced in her. But that they were directed at another member of the family seemed odd.

I did not get a moment to consider the thought. Angelina waved me forward so that I could speak with Mrs. Hewitt. I wish that I could write that I was not as reluctant to speak to the new widow as I was, but there was no excuse not to. As I approached, I realized that Mrs. Hewitt had asked Angelina to summon me, which did not ease my conscience in the least.

"Mrs. Wilcox, how good of you to come," Mrs. Hewitt said, choking on the words.

"Of course. I am happy to be at your service."

Mrs. Hewitt sighed in relief. "I am glad to hear that. Too many times, as you have hunted down certain criminals, have I avoided you, afraid that you were going to accuse me of some great evil. But now I must rely upon your skill and ability. Please, will you find the man who killed my husband?"

I swallowed, desperately trying to find something to say that would relieve me of the obligation to search out another killer. It did not help that a flash of glee lit up Angelina's eyes before she returned to her properly sober mien.

"Of course, Mrs. Hewitt," I finally said. "I can do no less."

It is a good thing that Angelina chose not to look at me at that moment, or it is entirely possible that I might have disgraced myself.

"Thank you, Mrs. Wilcox. I thank you from the bottom of my heart!"

I hesitated. "However, I will need to speak to you, as soon as tomorrow, perhaps? You may have some observations that might be useful. I would not wish to intrude upon your grief, but that the sooner we get to the bottom of this, the better."

"Oh, to be sure." Mrs. Hewitt grasped my hands. "Again, I cannot thank you enough."

"I shall call on you tomorrow, then."

I nodded at Angelina and took my leave, only to have Angelina follow me, catching me up near the gate to the cemetery.

"I'll thank you not to say anything," I said, glaring at her.

"I wasn't going to." Nonetheless, Angelina's eyes and her tone were merry. "But I thought you'd want to know that Mrs. Hewitt asked me to help with Mr. Hewitt's papers and all the details of the will and such. He left his entire estate to her."

I nodded. "Actually, I was aware of that last part. Last week, when we were discussing Mr. Hewitt's condition, I asked her how she would be set after his passing, and she assured me that the will was in excellent order and that she was the beneficiary."

"I also asked about life insurance. Mrs. Hewitt said that she didn't know if Mr. Hewitt even had a policy. She thinks he might have, but then asked if I would talk to Mr. Handley about it."

"She didn't know?" My eyebrows creased and I hurriedly uncreased them to prevent lines. "That is odd. She saw to all business matters for both the household and the manufactory. If there was a policy, she not only should have known about it, but seen to paying for it."

"As I thought, as well. However, she is not at her best at the moment."

"Indeed." I looked up the hill as Mr. Jessup and Mr. Judson slid close to Mrs. Hewitt. Behind them, Mr. Sutton spoke with the gravediggers. "Well, I must make my way home. I don't doubt someone will be calling me shortly and I'd best be wearing my work frock."

Back at my rancho, I hurried to my adobe, where Marisol helped me into my new blue work dress. It was a lovely frock of linen and wool. I almost hated to wear it, as it was quite neat, the color of the Los Angeles sky on one of our relentlessly sunny days, with box pleats at the back of the skirt and a simple bodice and cuffs that were, nonetheless, decorated with a somewhat deeper blue silk ribbon. I suppose I should have had it made of a darker color, as the various stains of wine and what patients left behind would soon sully it. But I found the color quite cheerful, in spite of my ambivalence about the weather and Los Angeles, in general.

I must add a word or two about Marisol Velasquez. She was a most excellent personal maid. But, alas, I had been spoiled by her predecessor, Juanita Alvarez Navarro. Juanita had been far more than a mere servant, but a dear friend, and remained a dear friend even after she left my service to marry the dashing young policeman, Ernesto Navarro.

Marisol, by contrast, was very quiet. Barely eighteen when she joined my household, she seemed to resist becoming part of it.

"They are all very kind," she'd told me a few months before the events I am relating. "But like my cousin Juanita, I will have to leave you all to marry and have a family of my own. It wouldn't do to form attachments."

I had to honor that. She was such an earnest, solemn little thing, with glossy, full black hair, and round face, as she was a trifle on the plump side. So, we seldom said much to each other, but I came to appreciate her deeply, as she was always where I needed her at the moment I needed her.

Nor did she complain about the often sorry state of my dresses at times. Los Angeles being what it was back then, rough and just beginning to civilize, dust was everywhere, and when there was mud, it often stuck to everything like glue. No matter how careful I was, and what aprons I wore, given my twin vocations as physician and winemaker, it was a constant struggle to keep myself clean. Marisol had not only learned many of Juanita's tricks to remove blood, wine and other stains, she had discovered some of her own. In short, she was becoming utterly indispensable.

By the time I was dressed, Olivia had our lunch ready, and I'd received a message that Mrs. Judson wished to avail herself of my services. It had struck me that she'd been absent from the funeral earlier, as well as the viewing the night before. I sent a message back to Mrs. Judson that I would be there at my earliest opportunity, then went to eat the lovely soup and bread that Olivia had prepared for us.

Ramon had the day off from his work at the Pico House restaurant and ate with us. As he teased his younger brothers and cousins, it occurred to me that I was not as certain as I would have liked about whether the street lamp had been lit or not. After all, how had the killer seen enough to shoot with such accuracy? That I had only been able to see a shadow seemed to indicate that the lamp had not been lit. Or if it wasn't, was it possible that someone's buggy lamps had been lit and close enough to shine on Mr. Hewitt, but blind me and Mrs. Hewitt?

"Ramon," I asked suddenly. "Pray forgive me for interrupting, but Saturday night, when you left me at the Social Hall, was the street lamp outside lit?"

"It was." Ramon nodded enthusiastically and grinned. "I couldn't help noting how many fine people were there."

"And what was her name?" Armando teased. He was Enrique's second oldest, and a fine lad of eighteen.

Sebastiano glowered at his son. "You'd best be behaving like a gentleman."

"Always, Papa." Ramon laughed. He was quite a good young man, but at twenty-one years old with a position of some importance at the Pico House and excellent prospects, he was feeling his oats, as they say.

"And when you came to get me," I continued. "Was the lamp lit then?"

Ramon's eyebrows rose. "No, it wasn't. It wasn't pitch black. A couple of buggies had their lamps lit, but there wasn't much light at all."

"Hm." I returned to musing.

Olivia groaned and Magdalena, Enrique's wife and the housekeeper, shook her head with a deep sigh. It was as if they knew what was in store. I sighed deeply.

"Yes, I am afraid I have been pulled into searching for another killer," I said. "Mrs. Hewitt asked quite plaintively for my help, and what could I say, but yes?"

"Of course you had to say yes," Magdalena said, shuddering.

Olivia, however, shook her finger at me. "You had best be as careful as possible. You make sure you carry your gun everywhere! It was bad enough that last time, when they brought you home with holes in your back."

"Basta, Olivia," Sebastiano said, tiredly. He was a tall man with black hair and beard threaded with silver. "She is not a foolish child."

Which was possibly the least helpful thing he could have said, mostly because Olivia was convinced that I did not have the sense God gave a goose. She went on at length about all the ways that I could not be trusted to take care of myself, speaking in rapid Spanish since she preferred that language to English. I ate, not able to counter a word she said, since, alas, I was not very good at taking care of myself and frequently missed meals, which was Olivia's especial bane.

I do speak Spanish fluently. I picked it up over the years, as the members of my household were as likely to speak in that tongue as in English, in which they were also fluent.

I walked into the pueblo that afternoon, as I had several stops I wished to make. It was yet another of the many annoyances foisted upon women of that time that we were forced to ride sidesaddle. Having to hoist myself on and off my roan mare, Daisy, multiple times, not to mention finding a place to tie her, made walking certainly more pleasant, if not more expeditious. In addition, my errands were not likely to take me out of the main part of the pueblo.

I went first to the shipping office to see if I could find out when the steamship Orizaba would be arriving. I had ordered quite a few medications from a company in San Francisco, and they had telegraphed the previous Saturday that the medications had arrived from the East Coast and that they would be on that particular boat.

My supplies of those medications were getting perilously low. I had thought I had ordered my medications in good time for the winter season. However, the reality of receiving anything that had to be shipped from just about anywhere was that those items that you needed the least would arrive well before they were needed, and the items that you needed the most would inevitably be delayed, usually beyond when you actually needed them, no matter how far in advance you ordered them.

I ascertained the arrival date of the steamship in question, but then, as I left the office, I happened upon Mr. Handley, the insurance agent, and Mr. Leander Wills on the street outside the shipping office, engaged in some discussion. The second they saw me, they stopped and doffed their hats.

"Good morning, Mrs. Wilcox," Mr. Handley said, smiling warmly. He replaced his hat over his somewhat unruly straw-colored hair, and adjusted his spectacles.

Mr. Wills smiled, as well, but the dark eyes behind his pince-nez glasses seemed anxious. He was a rather fastidious fellow, wearing only the best wool suits over his short and somewhat rotund form, with a clean-shaven chin – rather an oddity at the time. He, alas, had cause to be wary of me, as I had been forced to question his honesty in another matter some two years before.

"Good morning, Mr. Handley, Mr. Wills," I replied, smiling. "And how are you gentlemen today?"

"Quite well," Mr. Wills said, patting his bright orange silk vest.

Mr. Handley nodded. "Very well, Mrs. Wilcox. And you?"

"Fortunately, quite well."

The two men shifted and glanced at each other.

"Eh, Mrs. Wilcox, might I have a word with you privately?" Mr. Wills asked.

"Certainly, Mr. Wills," I said.

"Then I shall make my way back to my office." Mr. Handley tipped his hat toward us. "Good day, Mrs. Wilcox, Mr. Wills." He paused and removed his hat. "Mrs. Wilcox, will you join me there after you're done speaking with Mr. Wills?"

"By all means," I replied. "Unless, of course, I am called away."

"Of course." Mr. Handley bowed slightly, then turning, replaced his hat and scratched at the full beard on his chin as he moved away to the next block, where his office was located.

Mr. Wills turned toward me and sighed. "Mrs. Wilcox, I have a confession to make."

"Mr. Wills?" I stepped back in shock.

"I know you are searching for the evil person who murdered poor Mr. Hewitt." He coughed and held up his hands. "I did not! I swear it!"

"I had no reason to believe so," I said with a calm I did not feel.

"However." The little man sank into himself. "You have been so kind about not mentioning my little weakness. And I have been very good these past two years." He swallowed. "But I did enter into a game of chance with Mr. Hewitt some months back, and again, lost. It was, perhaps, a good thing that I did so. Eh, you may not have been the first to suggest that you would tell Mr. Judson or the justices about my problem."

"Nor have I been the last, I would imagine." I pressed my lips into a line.

Mr. Wills had a decided problem with gambling and failing to pay his debts.

"I'm afraid not." He sighed deeply. "Losing again set me back on the path of the righteous, I can assure you of that."

"Nonetheless," I said. "Why would you tell me about it? If you wish to make amends, perhaps it would be better to speak to Mrs. Hewitt about it."

"She is such a dainty, sweet thing." His next sigh came from the bottom of his soul. "I am afraid she would utterly despise me if I tried to make amends, and I could not bear that." He swallowed. "Not now, when I at last have hope."

He tipped his hat at me and hurried off down the street.

CHAPTER FOUR

There was no mistaking it. Mr. Wills had developed a deep affection for Mrs. Hewitt. I suppose I should have had some sympathy for the poor man's suffering over the poor widow. After all, unrequited love is quite painful, and up until the previous Saturday, Mr. Wills had to believe that his love would remain unrequited for an indefinite period of time. I looked back at him, wondering if he had, indeed, ended his suffering as such by ending the life of Mrs. Hewitt's husband.

However, I turned my attention to speaking with Mr. Handley, whose office was right there in the block next to me. I entered the building and made my way up to the second floor. He was waiting for me and ushered me past his clerks to his own office and seated me in the straight-back chair in his large, cluttered office.

"Now, how might I help you?" he asked, bustling to the chair behind his desk.

"I was under the impression that you wished me to help you," I said. "Or perhaps you had some other business for me?"

"No. No." Mr. Handley swallowed and adjusted his spectacles. "It's... It's a rather delicate matter, I'm afraid."

"How so?"

"I do not know how well you are acquainted with Mrs. Hewitt."

I watched him carefully. "Well enough to call her a friend, I suppose."

Mr. Handley's demeanor eased somewhat. "I had a most curious conversation with Mrs. Sutton just after lunch today."

"Ah." I smiled. "If I recall correctly, Mrs. Sutton had been asked to speak to you about any life insurance policy on Mr. Hewitt?"

"That is what she told me. I have no reason to question her sincerity, you understand."

"And yet?" I asked.

Mr. Handley winced slightly. "Therein lies my problem. Mrs. Wilcox, can I take you into my deepest confidence?"

I sat back in my chair, somewhat puzzled. "I dare say you might. Is this in regard to how the buggy manufactory is run?"

"Exactly!" Mr. Handley smiled and sank into his chair in relief. "One could hardly miss that Mr. Hewitt was seldom in any condition to conduct business. Obviously, Mr. Ledbetter dealt with much of it. But there were some things that he could not, such as the family's insurance policies. I dealt with Mrs. Hewitt personally, you see, and found her uncommonly astute." He suddenly frowned. "This is why I found it so odd that Mrs. Sutton was asking after the policy. After all, surely Mrs. Hewitt would have known about it. She dealt with all of those details for herself and her husband."

I sighed. "I had already thought of that, I'm afraid."

"But why would Mrs. Sutton be interested in a life insurance policy on Mr. Hewitt?"

"She is not." I glared at Mr. Handley. "I know you do not intend to impugn Mrs. Sutton's motives, but I am afraid that is exactly what you have done when you suggest Mrs. Sutton had any interest beyond helping a grieving widow in need. Furthermore, even the most astute of us do lose track of things in the face of great sorrow. If Mrs. Hewitt could not immediately remember which insurance policies she holds, then it is more than likely due to her grief, not to mention all the other things one must adjust and consider when one's beloved husband dies. It has not been that long ago since I faced the same situation, and I did not have a kindly undertaker's wife to help me in my hour of need."

Mr. Handley had the grace to cough and sputter. "I apologize. I do, indeed. That was, perhaps, ill-considered of me."

"It was, but we all make mistakes." I looked at him. "And did Mr. Hewitt have a life insurance policy?"

"Not with me, I'm afraid."

I briefly considered asking what the terms of such a policy might be, but decided not to, given the way Mr. Handley was jumping to conclusions.

"I might be able to find out," he said. "Along with the terms of such a policy. After all, if you are asking whether it exists, then one must draw the conclusion that you have an interest in knowing." He smiled rather triumphantly, then sat up righteously. "We must all do our part to find this terrible villain."

"Yes. We must." I forced a smile onto my face and rose.

Mr. Handley jumped to his feet and escorted me out of the insurance office to the hallway. I made my way back to the street, feeling quite out of sorts. I would have appreciated it if Mr. Handley had been as eager to help the year before when my two field hands had been horribly murdered.

The sound of someone coughing behind me reminded me that I needed to call on Mrs. Judson. Her note had mentioned a cold of some sort, and it was certainly the time of year for that particular bane of human existence. Nonetheless, it was seldom that serious, which was why I'd taken my time before going to her home.

It was a large, white-washed clapboard house with a wide veranda on two sides. I went to the front door, but the young Negro maid that answered looked at me, puzzled, and excused herself for a moment. I knew what had happened. Mrs. Judson held the annoying practice of making distinctions among the social classes of the pueblo. Intimate friends and others considered the upper tier of society in the pueblo, were to be admitted to the parlor right away. Those with whom Mrs. Judson was friendly, but in a lesser tier of society, were asked to wait while the maid answering the door went to see if Mrs. Judson was in. Under no circumstances was a tradesman to be admitted through the front door, and most in the pueblo knew they risked losing Mrs. Judson's trade if they knocked there first.

The criteria Mrs. Judson used to decide to which tier one belonged were vague, at best, and had been known to change unpredictably. I presented an exceptional challenge. As a physician and winemaker, I was little better than a tradesman. However, as a woman of considerable property, and as someone Mrs. Judson looked on as something of a friend but not an intimate one, meant that I warranted a request to wait and occasionally even immediate entry. The maid that had answered the door was clearly new to the household and had not been able to divine my social standing.

She returned a minute later, completely flustered, which led me to believe that she would be replaced in short order. Mrs. Judson was remarkably like her husband in assuming that her beliefs and preferences were universally understood and shared, despite considerable evidence to the contrary, as the constant flow of new household staff demonstrated.

I was shown upstairs to Mrs. Judson's bedroom, as the lady of the house had taken to her bed. Her cough was quite nasty.

"How long has this been going on?" I asked, removing my stethoscope from my bag.

"Yesterday morning." Mrs. Judson sniffed and dabbed at her nose with a lace-trimmed handkerchief. She was an average-sized woman with gray hair and wore a lovely cambric nightgown with cunning tucks and trimmed in lace.

"You sound as though you can't breathe through your nose."

"Not at all," she whimpered.

I listened to her chest, then checked for a fever. It was there, but seemed very mild. I also looked into her throat, but didn't see anything but evidence of some catarrh.

"Well, it's good news," I said. "I see no reason to believe that no matter how poorly you feel, you are not suffering from anything more serious than a cold."

Mrs. Judson let out a short whimper of protest. I held up my finger.

"I know you feel absolutely terrible," I said. "I do not understand what it is about colds that make one feel as if he were on Death's own doorstep. But it is very unlikely that you are."

Mrs. Judson coughed hard. "I don't think I have ever been this ill before." She coughed again. "But you are very reassuring, Mrs. Wilcox."

"It is still possible that you could develop a pneumonia, so it would be good for Mr. Judson to summon me should your fever go up and the cough gets worse."

"Assuming he even notices." Mrs. Judson coughed again. "He is running for the Common Council, you know."

"Yes. I saw that."

"He is so absorbed by that, he barely heard me sniffle this morning." Mrs. Judson sniffed with great difficulty, then blinked her eyes.

"I do not doubt that he is," I said, sympathetically. "Still, I would greatly like to speak with him in the near future."

Mrs. Judson swallowed. "About Mr. Hewitt?"

"I'm afraid so. Mrs. Hewitt asked me to inquire."

"Of course she did. I asked Mr. Judson to do so if she didn't."

As I had suspected earlier that day that she had, and I strongly suspected in that moment that Mrs. Judson had done more than ask, even as poorly as she was feeling.

"As he did," I said. "Alas, it was at the funeral, so I could not ask the questions I would have liked."

"Then feel free to insist that he speak with you. You have my blessing. That monster must be caught at all costs!"

Although I concurred that the villain needed catching, I could not help but notice that similar urgency had not been felt even as early as the previous spring when another innocent life had been taken. But because the victim had been an old Indian woman, few even noticed that she had died.

"Well," I said even so. "I expect that you will still be feeling poorly for the next few days, and the cough may even last longer. They sometimes do. Make sure you rinse your nose out with some warm salt water and have your cook make up a mustard plaster for your chest. I am afraid there is little else to be done."

"Mother had us hold our heads over a bowl of steaming water."

"That can also help." I packed my stethoscope into my bag. "If you are not feeling better by Friday, please call me."

"Friday? Oh, no! I am supposed to be at the meeting—" She stopped speaking suddenly.

"Meeting?" I looked at her, wondering.

"It's for the good of the town," Mrs. Judson said, still reluctant to say what it was about and hiding behind the righteousness of the cause.

"What meeting is that?"

"Eh..." Mrs. Judson coughed again, and while I did not wish to judge her, this time the source seemed to be convenience rather than her cold. "Mrs. Glassell. It's her new cause and I do believe that it might be needed."

"I did not know that she had a cause."

"Oh, yes. But I fear it is not one that you would approve of." Mrs. Judson flushed. "Temperance. Mrs. Glassell hopes to have a temperance revival meeting after the new year."

"Oh." I shrugged. "I concede that full temperance could be detrimental to my wine business, but the idea certainly has some merit."

"It does?"

"Some. However, I doubt it will happen, at least not here. And even if it does, I seriously doubt it will do any good. If there is one thing I have noticed about those in the grip of demon rum is that they always manage to get it, no matter what efforts you take to prevent that. Mr. Hewitt is a primary example. I assure you, Mrs. Hewitt saw to it that there were no spirits or wine in her house."

"I know she did. But one must do something. So many of our women and children suffer."

"Indeed, they do, which is why I believe the idea has some merit."

However, I did forebear to suggest my real thought was that women would be better served by supporting suffrage instead. Once we women had the vote, we would be able to also effect temperance or whatever other measures would be needed to protect ourselves from dissolute husbands.

As it turned out, I was right that our Noble Experiment with temperance would do little good. In fact, if the headlines we read are to be believed, it would seem that things have gotten even worse. But I digress, the fate of the elderly, I am told.

I left Mrs. Judson shortly thereafter and went to call on Mrs. Glassell, who was not "at home." I knew for a fact that she was inside the nice clapboard house with the large yard and carriage house at the back, because I heard her declare rather emphatically that she was not "at home" after the maid had left to inquire.

I did find it somewhat odd, however, that Mrs. Glassell did not wish to receive me. It is true that we were not friends, or even that friendly, unless I happened to be embroiled in an investigation. Then Mrs. Glassell was happy to speak with me and usually at length. Admittedly, her observations did not always help, but they didn't obfuscate the matter either. In addition, it was always possible that her constant gossiping might undercover something that I would need to find the killer. But I could hardly impose myself upon her and decided that I could put my time to better use.

The house being on a corner, I walked toward the back to go down the street back into the main part of the pueblo. As I passed by the Glassell's carriage house, I was hailed by Mr. Gluck. I had first known him as a general laborer, and he was a large man with blue eyes and wheat-colored hair and beard. He had been known for fighting in saloons, to the point where he'd needed surgery after a particularly bad fight one night. After he had recovered, he reformed completely and had not only given up fighting, he'd given up visiting saloons. I had been so impressed that I told him to give me as a reference, which he did when he'd sought employment with the Glassells.

"Hello, Mrs. Wilcox!" He smiled as he strode across the yard. "It is good to see you."

"Likewise, Mr. Gluck," I said, smiling. "How are you faring these days?"

"Very well."

"And your work goes well?"

At that, he sighed. "Not at the moment. But I am confident it shall work out well." He looked at me. "Mrs. Glassell is missing her carriage robe. It's a special one, wool with bright colors in stripes. But it is also very large so that Mrs. Glassell's gowns are fully covered."

Given that Mrs. Glassell was fairly stout, the robe must have been quite large, indeed.

"I'm sure you'll find it," I said soothingly. "Things go missing all the time."

"I know. But I do not wish to lose my position."

I smiled warmly. "Well, I am confident that it will turn up in good time. Good afternoon, Mr. Gluck."

"Good afternoon, Mrs. Wilcox."

I made my way down to the middle of the pueblo, feeling somewhat nettled. It seemed as though I was learning little more than to be annoyed at my fellow citizens for their complete disregard for the people who worked for them. I walked quickly, pondering my next task, but Fortune intervened in the form of an extended mule team outside of the warehouse next to the station depot.

I must amend the above, given the trouble that a station depot caused during the events I am about to relate. There was, in fact, a small railroad that ended in Los Angeles. It ran between the pueblo and somewhere near the port at San Pedro, although it could have been Wilmington. I had never bothered to ascertain where exactly it ran, my interest being more focused on whatever goods that I had ordered from San Francisco and when they would arrive in the pueblo.

However, some months or weeks before, the Southern Pacific Railroad had taken over our little line to the port and had only shortly before located a new depot for that line and the one that I had been given to understand would run all the way to San Francisco. Or perhaps we'd been told that it would run to New York or somewhere on the Eastern coast of our fair nation.

To be sure, I do not remember, nor did I make much note of it in my journals. I was vaguely aware that there may have been some sort of manipulation or downright skullduggery involved in where the rails would go. However, to the best of my knowledge, no one did anything that was outright illegal, and most of the men involved were utterly convinced that they were acting in the community's greater good. That they also made themselves fabulously wealthy at the expense of others? I find that harder to resolve, especially since I was one of the persons who ultimately benefited.

I walked past the mule team to see Mr. Wiley and Mr. Jessup, deep in conversation, next to the first of the two towering trucks. There may have been as many as twenty mules hitched to the first truck, with the second truck hitched behind the first. Both had rough wood boards for sides and were covered over with canvas. The mules nickered and snorted, apparently eager to be off, but I could see no sign of the teamsters that would be driving them.

"Good afternoon, Mrs. Wilcox!" Mr. Wiley smiled broadly and tipped his hat. He was small and rather gaunt, with sandy hair and beard.

I smiled at the agent. "Good afternoon, Mr. Wiley."

"Have you met Mr. Jessup?" Mr. Wiley asked.

"Not formally, I'm afraid." I smiled at the taller man. "Merely a greeting at the funeral this morning."

"Then may I present him to you?" Mr. Wiley turned slightly to the other man. "This is my shipping man, Mr.

Jessup, and a fine fellow. Mr. Jessup, this is Mrs. Wilcox, one of my best clients and an esteemed physician."

Mr. Jessup removed his hat and bowed slightly. "I am honored, Mrs. Wilcox. I have heard a great deal about the excellence of your wines and your skill in the healing arts."

"You are quite kind, Mr. Jessup. I have also heard many good things about you." I nodded. "In fact, you have been most kind to Mrs. Hewitt over these past two days and that terrible night. It was you who helped Mr. Hewitt to his buggy, wasn't it?"

"Yes, I did." He shifted, suddenly uncomfortable.

"Did you happen to see anybody else out there that night?"

He smiled. "I saw no one. It was very dark, as you know."

"It was. Well, thank you for speaking with me." I looked at both men. "I must be on my way. Good afternoon, gentlemen."

Quickly tipping their hats, they offered me the same, and I continued down the street. Not far away, I saw the buggy manufactory belonging to Mr. Medrano. I had not planned on speaking with him, but I decided that there was no reason not to.

I was fortunate to find him in his office on the first floor of the huge building filled with wood, sawdust, and men working. In the far corner of the building, there was a blast of heat from the forge as a blacksmith slammed his hammer again and again against a glowing bar on his anvil. Sunlight glinted around the gigantic bellows over the small fire pit nearby.

Mr. Medrano greeted me politely, then ushered me into the untidy room. There was a large wooden table covered over with various papers, several pencils of varying lengths, and a toppled over ink bottle that had been there for some time, for there was no ink in evidence on the tabletop. Mr. Medrano, an average-sized man, but for his rather brawny shoulders, immediately removed several bits of wood from the straight-backed chair in front of his desk, and offered me the seat.

"Now, how might I help you today, Mrs. Wilcox?" he asked, settling himself in a similar chair behind the table, then using his fingers to straighten his unruly dark hair and beard.

"I have been told that you were in the immediate neighborhood when poor Mr. Hewitt met his fate," I said. "I am hoping that you saw the villain who shot him or possibly saw something else that would lead us to the villain."

Mr. Medrano grinned. "And you do not think that I am the fellow?"

"I have nothing upon which to base such an accusation." I sat up straight, wondering if I would be able to get out of the office quickly.

"I did happen past that night." His smile only grew, yet there was something insincere about it. "But I only saw you and Mrs. Hewitt, and a couple of others." He thought about it for a moment. "There was the banker, and I believe the Glassells' horseman. And your young servant pulled up in your buggy shortly after the policemen left with the body."

"And how did you happen to be there so late at night?" I forced a smile onto my face in an effort to look less accusatory.

"My mother." Mr. Medrano placed his hand on his chest. "She has been feeling poorly these last few weeks, and I was visiting her."

"Poorly? What seems to be her complaint?"

"I would imagine the usual aches and pains of old age. She does have rheumatism and does not sleep well." He paused. "Actually, Mrs. Wilcox, would you mind visiting her? I will see to your fee."

He couldn't have said anything more endearing to me. However, something felt odd about his request.

"I should be able to visit in the morning," I said, smiling and rising. "Will that be soon enough?"

"Yes." He leaped to his feet. "That will be wonderful."

"Then please let her know that I shall arrive before ten o'clock."

"Thank you, Mrs. Wilcox."

"And to which address?"

He told me, then accompanied me out of the office and the building and bid me good afternoon. I left and headed back to my rancho, not entirely sure of what to make of the encounter. It was almost as if Mr. Medrano's words had been perfectly pitched to sound utterly blameless and everything I would want to hear from an innocent man, which only served to make me wonder what he was hiding. After all, he sounded as though he were courting me, and I knew better than to trust a man who was courting me.

Chapter Five

It was not unexpected, but I was rather put out when that night turned out to be almost as busy as a Saturday night. Once the votes were tabulated, the celebrations and the fights began. Elena Ortiz, Sebastiano's eldest daughter and already an excellent physician, helped me to no end as we stitched combatants back together. I had to do surgery on one fellow who'd been shot, and it did not help my mood the next morning when I got to the hospital run by the Sisters of Charity to find that the man had died during the night.

I arrived at Mrs. Medrano's adobe, which was not at all far from the social hall, at roughly half-past nine o'clock that morning, and was asked to enter at my first knock on the door. Inside, a weak lantern threw odd shadows on the whitewashed wall and over the room, cluttered with furniture and scraps of fabric.

"Pray forgive me for not getting up to let you in," said the old woman, sitting up on a long fainting couch.

It was almost impossible to see the wizened woman, what with the dim light and the dark blanket that covered her. Her shoulders were wrapped in a small, gaily colored quilt, and she had a work basket next to her.

"It's quite all right," I said. "I understand you are feeling quite poorly."

She sniffed. "Poor enough. But I am old, and of little use to anyone these days."

Her gnarled fingers continued to stitch two bright bits of calico together as she spoke.

"You seem to be keeping yourself busy."

"To what end?" She shook her head. "My stitching used to be so fine, perfectly straight. Now? Look at that!"

She held out the scraps for me to look at. The stitches were mostly even and straight, certainly far better than anything I could do, even though I did make rather neat sutures.

"It looks quite nice."

She snorted. "Not according to my daughter. She says that she can no longer sell our quilts, the stitching is so atrocious. She cuts the pieces for me and lets me work on them so that I can have something to do." She sighed as she took the needlework back from me. "I used to do such nice stitching."

"Given your rheumatism, I am amazed that you can hold a needle at all."

Mrs. Medrano winced and shrugged. "What else is a poor old woman to do? I've nothing else to support me."

"What about your son?"

"He does well enough, I suppose. I have food to eat."

I watched her carefully. "He told me that he spent Saturday night visiting with you."

"Hah! He came here roaring drunk sometime after dinner, then slept it off until close to midnight." The lamplit glinted in her eyes as a blank look came over her face. "My own flesh and blood. They have no use for me whatsoever, and do nothing but complain about what my support costs them. Never mind that I have worked my fingers into uselessness stitching to support them."

"Then let us look at your fingers and the rest of you," I said, quietly.

She let me examine her. She was quite clean, and her white hair had been neatly brushed and pinned. Nor did she have any bed sores, or odd bruises, or any other obvious sign of misuse. That didn't mean she hadn't been, merely that the signs of misuse were not present.

I gave her an unguent that contained both oil of wintergreen and ginger, as well as some willow bark for a tea. I briefly considered giving her some laudanum for her pain, but however efficacious laudanum was for pain, it also created other problems and was often given when it was not needed, especially to women. I decided, instead, to see how Mrs. Medrano would manage with the unguent and the willow bark tea.

I was about to go to the Hewitt home to speak with Mrs. Hewitt, but it so happened that I passed Mrs. Judson's house on the way and thought I might as well call on her. I'd intended to, as colds can grow worse unexpectedly. Fortunately, while she was still in bed, her cold had, happily, improved. She was quite out of temper, however.

"My poor husband!" she sniffed. "He lost the election! He is being very noble about it, but he is cut to the quick, I tell you."

"I can imagine," I said as soothingly as possible.

The loss couldn't have been much of a surprise, but that Mr. Judson believed himself to be held in higher esteem than he was.

"I hate to speak ill of the dead, but it had to have been that wretched Mr. Hewitt's fault." Mrs. Judson coughed again. "Poor Mrs. Hewitt. It will be a wonder if she's able to show her face in the pueblo after what her husband did. And that was after he said something utterly unspeakable to my husband that night."

"Did you hear what he said?"

"Oh, no. But Mrs. Carson made sure that I knew what had happened." Mrs. Judson sniffed. "Of course, one must make allowances for her after her terrible loss last summer. Still, it stung."

"I'm sure it did." I repacked my stethoscope and lozenges in my bag. "Well, Mrs. Judson, you seem on the way to recovery. I would recommend staying in bed and drinking lots of beef tea until your cough is gone."

"And I shall miss that meeting." Mrs. Judson shuddered. "Who knows what dreadful things they'll be saying without me there."

There was not much I could say to that. So, I collected my fee and left the house.

I was again about to go to Mrs. Hewitt's house when Mr. Handley hailed me from his horse. He reined in and quickly dismounted.

"We are well met, Mrs. Wilcox," he announced, doffing his hat. "I have found something out for you."

I offered a smile I did not feel. "And what is that, Mr. Handley?"

"There was a life insurance policy. It was written by Mr. G. Dawes, who, eh, no longer resides in the pueblo." He fidgeted with the horse's reins.

I shook my head. "I do not recall the man."

"You don't?" Mr. Handley's eyes opened wide. "Goodness gracious! They almost lynched the fellow. In any case, Mr. Alisal took over his office. He told me this morning that he'd found a legitimate policy that Mr. Dawes had written for Mr. Hewitt, but it had lapsed for non-payment of the premiums. Mr. Alisal said that he had thought about speaking to Mr. Hewitt about it, but decided if the man had let the policy lapse, he probably was not a good prospect in terms of doing business with him."

"How long ago did all this happen?" I asked.

"Oh…" Mr. Handley's brow creased as he thought. "The war had been over at least a year by the time Dawes left, maybe two years."

Our great nation having seen more than one war by this time, perhaps I should clarify that the war of which Mr. Handley spoke was the Civil War.

"That is very interesting, indeed," I said. "Have you told Mrs. Sutton all this? After all, she is the one who asked, on behalf of Mrs. Hewitt, no less."

Mr. Handley looked somewhat abashed. "Eh, no. I was just on my way to speak to her about it."

There have been those who, in my long life, have been prone to scoff (one of them exceedingly loudly) when I have disavowed any significant interest in gambling. And it is true that I do enjoy a game of chance now and again. That being written, I must point out that I do not bet indiscriminately. So when I write that I would not have placed a wager on Mr. Handley's actual intent to speak to Angelina, you can trust me that it was, indeed, an exceedingly unlikely event.

"Well," I said. "I will let Mrs. Sutton know that you have some information for her. Good day, Mr. Handley."

"The same to you, Mrs. Wilcox." Mr. Handley tipped his hat toward me, then replaced it.

I walked away quickly and made straight for the Hewitt home, which was next to the buggy manufactory. As I approached the buildings, Mr. Ledbetter came out of the house. He was quite a handsome fellow, of medium height and full shoulders. He smiled as he saw me and tipped his dusty hat.

I approached him and noted the tiny bits of sawdust clinging to his jacket, as well as his light brown beard and hair.

"Good morning, Mr. Ledbetter," I said. "How are you today?"

"Well enough." He looked back at the house and sighed. "How is Mrs. Hewitt?"

He shook his head. "She is so very brave."

"She is, indeed." I nodded.

"She says that you are trying to find this terrible villain."

"She did ask me to look into it." I tried not to frown. "Alas, I'm certain that tongues are wagging in the pueblo. Have you heard any ill reports?"

"How do you mean, Mrs. Wilcox?" Mr. Ledbetter looked confused.

"Rumors and the like." I watched him ponder this. "At a time like this, there must be all manner of questions about the manufactory, in particular."

Mr. Ledbetter winced, then sighed. "Of course, there are. But we both know that not much will change from when Mr. Hewitt was still alive."

"To be sure." I sighed and looked around, not sure how to re-phrase the question. "However, that is not, as yet, well known, and there might be some who would be interested."

"Oh, there are." Mr. Ledbetter snorted. "You might say that the buzzards are already gathering."

"I was afraid of that," I said. "Would you mind saying who these buzzards are? To better protect Mrs. Hewitt."

"Of course." Mr. Ledbetter frowned. "You may have already heard that Mr. Medrano has been wanting the buggy manufactory."

"I have. Is there anyone else?" I watched him carefully.

"Not I. I can assure you of that!" He shifted, uncomfortable.

"I did not think otherwise." I bit my lip. "Are there rumors that you do?"

"There are." Mr. Ledbetter pressed his lips together. "And others."

"Well," I said as soothingly as I could. "People will make the most unbecoming assumptions, and it can't be helped."

"It will be, if I have anything to say about it." Mr. Ledbetter's eyes flashed. "There are those who are trying to impugn my honor and not only mine, but Mrs. Hewitt's as well. I swear I will not let their vile epithets go unanswered!"

"I see." I shook my head. "It's a good thing that Mrs. Hewitt has you to stand up for her. However, I do not believe that she would want to you to go so far as to put yourself in need of my services. Nor do I. So, please be careful."

From there, I went to the door of the house and Mrs. Hewitt had me admitted immediately. She sat in her front parlor, her weeds thrown back from her face.

"Mrs. Wilcox, it is so good of you to come in my hour of need." Her face looked ashen, and her eyes remained very red from weeping.

"I am happy to do so."

She bade me sit on the sofa next to her chair. Both were covered in dark green velvet, but the sofa was also intricately carved on top. Tea and biscuits were quickly served by a young woman with dark, glossy hair and brown eyes.

"I saw you speaking with Mr. Ledbetter just now," she said, then smiled weakly. "He has been such a prop these past two days. These past few years. I do not know how we could have managed without him."

"So, you were friendly with him?"

Mrs. Hewitt sat up straight and glared at me.

"I most certainly was not!"

"Oh, dear!" I gasped. "I did not intend to imply anything but that you and your husband considered Mr. Ledbetter a friend. My apologies."

"No!" Mrs. Hewitt ducked her head, weeping copiously. "It is I who owes you an apology. Of course, you would not think anything so terrible, let alone ask me."

"I suppose I could have been more careful in my language." I reached over and patted her hand. "But was there a perfectly circumspect friendship?"

Mrs. Hewitt dabbed at her eyes, then chuckled softly. "Oh, no. Mr. Ledbetter is our foreman and an employee. My Thomas discouraged that kind of fraternization, possibly to forestall the rumor I feared you were implying."

"I do hope that you have not had to listen to any of that nonsense."

"One is never completely spared of that." Mrs. Hewitt snorted. "As we both know well. But, alas, what I have heard has not been very useful."

"Useful?" I looked at her, surprised. "How do you mean?"

"In terms of finding Thomas' killer, of course." A soft sob escaped her, but she quickly recovered herself. "He had his faults, without question. But he was kind, even when he was in his cups."

"That, I'm afraid, is the precise difficulty we're having." I took a sip of my tea and sighed. "He seemed largely inoffensive. But he must have angered somebody greatly that he was killed so."

"But who?"

I set my tea down on the table next to me. "Mrs. Hewitt, I would not for the world have you think that I suppose you to have done anything that is not blameless. However, there is one possible rumor that concerns me, and we must discuss it so that I may turn it away with as much certainty as possible."

Mrs. Hewitt looked straight ahead. "They're saying that I had him killed."

"Not yet." I sighed deeply. "But given what a trial Mr. Hewitt could be, I do not doubt that someone is considering it. Furthermore, there is my own bitter experience. When Mr. Wilcox was killed, there were those who joked that I had seen to its occurrence."

"But your Mr. Wilcox was struck by lightening." Mrs. Hewitt blinked. "And you were in church at the time. I remember. You were sitting next to me."

"I know. But that didn't stop the rumor. After all, what was my husband doing riding a horse on Sunday?"

"I must confess, I did wonder about that." Mrs. Hewitt shook her head. "I never saw him in church. But, still…"

"You had every reason to wonder." I picked up my teacup and looked sadly at it. "After all, what well-intentioned Christian man would go riding on the Sabbath except to take his wife to church?" I looked at her. "The reality was that Mr. Wilcox was anything but well-intentioned. Not to be unduly shocking, but he was riding from an illicit union with a married woman."

Mrs. Hewitt's eyes opened wide, and she gasped. "How terrible! I mean, after all, one comes to accept the occasional dalliance with the maid or at a house of ill-repute. But a married woman! How hideous. Poor Mrs. Wilcox! What a trial."

"My trial was short-lived," I said, trying not to smile. "And I have managed quite nicely since then."

"Well, I never in my life…" Mrs. Hewitt shook her head, then swallowed. "Pray forgive me if I am intruding, but why didn't you return to your home and family?"

"I…" I hesitated. "I don't entirely know. I wasn't sure how I would get home and…" I looked away, then shrugged. "I suppose I could have found a way. But I was not sure of my reception at home. You see, my father had found out about my medical degree and was quite upset. He threatened to put me out on the streets unless I did the decent thing and promptly marry Albert Wilcox, who was headed here to Los Angeles to see about furthering his father's business interests. My father has since informed me that he would welcome me back and allow me to practice medicine. But by the time he did, I had established myself here as a doctor." I winced. "And, in truth, it would be very difficult to practice at home. There is no shortage of physicians in Boston."

"Boston?"

"Where I am from."

"Oh, Mrs. Wilcox." Mrs. Hewitt sniffed and blinked her eyes. "I am honored that you have opened your heart to me."

"You have opened your heart to me many times." I smiled.

"Please. Call me Theodora."

"Thank you, Theodora. You must call me Maddie."

"Dear Maddie. What we have both gone through." Theodora dabbed at her eyes again. "Now, what were we discussing…? Oh, dear. That possible rumor." She sniffed. "Well, I can promise you that I would have never done anything to hurt my darling Thomas. Never. And besides, to what end would I have taken his life?" She began weeping again. "As you had pointed out, I was about to lose him, anyway."

"I know, dearest." I paused as she got control of herself again. "Could there be somebody who wishes to take over the manufactory?"

"That dreadful Mr. Medrano seems to think he should be the only buggy maker in town." Theodora wiped her eyes. "But what good would killing my Thomas do him? I still have daughters to raise. Why would I let go of my husband's business?"

"I suppose the assumption is that you'll remarry."

Theodora snorted. "I doubt it."

"Have you filed for the probate yet?" I asked. "If someone claims a debt against your husband's estate, that might give us someone we can look at."

"I was going to contact our attorney later today. Thank you for reminding me that I need to do so."

The maid appeared and handed Theodora a note. She looked at it and shook her head.

"Please thank him and tell him that I am not in and do not expect to be receiving for some time yet," Theodora told the maid. Then she turned to me and noted my raised eyebrows. "Mr. Jessup. He and Mr. Wills have been sending me notes, inquiring as to my well being." She sighed again. "Mr. Jessup was quite the prop during the funeral. But now I would just as soon be left alone."

"One often does at a time like this." I reached over and patted her hands.

I left shortly after, feeling rather unquiet in spirit. I did appreciate the new intimacy I had with Theodora, and it was well-rewarded over the years. However, I could not fathom why I was so unsettled.

I sighed as I made my way onto the Calle Principal, although at that time, many were starting to call it Main Street. In the distance, the mountains to the north of our valley stood dark green and light brown, with even darker spots under where several gray and white clouds floated against the brilliant blue sky. As I passed Harris & Jacoby's notions and bookstore, I saw Mr. Jacoby arranging a number of dolls around several prayer books, family bibles and other Christmas decorations.

Suddenly, I knew the root of my disquiet. I had no fondness for the pueblo. As I have often noted, it was remote and utterly lacking in cultural refinement, which might not have been so bad but that the streets were infested with violence. The population was largely made up of transient men who, with few ties to the community and little entertainment to be had beyond the many saloons and houses of ill repute, were frequently brawling and causing all manner of trouble.

True, I had made a good life for myself here and could do many things that as a woman in Boston I would not be able to do, even as a woman of property. More to the point, I had formed fast friendships not only with the members of my household on Rancho de Las Flores, but with Angelina, Regina, and several others. Regina, in particular, often worried that I would abandon the pueblo to go home to Boston.

However, around Christmas time, I began to miss my home city more keenly than normal. I know I am in the minority in my opinion, but I loved that first snowfall of the winter. I loved sleigh rides, and ice skating, and warm grog next to a roaring fire. But most of all, I missed my two sisters at that time of year.

I had told Theodora the truth about how I had come to Los Angeles, and about why I had stayed. But I did not tell her the full truth. There was another reason I had not strayed far from the pueblo, one I did not wish to acknowledge, even to myself.

Chapter Six

I made it back to the rancho in good time for lunch, which made Olivia exceedingly happy. She'd prepared an estafado, or stew, with mutton, for the previous Sunday's dinner, but had reserved enough to give us all lunch that day, which was a treat, indeed, given that the estafado generally tasted even better on the second or third day after it had been made.

I also had an invitation to tea with Mrs. Downey that afternoon. I sent my acceptance with Enrique and Magdalena's second youngest, Jaime, who was twelve at the time. Soon after eating, I went to get dressed for tea. I had a lovely dark green figured cotton tea dress and decided to wear that. Not only was it appropriate for a tea with the wife of our former governor, it wouldn't show stains if I were to be called away to see a patient. I walked to the Downey home and arrived in plenty of good time.

Mrs. John G. Downey was of average height, with a round figure, black hair and dark eyes, as befitted a woman of Mexican extraction. She was quite a pleasant woman, and very bright. She was also, by virtue of her husband's status in the pueblo, one of the more important members of our society, but nonetheless, was one of those rare creatures who has considerable status, but acted as if everyone else had the same. We were not bosom friends, but we were friendly and I was happy to go to tea.

Her maid, Mrs. Dunbar, admitted me to the front parlor. Mrs. Dunbar was of medium height, and plump, with dark eyes and hair. Mrs. Downey swept in, smiling, and greeted me warmly. Mrs. Dunbar appeared a moment later with tea and biscuits with cactus jelly, which she placed on a table between the ochre velvet sofa and a wine-colored chair. Mrs. Downey had me sit on the sofa and settled herself on the chair.

"Consuela," Mrs. Downey said as the maid turned to go. "Please stay. I'd like you to tell Mrs. Wilcox what you told me yesterday." Mrs. Downey turned to me. "I've heard that you are looking for the villain that killed Mr. Hewitt, and this might help."

Mrs. Dunbar looked around the room nervously, then sighed.

"It wasn't much," she said. "Mrs. Downey had me help with getting the food served at the party on Saturday. Others were there to clean up. So once all the food had been served, Mrs. Downey said I could go home."

"Consuela is a widow with a perfectly lovely little girl," Mrs. Downey said, pouring our tea.

"She stays with my landlady when I must work late." Mrs. Dunbar took my cup and handed it to me. "But Mrs. Downey lets me bring her here during the day."

"That's very kind of you, Mrs. Downey," I said.

Mrs. Downey shrugged and smiled. "As long as the governor is not around, it's not a problem. And it makes life easier for Consuela."

"So, what happened that night?" I asked.

Mrs. Dunbar took a deep breath. "It was just after midnight. I had gotten my cloak and had just left through the back door of the hall when I heard the gunshots go off. I hid up against the wall and someone ran past me into the hall. I didn't see who. I just heard the footsteps. But when I turned onto the street, I tripped over something. It was a very large carriage robe. I brought it home so that I could find out who owned it and asked Mrs. Downey about it yesterday afternoon."

"I see." I nibbled on a biscuit as I thought. "Mrs. Downey, do you know whose it was?"

"I'm afraid I don't. It could be anyone's." Mrs. Downey smiled at her maid. "Consuela, would you please fetch the robe?"

"Yes, ma'am." Mrs. Dunbar hurried from the room.

"Did you see anything of note that night?" I asked Mrs. Downey.

She frowned and sipped her tea. "Just Mrs. Glassell screaming that something terrible had happened, and that we were all going to be killed if this reckless gunfire was not stopped. She had come in through the back door less than a minute after the shots were fired. She even bumped into Mr. Jessup."

"Why was Mrs. Glassell coming from the back?"

Mrs. Downey flushed, then lowered her voice. "There's a necessary back there."

"Oh. Of course."

Mrs. Dunbar returned with the brightly striped carriage robe. It was big enough to have covered two of Mrs. Glassell's plump figure and quite heavy, being made of wool.

"I do believe I know whose this is," I said, getting up. "Mrs. Downey, I'd love to stay, but I think I'd best return it to its rightful owner right away."

"Oh, please." Mrs. Downey rose as well. "And please let me know how everything falls out."

"I will do my best," I said warmly.

It was not far to Mrs. Glassell's house, so I walked there, somehow managing not to get tangled up in the heavy robe. I had no doubt that it could easily have been the flapping cloak that I had seen shortly after poor Mr. Hewitt had so brutally met his end.

Fortunately, Mr. Gluck saw me coming and ran over to help me.

"This is it!" he gasped, overflowing with joy. "I'm saved!"

"I'm glad," I said, happily handing the robe over. "But I must ask a favor of you. Please make sure you keep an eye on it. I do not want it to go missing again, as it might be important in another matter."

"Of course, Mrs. Wilcox."

"Now, I think I will pay a call on your mistress."

Mr. Gluck shrugged and returned to the carriage house. I girded my loins, so to speak, as I was afraid, given that the robe belonged to Mrs. Glassell, she might have been the one to leave it on the street in front of the social hall.

I went to the front door of the house and knocked and again heard Mrs. Glassell loudly proclaim to her maid that she was not at home. There was little I could do about that, however, so I made my way back to the center of the pueblo.

As I passed Mr. Mahoney's saloon, I thought I might ask him a few questions. He had not been at the party at the social hall, not being of that part of society. However, the men of society did prefer his saloon, and I wanted to know if the grizzled saloon keeper had heard anything.

I went around to the back of the saloon, we women being denied entrance to such places. Let me amend that. Only certain types of women were admitted into saloons, and Mr. Mahoney adamantly refused entry to such. If I was admitted to the back of the place, it was because I sold Mr. Mahoney a goodly portion of my angelica, not to mention other wines that I made.

His daughter Alice showed me through the busy kitchen into the cluttered office. Mr. Mahoney sat on an empty whiskey crate and glared at the mountain of papers on his desk. He was a rangy fellow, with dark, graying hair and indifferently kept beard, and broad shoulders. Blinking his bright blue eyes, he looked up at me and smiled.

"Mrs. Wilcox, how good to see you," he said with the slight lilt of the Irish.

He leaped to his feet and pulled another pile of papers from the one chair in the tiny room. Sighing, he looked around for a place to set the papers while I balanced myself on the rickety chair.

"I should have your payment right here," he said, placing the papers in a precarious spot on the edge of his desk, then shifting some others to find something. "If I can find that invoice."

"I was not aware that you owed me anything," I said, trying not to laugh.

He paused and blinked. "I do believe you are right. And I am profoundly glad that you are one of my more honest suppliers." He frowned. "But why, then, are you here?"

I sighed. "It is regarding poor Mr. Hewitt's murder. I am hoping you have heard some talk about the matter that might help me find the killer."

"Ah." He smiled. "I should have known. Sadly, I have not heard much."

"I was afraid of that. He seemed quite the mild and amiable fellow."

"He was, indeed. That's the puzzle of it, it is." Mr. Mahoney settled himself on his crate. "Why would anybody want to hurt the poor man? I suppose there was the occasional bad deal, mostly due to his terrible memory. But most around here knew about it and were careful to do their business with Mr. Ledbetter."

"I don't doubt." I shifted, trying to keep my balance. "However, Mrs. Judson was quite annoyed with him. Apparently, Mr. Hewitt had said something rather dreadful to Mr. Judson."

Mr. Mahoney laughed. "From what I've heard, it wasn't anything that everyone else wasn't already saying. Mr. Hewitt simply said it to Mr. Judson's face."

"But what did he say?"

"Eh..." Mr. Mahoney shifted. "Nothing a lady should hear. Mr. Judson, however, was of the opinion that the comment cost him the election and said as much last night."

"And if everyone else was saying the same behind Mr. Judson's back, it probably did cost him the election. However, that was not Mr. Hewitt's fault."

"No. I would say not." Mr. Mahoney suddenly frowned. "Pray forgive me for changing the subject, but I do need another barrel of your claret. It's quite popular this time of year, and at least three different gentlemen have asked to host parties here in the coming weeks."

"Certainly. I shall have Sebastiano bring it to you."

I got up, thanked Mr. Mahoney for the order, then left.

I spent the rest of the day checking on patients. One, whose arm I'd set the week before, was doing quite nicely. Another had tuberculosis, or phthisis pulmonaria, as we called it in those days. Regrettably, there wasn't much to be done there, beyond keeping the poor fellow comfortable as he wasted away. The rest had various colds and catarrhs, which were quite common at that time of year, although two of them may have actually had influenza. But there was, fortunately, blessedly little pneumonia, or had been.

I made it home just in time for supper, which we ate in the big barracks building where everyone lived except myself, Sebastiano and Enrique, and their immediate families. I had my own adobe, which also housed the sick room and Marisol. Sebastiano had an adobe for himself, Olivia, and their five children (two of whom were actually adults), as did Enrique, Magdalena, and their six children.

We had quite a large group on the rancho. Rodolfo Sanchez and his wife, Anita, did not have any children, much to Anita's constant sorrow. Still, Anita had taken over the children's schooling, and cared for the babes that were too young to be educated. Hernan Mendoza was the other senior hand, and he was married to Maria, who helped Magdalena with the housekeeping. Hernan and Maria had four children, with the youngest, a girl, being barely five months old.

Our other five hands were not married as of yet. Pascual and Emilio Mendoza were brothers and cousins of Hernan. It was generally held among the group that Pascual had acquired a deep affection for Marisol, which was rather odd in that Marisol did not show the least sign of interest in Pascual. The Villa brothers, Manuel and Roberto, were not much older than Ramon Ortiz, although they were Enrique and Sebastiano's cousins, as was Angel Ortiz, who was also in his early twenties.

It was a pleasant meal with plenty of chatter and good food. As soon as we were all done eating, Anita called the eight children still of school age to the schoolroom, and Anita and I listened to their lessons from the day. Once the children were dismissed, Anita told me about her plans for the next day's schooling, which would help me should one or more of them accompany me on my rounds. Sebastiano's middle daughter, Elena, who was seventeen, usually did when she wasn't studying various medical texts. She was already almost better than I was when it came to delivering babies.

After seeing to the children and Anita, I retired to my study to write my notes in my journal, then indulged in a novel for an hour or so, until it was time for bed.

In the morning, Sebastiano, Enrique, and I were breaking our fast in the barracks and debating which small barrel of claret to send to Mr. Mahoney, when young Jane Hewitt was announced. She was about fifteen with her mother's fair coloring, although her blonde curls had been blown all about her head and her cheeks were flushed as if she'd run all the way to the rancho.

"Mrs. Wilcox," she gasped. "Mama asked me to come for you."

"Who's ill?" I asked, getting up from the table.

"No. We're all well. It's just that…" The young almost woman frowned, trying to remember the exact message. "Mama begs your pardon, but we had a visitor yesterday afternoon who upset her very much, and she would like the… the wisdom of your council." Jane blinked hard and swallowed. "She's quite beside herself."

"There, there, child," I said with a smile. "I'll come right now, if you'll but wait a moment while I fetch my bag."

Enrique and Sebastiano looked at each other and shook their heads.

"It looks like rain," Sebastiano said, getting up and hurrying out. "I'll get the buggy hitched."

"I'll have Armando drive," Enrique called after him.

"Isn't Armando at his job today?" I asked.

"Today is his day off," Enrique said. "Or he does not start until late this afternoon. I don't know which. His mother did not say, just that he would not get up right away." He sighed. "You know how these young boys are."

I chuckled in spite of myself. "I am afraid so. But will he be ready in the next few minutes?"

"He will if he doesn't want me to take a strap to him."

Enrique glared as he strode off to deal with his son. He was usually quite gentle with his children, to the point of almost being indulgent. However, there is something about older boys on the cusp of manhood that makes even the mildest of parents ready to resort to the lash. Ramon had not been any easier to deal with.

Nonetheless, when I emerged from my adobe with my leather bag slung crosswise across my person and Jane Hewitt at my side, Armando sat on the driver's seat of the buggy, blinking and yawning, but ready to go. The sky had gone a dark, flat gray that usually portended rain, and I very much hoped it would. We hadn't had any rain for months, and the pueblo's farms and ranchos sorely needed it.

We arrived in good time at the Hewitt home, and Jane went ahead of me into the whitewashed clapboard house. I asked Armando to put the top up on the buggy just in case the skies finally opened.

Inside, Theodora paced in her front parlor, wringing her hands. Jane's grandmother appeared with both Jane and her younger sisters in hand. It looked as though Jane had run a hairbrush through her curls, as they were far more orderly than they'd been.

"I'm taking the girls to school," Mrs. Perry announced.

And, indeed, the two older ones each had books and a slate strapped together in one hand and a lunch pail in the other.

"Thank you, Mother," Theodora said rather tonelessly.

We waited until the girls and their grandmother had left.

"I was told you had an unpleasant visitor yesterday?" I said when the two of us were alone.

Theodora gulped and swallowed back a sob. "Oh, dear. I am such a dreadful mess! I am not myself at all."

"It is to be expected," I said softly. "You have just suffered quite a loss."

"I have always prided myself on my strength. On my fortitude!" Theodora snapped.

And, indeed, she could be quite fierce when aroused.

"And you are still very strong. But even the strongest of us feel overwrought when we are beset with the worst."

Theodora took a deep breath and closed her eyes. "You are right. Please, sit down. Would you like some tea?"

"No, thank you. I'm quite all right as I am." I touched her hands. "Now, unburden yourself to me."

I settled onto the sofa as she sank into the nearby chair.

"Mr. Lowman," Theodora said. "He came by the manufactory yesterday afternoon. I was in and agreed to see him. He owns a livery stable. Over on Alameda Street."

I thought for a second. "Yes. I believe I have seen it."

"I would not have admitted him, but he is a good customer and needs new buggies with some regularity."

"I can imagine."

"He told me that he had purchased four buggies from Thomas sometime in September, but they have not been delivered. And Thomas promised that they would be before Thanksgiving!"

My eyes opened wide. "Am I to gather that you had no idea of this transaction?"

"None whatsoever. Neither has Mr. Ledbetter. The deal must have been struck in some saloon or other. It is certainly not the first time this has happened." Theodora pulled her handkerchief from her sleeve and worried it.

I couldn't help frowning. "And I was told yesterday that most men in the pueblo knew to conduct business with Mr. Ledbetter, thanks to Mr. Hewitt's problems with remembering things."

Theodora nodded. "They do. Which is why I cannot help but wonder if Mr. Lowman is trying to take advantage of me. He was quite forceful yesterday. I was afraid that he might strike me."

"Good Heavens!" I sat back in alarm. "What happened after that?"

"I sent him on his way, of course." Mrs. Hewitt blinked. "But he promised to return and keep returning until he got his buggies."

I thought. "Surely there must be some accounting somewhere that would note the receipt of funds for the buggies."

"I cannot find any extra funds." Theodora grew more agitated. "If Mr. Lowman gave Thomas any money, Thomas probably kept it and drank it up shortly thereafter." She blinked. "I seem to remember that he'd been drinking more that month and wondered at how he'd gotten the money."

"Oh, dear." I frowned. "Did Mr. Lowman say how much money he'd given Mr. Hewitt?"

"A hundred dollars, at least. That would be all we'd need to start the job."

"What other business do you have pending?"

"I'm not sure, but it may be that we are supposed to build the new fire truck. I wrote up a plan for the Common Council, and to the best of my knowledge, it was approved." Theodora shook her head. "I believe there are one or two other orders that are being worked on, but everything regarding the business is in the office at present, and I haven't been there since Saturday."

"Hm." I thought for a moment. "While I suspect it is likely that the matter fell out as you have supposed, it would be good for you to see if you can find any record of the payment from Mr. Lowman. Would you mind if I called on Mr. Lowman in the meantime?"

"Oh, would you!" Theodora gasped, then blinked again. "I would be ever so grateful. But I must warn you. He is utterly odious." She wrinkled her nose. "And odorous,

I might add. His breath smells as if he eats nothing but garlic."

I shuddered. "I doubt he does, but there are a lot of reasons why someone's breath is bad smelling." I got up. "I will make my way to his livery stable, then. But, please, go over your business records. It is possible that Mr. Lowman's is not the only anomaly and whichever one there is, that might point us to the killer."

Theodora sniffed. "You're right. Thank you again, Maddie. From the bottom of my heart. It's been bad enough seeing Mr. Wills on the street outside every day, and now Mr. Lowman." She shuddered. "All I want is to be left alone!"

I left quickly and made my way to the livery stable.

I could not recall having done business with Mr. Lowman, or any other livery stable for that matter. Let me amend that. If I had done business with a livery stable, someone else had transacted that business on my behalf. As I approached the old adobe barn and house, I began to feel grateful that I had a couple men in my household who could be expected to do business with Mr. Lowman for me.

I abhor the notion that women should be relegated to home and hearth, that our delicate sensibilities are not up to the harsher aspects of the world. As I have noted many times before, we women were subject to the stench of all sorts of noxious substances, and as wives and mothers dealt with them without complaint or much notice. As a physician, I dealt with still more. Nor was I at all unaware of what a stable smells like. I had one on my rancho, and while horses are not the most pleasantly fragrant of beasts, my horse and two mules did not reek.

As such, when I write that the stench of Mr. Lowman's livery stable was almost unendurable, you may be assured that it was that and more. I could not imagine how the man did business, as the smell indicated to me that he did not treat his beasts well, and yet, the stable was considered prosperous. As Theodora had warned me, the man was quite odoriferous as well, with several gaps in his teeth (which may have explained his terrible breath). He was a large, burly fellow, with dark hair, an unkempt beard, and an angry scowl on his face.

"Who are you?" he demanded of me as I stood in the large doorway to the stable.

I stepped back, startled by the abrupt address. "My name is Mrs. Wilcox."

"Oh. Yeah. You're that lady doctor who keeps making trouble for everyone."

I blinked. "I like to think that the only people I make trouble for are those who have made considerably worse trouble for others."

Mr. Lowman grunted. "What do you want?"

"I have been given to understand that you had a complaint against Mr. Hewitt, who was murdered this past Saturday."

"He owed me four buggies!" Mr. Lowman roared. "We shook on the deal."

I somehow managed to hold my ground. "Did you give him any money for them?"

"What kind of an idiot do you think I am? I'm not paying for work until it's done!"

"Forgive me, Mr. Lowman," I said, working very hard to smile at him. "I do believe that it is customary to offer a deposit toward such work at the time the deal is struck.

That way, the manufacturer is not burdened with buggies that he might not sell, and the buyer does not lose the cost of the buggies should the manufacturer not live up to his word."

"Oh, that." Mr. Lowman hemmed and hawed. "Yeah. I gave him a deposit. Like as not, he drank it up."

I did not want to suggest that he was quite probably right.

"Do you have a receipt?" I asked instead.

"Are you calling me a liar?" He advanced toward me, his eyes blazing.

I stepped back. "No, sir. I have every reason to believe that you are perfectly honorable. But we both know that not everyone is, and that there are those who would be happy to take gross advantage of a poor, grieving, newly made widow. It is out of tender concern for her welfare and that of her children that I asked."

Mr. Lowman shuffled uncomfortably, and it was gratifying to see that the man had some semblance of a conscience.

"I'll find the receipt," he finally grumbled. He looked at me. "I just want my buggies, is all. I need them and I don't like getting skinned by that Medrano fellow." Mr. Lowman snorted. "If you want to make trouble for somebody, why don't you make it for him? Like as not, he probably shot old Hewitt."

"And why do you say that?" I smiled again, feeling the strain of doing so.

"He likes shooting, and he hated old Hewitt." Mr. Lowman shrugged.

"Well, I will consider that, Mr. Lowman." I paused. "And just to be certain that you did not, can you tell me where you were Saturday night?"

"Here!" he snapped. "Where else?"

"Of course, Mr. Lowman."

All too eager to be away, I hurried off, fairly certain that Mr. Lowman had lied to me not only about the deposit, but about his whereabouts the night Mr. Hewitt was killed.

Chapter Seven

The promise of rain earlier that morning soon gave way to a shining sun without a drop fallen. Armando drove me to call on two of my patients, then back to the rancho for lunch. I spent the rest of that afternoon working on various chores about the place and mulling over what I had heard from Mr. Lowman.

The next morning, I had formulated something of a plan. I had Rodolfo saddle up Daisy to allow for the possibility that something might take me further afield than the main part of the pueblo. I could but hope.

For all there is a certain sameness to the weather in our fair region, it can be surprisingly fickle. It had seemed like rain was in the offing the day before, but that morning had dawned clear, with huge fluffy clouds scudding across the brilliant blue sky. There was a decided breeze, and I was grateful for my dark green linen and wool riding habit. It was quite cunning, as well as relatively warm, with velvet ruching on the bodice and velvet ruffles with satin ribbon on the bustle.

I called on Mrs. Medrano first. Her son, Mr. Medrano, admitted me to the dim room. His mother was still on the sofa, but had a different collection of quilts covering her.

"And how are you feeling today?" I asked her. "Did the unguent help?"

"To what end?" she grumbled. "I am left alone to keep myself company. My children have no use for me."

"And yet your son is standing right here."

"Bah!" The old woman closed her eyes. "He has no use for me. He only comes here when he gets drunk."

"Mama," Mr. Medrano said sadly. "You know I do not drink to excess."

"You are as bad as your father!"

Mr. Medrano sighed as I continued my examination. Again, Mrs. Medrano's hair was neatly combed and pinned. Her clothes were clean. But the jar of unguent was mostly full.

"How often are you using your unguent?" I asked.

"I cannot open the jar and my children will not open it for me," she said as her son rolled his eyes.

"Mama, I would like to speak with Mrs. Wilcox, then I will come and rub your hands."

Mrs. Medrano sniffed. I excused myself and followed Mr. Medrano out of the adobe.

"She is not telling the truth," he said.

"I'm afraid I believe that she is," I said.

"It is not! I swear!" Mr. Medrano's eyes grew wide, and he trembled with rage.

I held up my forefinger. "Perhaps I was not as clear as I could have been. She is telling what she believes to be the truth. That is the difficulty. It happens quite frequently, and it is very unsettling when it does. Alas, there is little to be done about it."

"I am not mistreating my mother!" Mr. Medrano snapped.

"I did not say that you are." I sighed. "That is the difficulty. Your mother believes that you do not pay her enough attention. Now, it is entirely possible that she would continue to say you were not, even if you were here every minute of every day. However, I am concerned that she has not used any of the unguent I gave her to ease her pain."

Mr. Medrano put his hand over his heart. "Mrs. Wilcox, I had no idea what that jar was for. She didn't tell me." He sighed. "She likes it when I rub her hands. But an unguent? That should be very helpful, I would think."

"It should be," I said. "And I also left some willow bark tea for her pain. It's quite easy to brew, and very mild. Just be aware that it has a very nasty taste, so adding it to some spirits might help. It will not do her much good if she does not drink it."

"To be sure." Mr. Medrano smiled, but there was no real warmth in it. "Mrs. Wilcox, you are an angel of mercy. Thank you."

He turned to go.

"Oh, Mr. Medrano, there is also the matter of my fee...?" I held out my hand.

"Oh! Of course!" He dug through his various pockets and pulled out a dollar coin.

"Thank you," I said, more happily than I felt. I debated for a moment, then decided to ask a question that had nagged at me from the night before. "I have been told that you like shooting."

"Who doesn't?" Mr. Medrano smiled and held out his hands. Then he stopped. "Is this about poor Mr. Hewitt? Of course it is, and you must ask. He was shot, after all. In fact, I was amazed that the man hit his target, it was so dark out. I barely saw anything, but what I told you on Monday."

"I do appreciate your candor, Mr. Medrano," I said. "Thank you and I must bid you good day."

I went over to Daisy and Mr. Medrano had the decency to help me onto my mount. From there, I headed toward the Calle Principal.

It is a good thing that I am a solid horsewoman. I heard the thunder of hooves first, then the wild neighing of frightened horses. I reined Daisy in just in time to keep her from rearing as a team of four horses pulling a wagon charged across our path. Three men, each riding a horse, chased after the rampaging team, struggling to get ahead of it.

Fearing the worst, I kicked Daisy into a trot and rode after the runaways and the men trying to subdue them. Runaway horses were not an uncommon occurrence in the pueblo, and such events often meant injuries or worse. Fortunately, the men were able to catch and subdue the team near the edge of the pueblo, and it looked as though the wagon was empty.

"Was anybody injured?" I asked as I rode up to the group.

"Oh, it's you, Mrs. Wilcox," called Mr. Navarro, the handsome policeman who had stolen my previous maid from my employ by marrying her the previous September. "The teamster got knocked over when the team bolted."

He said something to his fellows, then detached himself and his horse from the others and rode at a walk toward me. He was a finely turned out young man with dark, merry eyes, and black hair and beard. My Juanita was hardly the only woman in the pueblo who had been taken with him.

"I'll take you to him," Mr. Navarro said, easing his horse into a trot. "I have to find out how this happened, anyway."

The teamster, a large man with dark hair and beard, looked a little unsteady as he dusted off his battered suit and cursed loudly. He choked as he saw me dismounting nearby.

"My— My apologies, ma'am!" he yelped, reaching up to get his hat only to find that it was not on his head.

As he choked on the curse that sprang to his lips, I looked around at the ground and found a black, dusty felt hat that had seen better days a considerable time before.

I scooped it up and presented it to him. "There, there, sir. You have been sorely tried, and while I can't say that I like such language, it is nothing that I haven't heard before. Now. Are you hurt?"

"Mostly just my pride, ma'am." He coughed and blinked.

"Don't worry, Sam Pickens," Mr. Navarro said with a chuckle behind me. "This is Mrs. Wilcox, the lady doctor."

"Oh!" Mr. Pickens flushed a deep red.

"Did you hit your head when you fell?" I asked.

He backed away quickly. "I'm fine, ma'am. I'm fine!"

I decided that he did not look all that seriously injured and sighed.

"Very well, then." I looked at him a little severely. "If your head starts aching or you start to feel sick to your stomach or worse, I want you to send for me or Dr. Skillen at once. Head injuries can be worse than they seem at first."

"I'll do that, ma'am." Mr. Pickens slapped his hat against his leg to get the dust off of it.

"All right, Mr. Pickens," Mr. Navarro said. "What happened?"

"Blamed if I know." Mr. Pickens busied himself with trying to re-shape the battered felt of his hat. "I had just unloaded the wagon and was going to get on the box when the horses spooked and took off."

I did not bother to ask what had spooked the horses, as it was unlikely that I would get an answer. Being nervous creatures, even the steadiest of horses will run at the least cause.

"Whose wagon was it?" Mr. Navarro asked.

"One of Mr. Jessup's," Mr. Pickens replied, finally setting his hat on his head. "I was real surprised when the horses bolted. His horses are steadier than most. He takes them out hunting, and they get used to everything, especially gunshots."

My eyebrows rose. "Mr. Jessup likes shooting?"

"Oh, yeah," Mr. Pickens said with a grin. "He's a real crack shot. He takes me and the boys out hunting sometimes and we always know there's going to be a feast afterward. He always bags something. He can nail a rabbit in full run with a pistol."

"That's very interesting," I said. "Well, I am afraid that I must be on my way back to my rancho and lunch or my cook will be very displeased with me. Mr. Navarro, will you please offer Mrs. Navarro my best regards?"

"I will surely do so." He grinned merrily and helped me mount Daisy.

Both men tipped their hats, and I rode off.

Olivia had soup and bread ready, even though I was early for lunch. However, I had barely finished eating when I was called to deliver Señora Perez' latest child. I summoned Elena, and it was a good thing I did. Fortunately, both the mother and the baby, a very large but lovely girl, survived the ordeal, but it was a difficult delivery and took all afternoon and almost into the evening.

Olivia was not happy that both Elena and I were late for our dinners, although she did concede that we couldn't have abandoned a mother in the worst part of her labor. Still, she scolded both of us as we ate, especially as I had to leave shortly after to attend the meeting to establish a new library in the pueblo.

Sadly, it was as I expected in that many of the men made grand speeches and a committee was formed, which no doubt would mean there would be some showing off in terms of the donations, but the women would have to do most of the fundraising. And, as it turned out, that is exactly what happened over the course of the next several months.

I attempted to speak to Mrs. Glassell, but she scurried away before I could. So I went home and retreated to my study to write up my notes and consider the two notes I had received, one from Regina and one from Angelina.

Regina's note made me chuckle, in spite of her dreadful language. She did not have much to offer, but that Mr. Hewitt had loudly called Mr. Judson a pompous beast of burden the night of the party. But then went on to write that while almost no one said the same to the banker's face, most of the men referred to him that way behind his back. She also mentioned that while she hadn't seen much of Mr. Jessup, what she had seen had not impressed her.

"He seems quite taken with himself, especially with his ability to shoot," Regina wrote. "Which may or may not be significant. As we noted on Sunday, expertise with a gun is not an uncommon quality here in the pueblo, among the women as well as the men."

I turned to Angelina's note. Her comments were that no one seemed to know about Mr. Charles Hewitt, but that she would try to find out more. She also confirmed what Mr. Handley had told me about the insurance policy.

"I still think it's odd that Mrs. Hewitt knew nothing of it," Angelina wrote. "Even in her grief, she seems quite sensible, even seeing to Mr. Sutton's fees without me having to ask."

I sighed as I was forced to agree with Angelina. I desperately hoped that my newfound intimacy with Theodora was not blinding me to her possible guilt. I had been so blinded before and did not wish to repeat that particular mistake.

The next morning, in between checking on Mrs. Perez and her new daughter, and seeing another fellow who had broken his leg the week before, I tried to visit Mrs. Glassell. I was told that she was visiting Mrs. Carson, which I did not doubt. However, I also did not want Mrs. Carson present for the conference I wished to have with Mrs. Glassell. As I finished with the broken leg, I resolved to see Mrs. Glassell again. I was again on foot and saw the worthy lady walking toward her home. Alas, she saw me and hurried away in another direction. I chose not to follow her, but wondered a great deal at why she would be so assiduously avoiding me, and could not help but think about the abandoned carriage robe that Mrs. Dunbar had found.

I next visited Mrs. Judson, whose cold was much better, even though the cough remained stubborn. She had gotten dressed and rested comfortably on the sofa in her front parlor. Quilts and afghans were neatly tucked around her and a tea tray sat on the table next to the sofa.

"I simply couldn't stay in bed another day," she said, after coughing.

"I understand," I said, smiling. "You seem much better, and while your cough is still there, it seems much milder than it was. Have you been drinking your beef tea?"

Mrs. Judson made a face. "I feel as if I should grow hooves, I've drunk so much."

"That's good." I chuckled. "It seems to be having the desired effect. As long as you feel you have your usual strength, you can leave it aside. How is Mr. Judson?"

"As healthy as ever, but still in a foul temper, I'm afraid."

"I'm told by more than one person that he blames Mr. Hewitt's behavior at the party for losing the election."

Her eyes suddenly narrowed. "Why would you say that?"

"You did, I believe, the last time I saw you."

"My husband had nothing to do with Mr. Hewitt's death! He was helping the poor man."

"So I saw."

"He is innocent!" Poor Mrs. Judson broke down into a cough.

"I never said that I thought otherwise."

She sat up straight. "Is that all, then?"

"Yes. Let me know if you need me further."

She sniffed, and I made my way from the house.

Thinking that I had not checked on the Brownlow girls all week, I made my way to that house. Neither Mr. Brownlow nor his two eldest daughters were at home.

"Mr. Brownlow is at his office," Mrs. Ritter told me, as she placed little Ada on my lap. We sat in the front parlor, a comfortable room with a sofa and several chairs, and a stove in the corner radiating just enough warmth. "Pearl and Carrie are completely well and at school today. The exams are coming up, you know."

"Oh, yes." I smiled at Ada. "That is quite the event around here."

The school exams took place over the course of a week and were a public event that many in the pueblo attended whether they had children in the schools or not. I did not enjoy watching them and made a point of not going.

"Pearl is getting worried, but she can recite her lessons quite fluently."

"Miss Pearl has little to worry about." I made a face at Ada, who laughed quite charmingly. "The teachers all know that happy parents and civic leaders mean more sup-port for the schools, so they show each child to their best advantage. So unless Miss Pearl insists on being completely slothful, she cannot fail."

Mrs. Ritter nodded. "Still, she wants to do her best for her father."

"Which is as it should be." I looked into Ada's throat, but it was clear and the little girl scrambled off my lap to run about the room. "This one is also completely recov-ered. Thank you, Mrs. Ritter."

"No." She blinked her eyes as I stood up. "Thank you, Mrs. Wilcox. You are so good to our girls."

"You are kind to say so." I smiled. "And I really must be on my way."

I went back to the rancho for lunch, then had Daisy saddled, and paid a few more calls on patients.

The next day was Saturday. I will not say that I dreaded Saturday nights, but they were, without question, the most difficult night of the week. Wages were generally distributed on Saturdays, which meant that men with little else to do would fill the many brothels and saloons that we had in the pueblo, and drink to excess, then start to fight. Such fights usually resulted in all manner of injuries, and even the occasional death.

While I bemoaned the miserable violence of the place, I must confess that sewing the combatants back together did present an invigorating challenge at times. Fortunately, few Saturday nights were as heart-wrenching as that Saturday proved to be.

There were several physicians in the pueblo, including one fusty old fellow who had the temerity to insist that his patients go to him at his office. However, there were three of us who had come to agree not only on our respective methods, but that if we were going to keep a large number of drunken fools bent on killing each other from actually succeeding, then we needed a plan.

Dr. Skillen was a homeopath, and his remedies were as effective as most others at the time. Doc MacKenzie had no medical degree, but many, many years of practice. Both had grudgingly come to accept me as their colleague, although Dr. Skillen continued to believe that a woman performing surgery on a man was unseemly. Still, he couldn't complain because he knew I was a much better surgeon than he was.

Our plan was simple. As the surgeon, I waited with Elena at St. Vincent's Hospital, where the good sisters had allowed me a small room with lots of light and that I might wash with carbolic acid to keep the room as sterile as possible. Sterile surgery was still very new then and not completely trusted. But I like to think that people in the pueblo had begun to notice that my patients were more likely to survive.

That Saturday, I was somewhat apprehensive. My stock of carbolic acid was running low, and while I had good reason to believe fresh supplies were on their way and would arrive at the port near Wilmington the next day, I still had my most difficult night to get through.

I did not get very long to brood over it. Shortly after five o'clock, my first patient arrived on a litter. It was Mrs. Dunbar, Mrs. Downey's maid. She had two gunshot wounds, one in the right side of her chest, and another in her right shoulder. Her condition was dire, but she was alive.

"Please," she gasped as they laid her on my operating table.

"It's all right, Mrs. Dunbar," I told her. "I'm here and I'll take good care of you."

"My baby. Shirley."

"We'll see that she is taken care of, too. Now, rest."

"No. Keep her from Mr. Dunbar." She clawed at my hand. "Promise!"

"I promise I will keep her safe. On my life. Now, rest. I will get you some morphine for the pain, then give you some ether."

But as I turned to get the syringe of morphine, the poor woman breathed her last.

CHAPTER EIGHT

I t is the difficult truth of being a physician that you are going to lose patients. Indeed, in my early practice, before I read Mr. Lister's wonderful article on germs and keeping things sterile during surgery, I lost more than I saved. Nonetheless, I do not like losing patients, and I was most infuriated when Consuela Dunbar died, even though there had been no way to save her.

"Who could have done such a horrible thing to a poor widow with a child!" I all but shrieked at Angelina later that night.

Angelina held the child in question. Little Shirley was about three years old, with a round cherubic face, wide, dark eyes, and long glossy black hair that curled becomingly. The poor babe was finally asleep after several hours of crying for her mama. Angelina had held her the entire time, I was told. Unfortunately, I'd had to go back to work, but the casualties were relatively light, and I'd cut and stitched with my mind elsewhere.

As soon as I could, I went to the funeral parlor and Angelina's study. It was a cozy room with a sofa and large wing-backed chair, where Angelina had settled with the babe. I paced relentlessly as Angelina told me what had happened.

Shirley and her mother had been going home from Mrs. Downey's when Mrs. Dunbar decided to stop at one of the shops on the Calle Primavera. Angelina was also on the street at the time, not far from Mr. Carson's stationery store. No one knew where the shots had come from. Angelina had seen to taking care of little Shirley.

"It could have been anybody," Angelina said wearily. Her heart was at least as heavy as mine. "I saw Mrs. Glassell walking toward Mr. Carson's store. There was that livery man who smells so awful."

"Mr. Lowman."

"Yes. And Mr. Medrano, too. And Mr. Judson."

"It may even have been somebody you didn't see." I shuddered. "Isn't there an alley between those two blocks there?"

Blocks were the large buildings that housed shops and offices.

"Yes. And several barrels in the front of that general store in the other block near the alley."

I sighed, then touched the girl's soft cheek. "The poor little angel. She's an orphan, Angelina, and for what reason? Her mother was a servant, simply trying to provide for herself and her child, and only able to keep the child with her thanks to the kindness of her employer. Why would somebody have wanted to kill her?" I sighed again, this time deeply and profoundly. "And we already have Mr. Hewitt's killer to find."

"Maddie." Angelina swallowed and creased her brow. "Didn't you say that Mrs. Dunbar may have seen or was there when Mr. Hewitt was shot?"

I thought about it. "She was in the immediate area and found a discarded carriage robe that turned out to be Mrs. Glassell's."

"Oh, my." Angelina's eyebrows rose. "And you wrote me a note earlier today that Mrs. Glassell will not talk to you. Maddie, could this be related to Mr. Hewitt's killing? Is it possible that the man or woman who killed Mr. Hewitt thought that Mrs. Dunbar saw something significant and killed her to keep her from telling us?"

"But she didn't see anything!" The pitch of my voice rose alarmingly high.

"That wouldn't matter if the killer thought she had."

"How would the killer have known?"

"I have no idea." Angelina shrugged. "At least, not right now."

I stopped. "Did you see Mrs. Hewitt anywhere this afternoon?"

"No. She's still in deep mourning and not leaving her house."

"On the other hand, if she's paying someone to do these nefarious deeds, she wouldn't need to." I shook my head, attempting to clear it. I looked at little Shirley again. "I promised to keep her safe."

"And allowing me to care for her will keep that promise." Angelina smiled, but her eyes were full of pleading.

The reason Angelina and Mr. Sutton did not have children was because they had already lost three and all Mr. Sutton had told me was that he could not give her more. I did not know why, but had refrained from asking.

I smiled softly at Angelina. "I will trust you then. She seems quite a lovely child."

Angelina smiled at the babe in her lap, her eyes filling. "Yes. She is."

I went home after that. Elena was still quite sad the next morning about Mrs. Dunbar, but I had to remind her that such things happened, even as my own heart broke. I was not in any mood to deal with Reverend Elmwood's usual fulminations, but while he chose to preach on something utterly inane (it had to be because I failed to note the actual topic in my journal), I was not comforted.

As I left the church, I saw Theodora with her mother and daughters and went over to them.

"I am so glad you're here," I said, clasping Theodora's hands.

She shrugged under her widow's weeds. "One must."

She looked over at her mother, who swept the girls away from us.

"How are you managing?" I asked softly.

"Not well." Theodora choked. "But what else is there to do? I had thought I would know how to deal with this since we were expecting him to expire. But this..."

"I understand." I looked around. "Have you heard about the other tragic event last night?"

"Another one?"

"Yes. Mrs. Dunbar. She was a widow in the service of Mrs. Downey."

It was, perhaps, irrational of me, but I felt rather annoyed that I could not see Theodora's face under the heavy black veil.

"No one has said anything to me about it," Theodora said. "What happened?"

I explained as succinctly as I could, and Theodora shuddered.

"I do believe Mrs. Glassell is right," she said. "There is far too much random gunfire in the town. Something must be done or civilized people will not want to come here."

"I agree," I said, although I did not entirely agree with her.

I was fully in concert with the idea that something need-ed to be done about the violence. However, I could not imagine anyone actually wanting to come to Los Angeles, my antipathy for the place still being quite strong.

I took Theodora's hand. "Have you, by any chance, found a record of Mr. Lowman's deposit?"

"I'm afraid not. There is nothing. I checked every-where." She sighed.

"I did speak with him on Wednesday." I frowned. "He insists that he gave Mr. Hewitt some money, but could not tell me how much. I believe you said he didn't say so, but that it would have been a hundred dollars."

The black veils twitched. "He did not say how much money he'd given Thomas. I just assumed it would have been the customary amount."

"Then we have good cause to be suspicious regard-ing Mr. Lowman's claim." I looked around at the other churchgoers as they finished greeting their neighbors and friends. "Let us be on guard, then. I will speak to Mr. Lomax, the policeman, about Mr. Lowman. Perhaps that will help."

"I do hope so. Thank you, Maddie."

As I turned from Theodora, I saw Mr. Brownlow speak-ing to Mrs. Ritter, who then took the three girls with her toward their home. Mr. Brownlow approached me with a warm smile.

"Mrs. Wilcox!" He doffed his hat. "It is indeed a pleasure to see you this morning."

"Thank you, Mr. Brownlow. Happy to see you, as well."

He offered his arm. "Might I see you to your home this morning?"

"It's very kind of you to offer, but it's not necessary." I smiled at him.

"It would be my pleasure." He bowed slightly.

I sighed, not sure how to respond. Even as I had absolutely no use for a husband (and still do not), I was not insensible to the pleasures of being courted. Indeed, I occasionally encouraged it. At the same time, when a man in the pueblo began to pay court to me, it was generally with a view to furthering his own interests. Mr. Brownlow looked so hopeful, and his smile was quite winning.

"I cannot encourage you, Mr. Brownlow," I said softly.

He chuckled. "Then I stand warned." He replaced his hat. "Can you at least accept my friendship? Perhaps I can convince you to change your mind."

"I am afraid not." I laughed. "I assure you, Mr. Brownlow, many in the pueblo have tried offering me their friendship in the hopes of changing my mind, only to find that my mind is quite firmly made up."

"Then it is I who may choose whether or not my heart will be broken, and I will choose to take the risk." His smile softened. "You are a very charming woman and my daughters like you a great deal."

I could not help but smile ruefully. "Very well. You have been warned and will have no cause to complain when your attentions are not returned. As for walking me home today, I am afraid I had a very trying night and would prefer to be alone with my thoughts."

"Oh." He looked puzzled for a moment, but then bowed. "As you wish, Mrs. Wilcox."

"Good day, Mr. Brownlow." I smiled again, then started down the road.

I did want to be alone with my thoughts. Angelina's idea that Mrs. Dunbar was shot to hide the person who killed Mr. Hewitt preyed on my mind. However, as I walked toward my rancho, I could not help but wonder what Mr. Brownlow's true objective was.

He was exceedingly charming, and I could not help but believe that his motives were comparatively pure. He was seeking to further his own interests in some way. I was not so charmed as to believe otherwise. But he did not seem to have the usual designs upon my property or my person. There was little to make of it, so I reminded myself that I had other, far more urgent matters to consider, and picked up my pace so that I would not delay my household's dinner.

I was the lone Protestant in my household. Everyone else was Catholic. Given their practice to fast from midnight on before going to their mass, it made my tardiness on Sunday mornings highly unpopular, as no one wanted to wait for their dinner. As I approached the yard gate, the younger children cheered when they saw me. I was quickly escorted to the barracks, and we commenced our Sunday meal.

I had hoped to spend that afternoon resting and writing letters and other such relaxing chores, and did get my usual letter to my sister finished, when I was summoned to the bedside of my phthisis patient.

He was at his end, so there was little to do but wait for his children to say goodbye, then comfort his wife. Fortunately, one of the priests was there to tend to the family. I left the adobe feeling quite out of sorts and powerless.

It was quite late and dark had fallen. I knew I would get a scolding from Olivia and felt as though I deserved it. Enrique had sent his son Jaime after me with a lantern, and the two of us made our way down the street, only to be hailed by Mr. Lomax.

He tipped his hat and smiled. "Good evening, Mrs. Wilcox. I'm glad I spotted you."

"Is everyone well?"

"Mostly. Hannah's cold is better, but now Eli and Rachel have it." He sniffled a little, himself.

"It is the way of it. But what do you need?"

"It's something I found," he said, then looked around. "We're not far from the jail office. Do you mind? I'll walk you home."

I looked at my young escort. "Jaime, please tell your tía that I'll be on my way shortly and in the company of Mr. Lomax."

Jaime said he would and ran off back toward the rancho.

Mr. Lomax took me to the jail and one of the two desks in front of the cells.

"I locked it in my desk," he explained, unlocking said desk and opening a bottom drawer. "So the other fellows won't see it and take it."

"Take what?"

Mr. Lomax pulled out a very large and very handsome six-shooter pistol. The handle was a dark mother-of-pearl, and the barrel was a well-polished silver engraved with scroll-work.

"I found this behind some barrels next to the alley be-tween those two blocks on Spring Street," he said.

Or as I called it, the Calle Primavera.

"Who would have left a beautiful piece like this?" I asked.

"Somebody who had just used it and didn't want to be seen going back for it."

"You mean Mrs. Dunbar's killer." I gasped. "You believe that was the gun that was used to kill her."

"I do so." Mr. Lomax shrugged and put the gun back into the drawer and locked the desk. As he continued speaking, he escorted me from the office and locked the building. "Of course, the fellow might not have missed it right away, and I found it before he could."

"Or she could have." I thought about it. "Could the killer have hidden behind the barrels?"

"Easily."

The gas street lamps had been lit and gave off a gentle, golden glow of lit spots along the Calle Primavera. Mr. Lomax walked at my side, forbearing to take my arm, although he could have in all decency.

"But why would the killer have left the gun?" I asked. "I would think he would have wanted to keep something so fine."

Mr. Lomax smiled and shrugged. "I'm guessing he thought he'd holstered it and it dropped instead. It doesn't happen often, but I have seen it before."

I thought about Mrs. Dunbar's wounds. "Only two shots hit Mrs. Dunbar, and they were not as close together as the ones that hit Mr. Hewitt."

"Folks told me they only heard two shots." Mr. Lomax pointed out. "And she was across the street and down a ways from where the barrels were."

He pointed at the opening between two large blocks where four barrels sat near the opening to a grocery store.

"Which would indicate that we are still looking for someone with excellent shooting skills," I said as we moved on toward Alameda Street.

Mr. Lomax nodded. "I would say so. But there's plenty of folks in the pueblo who shoot well. You wouldn't think it, but Mr. Judson is pretty good with a gun. So is that notary, Mr. Wills, and Mr. Handley isn't bad either."

"What about Mr. Medrano or Mr. Lowman?"

"Lowman?" Mr. Lomax shuddered. "I would not want to be in a gunfight with him. That man draws fast and hits his target, and he's meaner than a rattlesnake."

"And he has been giving Mrs. Hewitt some trouble about a deal that he claims he made with Mr. Hewitt."

Mr. Lomax shrugged. "As for Medrano, don't know him. Haven't heard much except that he wanted Mr. Hewitt's business."

I gazed ahead. "The problem is, as you pointed out, there are any number of people in the pueblo who shoot well. Nor does this mean that the man who shot Mrs. Dunbar is the same as the one who shot Mr. Hewitt."

"True." Mr. Lomax touched my elbow as I stumbled over a rut in the dirt street. "It could even have been someone with a grudge against the governor. Plenty of folks are not happy with him regarding the railroad."

"You might have a point." I sighed and shook my head. "But I'm not sure that it entirely makes sense. I'm certain that Governor Downey, like most men of his ilk, is barely cognizant of his household staff. How would killing his servant harm him?"

"Doesn't have to make sense."

I thought for a moment, then tried to see the gun in my mind.

"Is it possible that the owner of the pistol does not know that you collected it?" I asked.

"More than likely, I'd say." Mr. Lomax looked at me. "Are you thinking that we should be looking out for somebody missing a six-shooter?"

"It does seem as if it might be a worthwhile endeavor." I frowned. "And perhaps it would be best if we did not mention that you found or have it."

Mr. Lomax smiled and nodded. "I had a feeling you might think that. I haven't said anything."

We turned off of Alameda Street onto the road that led to Rancho de las Flores. Darkness enveloped us. The waxing half moon shone around several clouds, which also blocked some of the starlight. The air had the crisp nip of a Boston fall.

I couldn't stop the profound sorrow that welled up in me. Back home, if there hadn't been snow, there soon would be. Back home, there was little likelihood that a young widow would be wantonly shot on the street, leaving her daughter an orphan. Back home, those people who excelled at shooting did so because they enjoyed the sport, not because it was needed for self-defense.

I was, perhaps, not being fair to the pueblo. People in Boston got murdered, many times for the same reasons as they did here. But at that moment, I was badly homesick.

A faint light gleamed ahead of us, the lantern at the gate of the rancho. As Mr. Lomax and I approached, Bella and Pancho, the two rancho hounds, began barking loudly. Rodolfo came up to the gate and opened it. I offered Mr. Lomax a ride back to his house as soon as we could get the buggy hitched, but Mr. Lomax declined the offer, tipped his hat, and offered me a good night.

The next morning dawned cloudy, but I'd had an idea as I tossed sleepless during the wee hours of the morning. Donning my green riding habit, I, nonetheless, walked into the pueblo. Mr. Wiley happily pointed me in the direction of Mr. Jessup's office. I had not spoken to Mr. Judson, but given my latest encounter with Mrs. Judson, I seriously doubted that I would be able to speak to him in the near future.

Mr. Jessup was kind enough to see me right away.

"How might I help you, Mrs. Wilcox?" he asked as he seated me in front of the huge oaken desk, covered with papers and ledgers in neat stacks.

"I know I asked you if you saw anybody near Mr. Hewitt's buggy, but I failed to ask whether you'd seen Mr. Judson between the time you'd helped Mr. Hewitt and the time the shots went off."

Mr. Jessup sat back and thought. "I do not believe I did. Why do you ask?"

"I cannot say. You did hear about the tragic shooting Saturday night, didn't you?"

Mr. Jessup frowned. "Eh, no, I didn't. I was not in Los Angeles at the time."

"Oh?" I smiled. "Where were you?"

"San Buenaventura." He smiled expansively. "I left on Friday night's stage and only returned this morning."

"Oh. Well, it was most tragic. A poor, innocent woman."

"How terrible." Mr. Jessup shook his head. "We really need to do something about the violence on the streets in the pueblo."

"We do, indeed." I got up. "Well, thank you, Mr. Jessup. I appreciate your time."

He rose also and escorted me out of the building. I could not help but feel annoyed. The fact that Mr. Jessup had not seen Mr. Judson right before the shooting meant absolutely nothing. It simply made it possible that Mr. Judson had shot Mr. Hewitt. That seemed terribly unlikely, given Mr. Judson's adherence to good morals. But I had heard of others who were quite vocal about being upright, yet who would do terrible things in a moment of weakness.

After that, I needed to attend Mrs. Dunbar's funeral. Mrs. Downey was kind enough to attend, as did Mrs. Dunbar's landlady. But there was no one else besides Angelina, the baby, and Mr. Sutton at the graveside, presided over by Father Gilberto from the Plaza Church. Angelina held little Shirley, who didn't quite understand what was going on, but cried piteously, nonetheless.

As we left, I held Mrs. Downey back.

"Is it possible that someone was using harm to Mrs. Dunbar as an excuse to hurt your husband?" I asked her.

Mrs. Downey's eyes opened wide in shock. "That makes no sense whatsoever! I am not so gullible as to believe that the governor is universally loved. But what good would it do to harm Mrs. Dunbar?"

"I have no idea, unless the man threatening him wanted to frighten him first." I shuddered.

"That could be." Mrs. Downey pressed her lips together. "But I think not. We have been threatened before, and I can always tell because John gets very worried and insists on hiring men to guard me. I have seen none of that."

"If you do, would you be so kind as to let me know immediately?" I asked.

She agreed, and I excused myself to hurry ahead down the Calle de Eternidad after the landlady.

Her name was Mrs. Gutierrez, and she was a tiny woman, wizened, with eyes that often closed as she thought.

"I wish I could help you, Señora Wilcox," she said in Spanish. "But I did not see anyone." She suddenly frowned and her eyes drifted shut. "No, I did not see him, but someone was watching the house in the days before poor Señora Dunbar was murdered. Not all the time, but often enough."

"I see." I blinked back tears. "Thank you, Señora. If you see someone watching your house again, please let me know."

The old woman shrugged, then shuffled on her way.

Chapter Nine

After the funeral, I visited some patients, then headed back to the rancho for lunch, only to find Mr. Lomax there, waiting for me.

The telegram that Mr. Lomax had brought left me dumbfounded.

"I don't understand," I said.

Mr. Lomax took a deep breath. "I wired the sheriff up there, as I was told that was where Mrs. Dunbar is from. I was hoping to find some relatives to care for the little girl."

"I am so glad that you thought of that," I said, feeling rather abashed that I had not thought to do so. I looked at the telegram. "She warned me against a Mr. Dunbar. I thought it was her husband's father. And now we have a man with that name demanding that we bring him his daughter? I was under the impression that Mrs. Dunbar was a widow."

"As was I." Mr. Lomax shifted. "That's why I wired back. Turns out, she's not a widow. But we might want to think twice about turning the child over. Sheriff there says that Dunbar is a ne'er-do-well, in jail all the time. Drinks up whatever money he makes."

"Oh, dear." I took the second telegram and looked it over. "Hardly a felicitous situation for a young babe."

Mr. Lomax could not help but agree. I sent two of our rancho boys with notes to Angelina and Regina even before Mr. Lomax could leave. The women arrived promptly and were aghast at the news.

"What are we to do?" I asked as I paced in my study.

Anita had taken little Shirley to play with the other children.

"We cannot send that poor babe to such an evil man!" Angelina stood with her hands on her hips. "You promised her mother that you would keep the child safe."

"I agree," said Regina. "You cannot break a promise made to a woman on her deathbed."

"But what about the child?" My eyes filled. "Would it be a kindness to deprive her of her only relative?"

"If he is such a monster, it would be the only kind and decent thing to do," Angelina snapped.

Regina sighed. "However, I understand Maddie's dilemma. We do not know for certain that this man is not a kind and loving father, even if he is a wastrel."

"True." Angelina pressed her lips together.

"In addition, there might be another loving relative who would embrace the child," I said. "We didn't know about her husband. Perhaps there is an aunt or grandparent who would care for her in the right way."

Angelina blew her breath out. "Then we must go to San Buenaventura and find out."

My stomach twisted. "We could write letters."

"The woman asked you to protect the child from this man we now believe to be the child's father!" Angelina's pacing took on a frenetic energy. "I am not trusting any letters. You know how people write glowing reports to achieve what they want. I want to meet these people and talk to them. It is the only way to ensure Shirley's safety."

"I'm afraid she's right," Regina said, a languid counterpoint to Angelina's agitation. "Alas, I cannot go. There is no one else to run my business. And Angelina cannot travel alone. Could Mr. Sutton go with you?"

Angelina shook her head. "He has our business to tend to, and a funeral to lead tomorrow."

They both looked at me. I swallowed.

"What about my patients?" I asked.

"You have Doctor Skillen and Doctor Wang," Angelina said, glaring at me with her arms folded.

Regina looked at me with her eyes narrowed. "There is more to your reluctance than meets the eye."

"I do not know why you would say that." I swallowed and flopped into my desk chair.

Regina stood. "Madeline Franklin Wilcox, in the entire time of our association, I have never seen you balk at a challenge. Perhaps hedge occasionally, but not balk."

"I haven't either." Angelina walked up and stood over me. "What is your real reason for not wanting to go to San Buenaventura?"

"It is quite humiliating," I said, making a face and blinking back tears. "I do not travel well, it seems."

"What do you mean?" Angelina asked.

"It is not as bad on a train, but still happens. On a boat or stagecoach…" I shook my head. "I get horribly sick. When Mr. Wilcox dragged me out here in Eighteen-Sixty, we took the Overland Stage from St. Louis." I shuddered as the tears fell. "I have told you before that my husband was not a kind man and treated me dreadfully. As we traveled, he made fun of me the entire time, and even became angry and struck me. But I was truly ill and came very close to dying. I could hardly eat anything."

Regina snorted. "Oh, the food was dreadful!"

"You took the stage, too?" Angelina asked.

"A year or so before Maddie did." Regina shuddered. "I do not get in the least bit sick in any conveyance, and it was still a miserable experience. Crowded into that tiny space, having to get out every two hours or so, then cramming myself back in. Then hard tack and brackish water to subsist upon. The only good part about it was that it only took three weeks or so to get here."

"And I was newly married to a man who had no regard nor kindness for me." I pulled my handkerchief from my sleeve and dabbed at my eyes. "But that is the real reason why I remained in Los Angeles. True, given how my father had forced me to marry Mr. Wilcox, I could not have been assured of a welcome home. However, I do not dare leave lest the journey kill me!"

Angelina chuckled as she held me close to her. "Dear, dear Maddie. Of course you are afraid. But I am not your miserable excuse for a husband, and I would not dream of chiding you for something you cannot help. And I know well the feeling. I do not do well on stagecoaches myself. But this is for Shirley's welfare, and we'll only be on the coach overnight. We can both survive that."

"We can but hope," I said with a sigh. I dabbed at my eyes one more time.

Regina looked through the newspaper that I'd left unread on my desk.

"The stage leaves the Wells Fargo office at six p.m." She frowned. "That does not give us much time."

We fell to, making plans and arrangements. Regina insisted on paying for our fares, although she declined to make the actual purchase. She was rather sensitive to the judgments of pueblo society and seldom acknowledged any connection to Angelina and me lest we be tainted.

Olivia heard our flustering and came into the study. I explained about the sudden trip. Olivia's already solemn face grew even more pained.

"Who knows you are going away?" she scolded.

"What do you mean?"

She broke into Spanish, gesturing frenetically. "There are all manner of robbers and bad men out there on the road. You are looking for another killer. You do not think that if this killer hears that you will be on a stagecoach, he will not make like such a bandit and find a way to do away with you? This is why we say you do not take care of yourself! This is why we worry so much about you."

Angelina laughed, then translated for Regina, who looked at me.

"I'm afraid Mrs. Ortiz is right," Regina said. "But who...? Ah. I know. I will see to it and no one will be any the wiser until you actually get on the coach. But there's not much we can do about that."

"I'd best put together a basket then," Olivia muttered. "You will need food and drink."

"Olivia," I said hesitantly. "I do not think either Angelina or I will be able to consume much."

Regina. "Oh, dear. Your weak stomachs." She looked at Olivia. "Both Mrs. Wilcox and Mrs. Sutton are made quite ill by traveling on a stagecoach."

"It's because you do not eat!" Olivia snapped and went straight to the kitchen.

Anita and Magdalena agreed to take care of Shirley. Surprisingly, Anita was somewhat reluctant to do so, but I did not find out why until later.

Elena heard from her mother about my little problem and thought of a solution so patently obvious that I blush to disclose that I hadn't thought of it myself.

Regina and Angelina had just barely gone to their tasks when Dr. Wang Fu arrived at the rancho. He wore his black hair in the Western style, although he did keep his narrow mustache over his shaved chin, and had on a nice brown wool suit.

"Miss Elena sent for me." He smiled gently. "She says you get sick on coaches."

"Oh, Fu!" My eyes filled again. "I am so glad to see you."

Fu, like the vast majority of Chinese, held to the custom of speaking his family name first, then his given one. It was a curious custom, but I was happy to honor it, especially as we claimed the intimacy of good friends.

"I have nostrum here." He held up a flask about the size of a book and his dark eyes twinkled. "So, you don't have to cut yourself open."

I laughed as I took the flask. We each had tremendous respect for the other's methods, but poked fun at each other, nonetheless.

"Thank you for sparing me that trouble." My brow creased. "It doesn't look like there's a great deal here. Will there be enough for the trip back?"

"There should be. And extra," Fu said. He turned serious. "But drink it before you go. It work better that way."

I thanked him handsomely. For all I teased Fu by calling his potions and teas nostrums, his preparations were exceptionally efficacious. He had no specific formulas, but prepared each one for his patient's exact condition using some mysterious method that he was never able to explain.

He had barely left when I had another caller. I would have told Magdalena to send Mr. Brownlow away, but I had answered the door when he knocked.

"I hope that I am not intruding?" he asked, his hat in his hands.

"Not intruding as such, Mr. Brownlow." I made a face. "But now is not a good time, I'm afraid." I looked around for my hat and my leather bag. "I must get to the train depot. The train from Wilmington should be in with my supplies. I have the wire from San Francisco that they were on the Orizaba."

"Oh, no. Haven't you heard?"

"Heard what?"

"The Orizaba. It was in this morning's paper."

I closed my eyes and groaned. "Which I have not yet read." I looked at him shifting on the doorstep. "Oh, come in, Mr. Brownlow. Now, is the ship sunk?"

"No, ma'am. A mechanical difficulty is all, thank God. There were over three-hundred passengers on board. They arrived yesterday morning in Santa Barbara. All that is needed is some way to bring those passengers who live here home."

"I suppose that's good news." I went back to pacing my front parlor. "But my supplies. I'm dreadfully short of carbolic acid." I shook my head. "Well, we'll find out in a few days or so what's to be done with the freight. I have a journey to take in the meantime."

"A journey, Mrs. Wilcox?" Mr. Brownlow's eye glimmered hopefully.

"Yes, and I must concentrate on my preparations and packing, I'm afraid."

"Would you do me the honor of allowing me to be your escort?"

"What?" I turned on him, Olivia's warning ringing in my ears. "No, thank you. I will not be unaccompanied."

"Oh." He looked quite crestfallen.

I sighed, feeling guilty for some reason. "But if you wish to call on me after I return, I suppose that will be all right."

He brightened. "Thank you, Mrs. Wilcox. I look forward to it."

"Now, if you'll excuse me, I really must tend to my packing."

I got him outside and had Rodolfo escort him to the rancho gate.

I was ready when Mr. Sutton pulled up in their buggy to drive Angelina and me to the Wells Fargo office, from where the stage would leave. I wore my dark green riding habit, having little else to travel in, and Angelina wore a similar suit. Neither of us carried more than a small satchel each. I had my usual leather bag as well. And there was the huge basket of food that Olivia insisted we take. Poor Mr. Sutton, who looked exceptionally somber in the best of moods, looked positively morose.

We got to the stage office in good time to claim our tickets from Mr. Lomax. He smiled slyly, as he had known very well why Regina had asked him to make the purchase. I remembered just in time to drink some of Fu's preparation and made sure Angelina drank some as well. It tasted foul, as so many of his preparations did, but I had great hopes for it. Angelina and Mr. Sutton stood close to each other, whispering quietly between themselves.

When the stage pulled up, lanterns glowing in the winter dusk, I was somewhat disheartened to see that it was a mud wagon. Granted, a regular Concord stage was only marginally more comfortable, but it was a margin I would have relished. The mud wagon had a bench seat backed up against the driver's box, which faced to the back, a simple bench with a leather strap across for a back support facing forward in the middle of the coach, and a third bench, facing forward, at the back of the coach. The roof, such as it was, was merely a canvas tarpaulin, and the windows only had canvas coverings to keep the dirt out. I shivered a little in the winter chill, but knew it would be warm enough once all seven of us who were waiting were aboard.

The coachman, or jee-who, as they were called at the time, insisted that as ladies, Angelina and I took our choice of seat, and we chose the middle one, happy that we each could be next to a window. The coach, when full, could hold nine people, plus an extra man on top with the jee-who. I wondered that more people were not on board, but didn't question it.

One of the men waiting with us chose to ride on top. Two others faced us, and one very fat man sat behind us. Angelina and I were about to exchange greetings with the men in front of us, but one closed his eyes and fell asleep even before the jee-who mounted the box. The other sighed deeply and glared out the window.

Angelina and I glanced at each other, shifted the food basket between us, and shrugged. The coach rocked a little as first the passenger, then the jee-who mounted the box. The jee-who cracked his lash over the team of six horses, and with a great deal of creaking, groaning, and rocking, the coach moved ahead into the night.

The only good thing I can say about that miserable trip was neither Angelina nor I disgraced ourselves. That would have been too horrifying. But, oh, we felt miserable. The coach rocked and pitched like a toy boat on rough seas, even with the horses at a walk because of the darkness. Even worse were the bone-jarring jolts as the coach went over one pothole or another. The leather strap provided little comfort or support. Angelina and I kept our faces to the windows not only in case the worst happened, but because it seemed to help with the nausea.

We stopped every two hours or so to change horses. Angelina and I briefly debated getting off the stage for a few moments, but decided to remain in our seats, as the stage office men were very efficient in their work and we feared being left behind. In fact, the man who had glared out the window did get left behind in San Fernando, I believe, when he exited and did not return promptly.

In spite of our wretched condition, Angelina and I did try to sleep, leaning our heads against the side of the stage. However, we were kept awake by the loud snores of the man behind us.

"How does he sleep?" Angelina asked late into the night.

I had no idea of the hour, nor how the man managed to keep snoring so loudly. Eventually, sheer exhaustion overwhelmed both of us, and I finally awoke as we pulled into yet another station and saw the glimmer of dawn out of the window on my right. Fresh cold air wafted into the coach.

"Where are we?" Angelina muttered.

"I have no idea," I replied just as softly.

We continued on the road for some hours more. I am not sure how many. The sky was dark with clouds and the wind began to blow into the windows, bitterly cold. Angelina and I managed to sip some of the cold soup that Olivia had sent with us, then each ate one of the small loaves of bread. We offered to share, but the two men in the coach with us declined.

Finally, we crested a hill from which we could see the ocean. A minute later, the stage stopped, and as the station men hurried to change the horses, the jee-who got down from the box and helped Angelina and me from the stage. I was chilled to the bone and my lower limbs shook as I stood for the first time in many hours and dizziness wafted over me. Angelina looked as though she felt the same.

The sun had fully risen and what I saw before me seemed rather bleak, indeed. The mission was before us, and quite an impressive edifice, with white plaster walls. However, there was not much more to the city of San Buenaventura than a rough collection of adobes. There were a few frame houses and even a block or two, but not much more than that.

"It reminds me of Los Angeles when I first saw it," I said. "It's hard to fathom, but our little pueblo has, indeed, grown quite a bit in the past twelve years."

"At least it should be easier to find out if Mrs. Dunbar has any relatives," Angelina said, filled with the same dismay I felt.

We went into the stage office to find out what time the coach returning to Los Angeles would arrive, and were told it would in two hours.

"We'd best make haste then," I said to Angelina.

We were able to leave our satchels and the food basket in the care of the station agent, and, after getting the directions, made our way to the county sheriff's office.

It was housed in a relatively new adobe, with white-washed walls and a tile roof. The sheriff was a lean man, I do not recall his name, with a neatly trimmed beard that was dark brown. He sniffed a little as if he had a cold, though.

"Sir, we are here seeking relatives of a Mrs. Consuela Dunbar," I told him.

"You got the kid?" he asked.

"Not with us," Angelina said.

The sheriff looked at a door in the side wall of the office. "Good thing."

We could not help but be a little shocked that a man would withhold another man's child from him.

"Hey! Who's out there?" someone cried from the back. "Is someone going to bring me my girl? Hey!"

"Is that Mr. Dunbar?" I asked.

"I am afraid so, ma'am."

There was a great deal of clattering from the jail within.

"I got my rights! You can't keep my girl from me."

"He's been screaming like that since I told him about his wife being killed yesterday morning." The sheriff shook his head.

"We didn't know that she was still married," I said. "We were under the impression that she was a widow."

"That was a smart move on her part."

"We're here looking for other relatives," Angelina said.

The sheriff shook his head. "She didn't have any, except her mother, and she died before the baby was born."

"What about Mr. Dunbar's relatives?" Angelina asked.

"Don't know of any." The sheriff smiled bitterly as more clattering erupted from inside the jail. "I'm not sure as I'd trust them, anyway. Mr. Dunbar came here about six years ago to work in the Sespe oil fields. When a fellow gets that drunk and causes as much trouble as Dunbar does, then like as not, he comes from that kind of family."

"Might I see him?" Angelina asked.

The sheriff stepped back. "Why would you want to?"

Angelina folded her arms across her chest. "I would not want it said that we did not give the man every chance to prove himself."

Shaking his head, the sheriff admitted Angelina to the back room. A minute later, Mr. Dunbar screamed loudly.

"You can't do this! You can't! Give me my daughter."

Angelina hurried from the room with the sheriff behind her.

"What happened?" I asked.

"He tried to attack the lady." The sheriff locked the door.

"I believe we have given him every chance," Angelina said simply.

"Indeed," I said and turned to the sheriff. "Do you know where Mrs. Dunbar lived?"

The sheriff gave us directions to another, much smaller and less well-kept adobe on the edge of town. The house was owned by a small, graying Mexican woman who had nothing good to say about Mr. Dunbar.

"He beat that poor woman," she said in Spanish. "He beat her almost to death. He even struck the poor baby. It's a miracle he didn't kill her."

We listened to her continue for several more minutes in that vein, then asked if Mrs. Dunbar had any relatives in the pueblo.

"Her mother is dead, and it's a good thing," the woman said, spitting on the ground. "She ran a saloon, a nasty one, and forced her daughter to work there. The old woman, she auctioned her daughter off. Mr. Dunbar won and made her life a misery. I was the one who told her to go and helped her get on the stage. I told her to go to San Diego. I don't know why she didn't."

"Maybe she didn't want anyone to know where she was," Angelina said. "And if she went to San Diego, then you would know that was where she'd gone."

"Bah! I would not tell that monster. I don't even let him live here anymore."

We bade her good day, then hurried back to the center of the town, as we had discussed the night before, and found there a rather nice hotel in a small block not far from the mission. I approached the front desk, a large dark oak affair in an airy whitewashed room featuring two worn but clean chairs upholstered in needlepoint. The man behind the desk wore an exceptionally long, dark beard, although his hair was cut short and freshly slicked down with some sort of pomade.

"I have no rooms, ladies," he grumbled.

"We do not want one," I replied, smiling as kindly as I could. "We are trying to find out if a certain gentleman spent this past Saturday night at your fine hotel. A Mr. Jessup."

The man squinted at me. "The fellow that owns the shipping company?"

"Yes. Him."

"Why are you asking after him?"

I chuckled a little nervously. "He has been paying his attentions to my dear sister, and since she knew that I would be traveling through here, she asked that I inquire about him."

"Is she a Mrs. Hewitt?"

"Why, yes!" I smiled, then put on a sad look. "She was recently widowed."

"Sad for her, but good for him." The man almost smiled. "He's been hankering after her for quite a while, to hear him tell it. Well, you can put your sister's fears to rest. He's a fine fellow."

"So he was here this past Saturday."

"Don't know." The man's face creased. "I didn't see him. But that don't mean nothing. He's got a couple friends in town that he usually stays with. Sometimes the fellows come in here for a dinner. Sometimes they don't. But if he said he was in town, then he probably was. He's got no reason to say that he weren't."

"So very kind of you, sir," I said, not sure what to think of it. "Good day."

Angelina and I hurried back to the stage station in the hopes of catching the stage back to Los Angeles.

Chapter Ten

The ill-fated steamship Orizaba was to make our lives even more difficult than I had imagined after hearing that my medical supplies were aboard. Angelina and I got to the stage office in plenty of time for the southbound stagecoach. But the coach was overflowing with passengers from the steamship. At least, the stage company and the steamship company had arranged for extra stages and wagons to get as many of the passengers currently left adrift in Santa Barbara back to Los Angeles and other points south.

"What do you make of that hotel man?" I asked Angelina as we settled onto a bench to wait for the next coach.

"If it were my sister, I wouldn't take his word regarding Mr. Jessup." She frowned. "But that's not because I think the hotel man was dishonest. Or that Mr. Jessup wasn't here on Saturday. The hotel man probably thinks that anybody who doesn't start fights and pays his bill is a fine fellow."

I had to chuckle at that. "Too true." I looked down the rutted street toward the new pier down below, and the road just beyond that. "It's a pity we can't spend our waiting time trying to find Mr. Jessup's friends. But I do not want to chance missing the first available coach."

"I think I see one coming."

It was, indeed, another coach, but it, too, was over-full with passengers trying to get home from their sea voyage.

Finally, sometime before three o'clock in the afternoon, a wagon rolled into the station, laden with still more ship passengers in the wagon's bed, although these were exclusively men who had sent the women ahead in covered conveyances. The driver looked somewhat familiar, but I could not remember who he was. He, however, remembered me and smiled broadly as he got down off the box. He spoke briefly to the men changing the four horses hitched to the wagon with a set of mules, then walked over to me and tipped his hat.

"How do you do, Mrs. Wilcox," he said, grinning. "What brings you up to San Buenaventura?"

"I am making some inquiries for a friend." I had seen the man recently, but thanks to my exhaustion, I could not remember where or how. I gestured toward Angelina. "Do you know Mrs. Sutton?"

"'Fraid not, ma'am." The man took off his hat and nodded. "I'm Mr. Pickens."

Mr. Pickens! Of course, the poor unfortunate whose horses had spooked the week before.

"Nice to meet you," Angelina said, a tired smile on her face.

"It is good to see you looking well," I said to him.

He laughed. "I was a sight, wasn't I? And speaking of, you ladies look tuckered out."

"It was a long night getting here," I said. "And now that we have finished our business, we need to get back to Los Angeles as soon as possible."

He looked at the weary men in the bed of the wagon, then back at us.

"Well. I can't leave you ladies here."

"Mr. Pickens, we couldn't force those poor men from their seats," I said, wishing very much that we could.

"You aren't getting home tonight any other way," he said with a sigh. "There's still a crowd of people that were waiting in Santa Barbara when I came through. Hey, fellows! We got two ladies here that are stranded and need to go back to Los Angeles. I need two of you to ride up top with me." He looked at Angelina and me. "I have to wire for some extra horses ahead. You get yourselves ready."

Angelina bounced up. "I have to wire my husband."

We followed Mr. Pickens inside the stage office, where there was a telegraph machine. He made Angelina send her wire first and as we waited for her to do so, he smiled again at me.

"It's no trouble having you ladies along," he explained. "And it won't be that uncomfortable. Mr. Jessup, it's his wagon. He sent me up to Santa Barbara on Sunday, figuring they'd need some extra wagons for the freight. But they needed the wagon for the passengers more. And that wagon has benches you can sit on. Mr. Jessup has me and a couple of the fellows ride up here with him a lot of times, and we take turns driving so that we can keep going at night. One drives while the others sleep on the benches. Mr. Jessup doesn't like taking the stage if he can avoid it."

Angelina finished her wire, and Mr. Pickens hurried to the counter to send his. When we came back outside to the wagon, two men I didn't know sat up on the bench. The other men helped us into the wagon bed. Mr. Pickens was as good as his word and there were two benches on each side of the wagon. Angelina and I each drank the last of Wang Fu's potion. I sat next to Mr. Lyons, Mr. Wiley's employee. Or perhaps they were partners at that point. He was a small, wiry man with dark brown hair and neatly trimmed beard. Mr. Lyons and another passenger on the steamship talked endlessly of their travails aboard the ship, while Angelina and I tried not to disgrace ourselves. Not being cooped up in a coach did help in that regard. We also shared the contents of the basket and those were eagerly accepted.

It must be acknowledged that trying to get home on a stranded steamer was probably worse than even the misery that Angelina and I endured on the trip, a misery that was only compounded by the fact that it had served only to find that we had been correct in our assumptions about the welfare of the child all along. But as Angelina pointed out, it was the only way we could have been certain. We conferred on what to do about little Shirley upon our arrival and both decided that we would arrive far too late to wake the babe and move her. As for what we had found out about Mr. Jessup, we had no idea what to make of that, even assuming it was true.

"It does seem interesting to me that the hotel man knew about Mr. Jessup's interest in Mrs. Hewitt," I told Angelina as the sun set that afternoon.

She made a face. "For all men chastise women for being gossips, they are just as bad, if not worse than we are. It would not take much to get such a confession out of Mr. Jessup if he indulged in too much wine over dinner."

"Too true." I sighed. "Nor does it mean that Mr. Jessup likely killed Mr. Hewitt, let alone Mrs. Dunbar."

We arrived in Los Angeles in the wee hours of the morning, well past the time that lamps were required to be lit. There were four buggies waiting when we arrived. I was not surprised to see Mr. Sutton there, looking dour as always. But Mr. Brownlow also waited in another buggy. The two others waited for the other passengers.

"Where is Mr. Ortiz?" I asked as Mr. Brownlow approached.

"I insisted on the privilege of escorting you home," he said simply.

Alas, I was so exhausted at that point that I allowed him to drive me home, all the while discouraging him as best I could. Sebastiano, however, was waiting at the gate as Mr. Brownlow pulled up.

"Thank you, Mr. Brownlow," Sebastiano said, helping me from the buggy. "Your luggage, Maddie?"

"Here," I gasped, then turned to Mr. Brownlow. "Thank you, sir."

"It was my pleasure," he said, smiling in the light on the gatepost.

Sebastiano pulled my satchel and leather bag from the buggy. I held onto the food basket and got out without help. Sebastiano yawned and shook his head as Mr. Brownlow snapped the reins and his buggy moved away.

"You've got another one after you," Sebastiano grumbled as he shut the rancho gate. "He came by at least three times this afternoon."

"Oh, bother. I am doing my best to discourage him." I shivered in the chilled air. It was warmer than it had been that morning in San Buenaventura, but still very nippy.

"Olivia does not think you should." Sebastiano blew out the lamp on the gatepost, and picked up a lantern nearby.

I snorted. "He probably wants my land. I cannot imagine why these fellows continue to think that I cannot see past their avarice."

Sebastiano handed me my satchel and leather bag, then took the food basket from me.

"Empty," he said, hefting it. "Olivia will be pleased."

"I'm glad." I sighed at the door to my adobe. A lamp burned in the front window. "Thank you, Sebastiano. I very much appreciate you getting up at this ridiculous hour."

He shrugged and went on to his adobe, some paces away. Marisol, yawning and wearing a nightdress, was, nonetheless, at the door as I opened it. She helped me into my room and out of my riding habit, and we were both in bed minutes later.

I woke later than usual, feeling only somewhat refreshed. The dizziness from the trip had finally left me, but I had not had nearly enough sleep. I donned my blue work dress and went out to the barracks to break my fast. Olivia saw me come in and quickly brought me a bowl of soup.

"You ate all your food," she said. "It helped, didn't it?"

"Yes," I said simply.

The food had helped, so I was not specifically telling an untruth, but it had helped with the atmosphere in the return coach rather than filling our bellies. We did try to eat some of the dried sausage, but after one bite, I nearly disgraced myself. Angelina managed two bites before choosing decorum over being fed.

Anita brought little Shirley over to say hello. The little girl was rather sweet, but still very fretful. I told Anita that Angelina and I would have a conference later that afternoon to discuss who would care for the child, and invited her to join us.

After I had finished eating, I made my way on foot into the pueblo to find out what had happened to the freight on board the disabled steamship. I landed at the railway depot. The mail had, at least, been delivered and I had a letter from my sister Carrie. I slid that in my pocket, hoping that I would get a chance before long to sit down and enjoy it.

There was a small group of men outside of the office at the depot, many of them merchants in the pueblo, and there was a great deal of grumbling among them. Mr. Wiley saw me and broke away from the group.

"Good day, Mrs. Wilcox," he said, smiling and doffing his hat.

"What is going on?" I asked, nodding toward the group of men.

"We all have freight on the Orizaba." Mr. Wiley looked down at his feet and shuffled them. "The steamship company has declared that the breakdown of the ship was the result of mere chance, an act of God, if you will, rather than a defect on their part. Therefore, the rescue of the vessel has become a salvage operation, and they are demanding a fifteen percent deposit based on our invoices, against the value of our freight, to cover the cost of the salvage operation."

"But..." I am afraid I gaped at that bit of news. "That's robbery of the worst sort!"

"They will not release any of the freight until we have all paid." Mr. Wiley shuffled his feet again. "We have decided to stand together and refuse."

"Oh, no!"

"My dear Mrs. Wilcox!" Mr. Wiley whipped his hat onto his head, then stood ready to catch me lest I collapse from the vapors.

That is what I presumed he was attempting to do. Not being one to suffer so, I merely took a deep breath and shook with my fury.

"I have medical supplies among that freight," I said. "I agree. Your cause is just. But how am I supposed to do surgery without carbolic acid, I ask you? I have laudanum and morphine on board, and a host of other drugs that I sorely need. The company is endangering the health and well-being of the citizens of Los Angeles!"

I strode forward and pushed through the crowd of men into the depot. The shipping agent, a stern-visaged man with a medium brown beard and waxed mustache, and wearing a finely cut and immaculate suit, sat at a table that had been set up in the waiting room.

"I demand my freight," I told him sternly. "Those are medical supplies that are sorely needed. The sheer effrontery of demanding such an assessment of people who have already paid for those goods! It's appalling."

"Well, madam, if you will be so good as to produce your invoice and pay the fifteen percent, I may be able to release your goods."

"No!" I stamped my foot for good measure. "How dare you take advantage of a mishap to fleece the good people of this pueblo?"

He swallowed briefly, but did not waver. "I am afraid I cannot do that, madam. However, if you produce the doctor and the money—"

"I am the doctor!" I snapped. "I ordered those supplies to take care of my patients."

He gaped. "You?"

"Why is it so hard to believe that a woman can be a doctor?" I folded my arms across my chest. "Never mind. I do not need your foolish prejudices. I need my freight and I need it now."

He sighed. "Madam, I cannot do that, and will not do that."

"Then I will see you in court!"

I swept from the room to find the gaggle of men watching me, and it looked as though several of them were trying not to laugh.

"We must hire an attorney," I told them.

"I suppose we could speak to Mr. Meyers," Mr. Carson said. He was a rotund man, newly gone gray, thanks to the loss of his and Mrs. Carson's daughter the summer before.

The others grumbled, but agreed.

"I will be happy to contribute to the fee," I said.

"No, no, Mrs. Wilcox. Allow us to see to the fee." Mr. Wiley took my arm, and smiling, led me away from the group. "You have life-saving supplies on board, supplies that, as you pointed out, are sorely needed for the health and well-being of our citizens."

I looked at him, completely at a loss. "Mr. Wiley, it is my preference to act in good faith, like the conscientious woman of business that I am. Nor am I one to shirk my duty in a needed endeavor."

"We will take that into account, Mrs. Wilcox." He patted my arm and looked as if he were about to tell me not to worry my pretty little head about it. Fortunately, he knew well how little I thought of that particular phrase. "You know how judges are, never willing to take a woman's word into account, even the word of a woman as astute as you are. Why don't I call on you with regular reports of what actions are taken?"

"If you insist." My eyes narrowed, but Mr. Wiley patted my arm again, then left to join the other men.

He and I had always been friendly, and I will confess to a certain fondness for the fellow. But there was something decidedly odd about his friendliness that day. It was almost as if he were courting me, yet he knew well the futility of that, and had been very clear that he did not wish to marry me.

I walked back to the center of the pueblo, utterly puzzled. Near the block where Mr. Wiley's office was, Mr. Lyons saw me and hurried over.

"Mrs. Wilcox!" He smiled winningly and tipped his hat.

"How do you do, Mr. Lyons?" I asked, pleasantly.

"Very well. I see that you have recovered from our journey yesterday."

"I have, for the most part." I looked at him. "As you have. I just now saw Mr. Wiley at the train depot."

"Ah. About the deposit for the Orizaba." Mr. Lyons looked rather darkly in that direction. "Highway robbery is what it is."

"Indeed. The last I heard, they were talking about engaging an attorney."

Mr. Lyons smiled at me. "Do you think that's the best way to handle this?"

"Of course." I looked at him, even more puzzled. "What other recourse do we have? And I have much needed medical supplies on board. I need them as soon as possible."

"I suppose that would be the case." He straightened his hat, then looked around. "Might I walk you to your next destination?"

"That's very kind of you, Mr. Lyons, but I think not." I smiled nonetheless. "I am afraid the journey yesterday and this new problem with the steamship have both put me quite out of temper."

Mr. Lyons tipped his hat again. "Very well, then. I hope to see you again soon."

I sighed as he made his way down the street. I quickly came to the conclusion that Mr. Wiley and Mr. Lyons were in concert on something that they wanted from me, or had some other trick up their sleeves. Which made no sense whatsoever because while they were very astute business-men, they were not, as a rule, devious. Plenty of other men were, but not these two. If anything, we enjoyed a rather open and honest communication.

I decided to put it aside, on the assumption that they would tell me what they wanted soon enough. I made my way to a dispensary in the hopes of finding at least some of the drugs I needed, only to find that Señor Lopez was in almost as dire a straights as I was.

"I say we just pay the deposit," he grumbled. "The steamship company will get it out of our hides one way or another."

"That is very probably true," I sighed. "However, giving in like that only encourages the fiends."

Señor Lopez sighed deeply. "There are times when you cannot win either way."

I bid him a good day, knowing full well that he was right.

My two greatest failings have always been my vanity and my temper, and by then, my temper was flaring badly. However justified my anger was, I did not want to give in to it and find myself engaging in an ill-considered action. But that did leave me wondering what to do next. Mrs. Gutier-rez had said that someone had been watching her home before poor Mrs. Dunbar had been shot. It did not take long to find out which was Mrs. Gutierrez's adobe, and I headed to the neighborhood at once. Fortunately, the old woman's adobe was across the road from the Vasquez farm on the south side of the pueblo.

The main adobe of the farm sat nestled among three groves of orange, walnut, and olive trees. Bee hives were stacked at the opening of the orange grove, and the senior Mrs. Vasquez was justifiably proud of her honey. She was a stout woman, with gray hair that constantly struggled loose of its pins. Her husband, Baldo Vasquez, had died the year before, and while she sincerely grieved him, she remained full of life and vigor. Her son, who was married with four children, had taken over the farm even before his father had passed away, and the younger Mrs. Vasquez was very fond of her mother-in-law, and very appreciative of the older woman's help.

The senior Mrs. Vasquez was baking bread that morning when I arrived. She wiped her hands on her apron, then bustled about, fetching pan dulces topped with her lovely honey and tea.

"I am so glad you are here, Señora Wilcox," she said as she poured for us both, then flopped into a chair across the worktable from me. "I have an excuse to get off my feet for a little while."

Mrs. Vasquez invariably spoke to me in English, even though she knew that I spoke Spanish.

"I see you're quite busy," I replied, after sipping some tea.

"Always!" Mrs. Vasquez laughed. "And this time of year, especially so. So much food to prepare for the Navidad.

We will have the whole family here, and it will be quite a party.”

“I can imagine.” I looked out the window at the rather run-down adobe across the way. “Are you friendly with Mrs. Gutierrez?”

“Oh, yes. We talk all the time. Poor thing is all alone now, what with Señora Dunbar gone and the child taken to her relatives.”

“Not quite to her relatives. The little girl is residing on my rancho, even now.”

“Ah. Well, poor Señora Gutierrez, she needs to find a new boarder because she is so frail and has no other relatives to take care of her. A rough man would not be good for her.” Mrs. Vasquez sighed and shook her head. “Do you know of anyone?”

“I am afraid I do not.” I nibbled on a pan dulce. “I have another concern, though. Mrs. Gutierrez said that she saw someone watching her adobe in the days before Mrs. Dunbar’s death.”

“Not just watching her adobe, but following Señora Dunbar.” Mrs. Vasquez leaned forward. “I did not see much, just shadows. In fact, it was I who told Señora Gutierrez about the stranger. I wanted her to warn Señora Dunbar, but what was the poor woman to do? She had to go back and forth to her work. It was a terrible thing to happen. Why would somebody kill a poor widow and leave her child alone? What a terrible monster.”

“Yes, I agree. I simply wish you had seen something that would help us find the monster in question.”

“None of us did. But he was there.” Mrs. Vasquez sat back and tried to pin a stray lock back in place. “Or maybe it was a woman. I saw something flapping, like a cloak or a dress, but nothing else. Señora Gutierrez. She may be frail, but her mind is as sharp as ever. You can trust what she says."

"Well, thank you for confirming that," I said, even though it was small comfort.

I stayed a few minutes longer to finish my pan dulce, then thanked Mrs. Vasquez again, and left. I headed through the main part of the pueblo to return to my rancho. Mr. Handley saw me as I walked down the Calle Principal and hailed me.

"It is so good to see you, Mrs. Wilcox," he said, sweeping his hat off with an elegant bow.

"Good to see you, as well, Mr. Handley." I forced a smile to my lips, wondering what on earth he was doing.

"I have news. That insurance company that Mr. Hewitt had the policy with?" Mr. Handley proudly puffed out his chest. "It is no longer in business."

"I do not see how that makes a difference," I said slowly. "The policy had lapsed."

Mr. Handley opened his mouth, then closed it. "I am telling this badly. The important point is that none of my colleagues here in the pueblo write life insurance with another company. I do not know why. They are quite beside themselves. We only found out about it yesterday, but it happened last week. There will be any number of lawsuits over this. It's why I am glad that I do not write life insurance." He chortled. "Seems silly to insure against something that will happen to us all."

"It's quite useful for widows with young children, though."

"Oh. Yes." Bemused, Mr. Handley blinked. "It would be. Thank you for pointing that out, Mrs. Wilcox. Well, may I accompany you home or to your next call?"

"No, thank you, Mr. Handley."

I walked off, feeling rather peeved. It was not unusual for men on the street to tip their hats and nod as I passed by them. It was simple courtesy, and for the vast majority of those men, that was all they were interested in. But that day, several men took off their hats and hailed me in quite a friendly manner. It was bewildering. They all wanted something, that was plain enough to see. But I wondered what it could be. My rancho and winery were fairly prosperous, but not so prosperous, I had heard whispered, that men in the pueblo thought it was worth having to deal with me.

I was so absorbed by my pondering that I nearly ran into Mr. Medrano.

"We are well met, Mrs. Wilcox," he said, sweeping his hat from his head.

"What do you want?" I snapped in spite of myself, then gasped. "Pray accept my apologies, Mr. Medrano. I have been sorely pressed this morning, but I have no right to take it out on you."

His smile, yet again, held no warmth. "I understand completely, ma'am. I, too, have been sorely tried these past two days. I heard you had left the pueblo, so perhaps you don't know that there was a fire in my shop the other evening."

"I'm so very sorry, Mr. Medrano."

"I am hoping for your wisdom and counsel." He tried looking earnest and just barely failed. "I am afraid that

Mrs. Hewitt may have started it. Or had someone start it for her."

"Why would she do that?" I asked, stepping back in shock.

"Then she would be the only buggy manufactory in the pueblo. She would have sole control over the custom."

"She has expressed no such interest to me, sir." I glared at him. "And we have been in some conversation over the past week." My eyes narrowed. "However, I have heard that you desire the same end."

Mr. Medrano chuckled. "Of course. Who wouldn't? It is how business is done, as I am sure that you, being such an astute woman of business, would understand."

"Mr. Medrano, I do understand, but cannot countenance such aims." I paused, suddenly worried that Theodora might have done something so rash. If she had killed her husband, why not seek to drive out her competitor?

"Well, I must be off," Mr. Medrano smiled again as Mr. McKinley, a land agent I had even less liking for, greeted me with a tip of his hat. "I need to check the land registries. I want to verify my boundaries."

"To what?" I asked.

"I have a plot of land not far from the Molina de las Huertas."

"Are you planning on selling it?"

"Of course!" He suddenly laughed. "Haven't you heard? There was a defect in the title to the land the Southern Pacific had wanted to buy for the new train depot. They've decided that they do not want to wait to resolve it, but instead wish to purchase another plot of land in the immediate vicinity."

"Oh." I shook my head and moved off. "I must be off as well. Good day, Mr. Medrano."

He tipped his hat and headed toward the Clocktower Courthouse, where the land registries were. I turned back to go home, only to remember that I had a significant plot of land next to the Molina de las Huertas. Suddenly, I knew the reason for my sudden and otherwise unaccountable popularity.

Chapter Eleven

If I was furious over the turn of events, my household, I am afraid, found the situation quite amusing.

"You should take advantage of it, Maddie," Magdalena giggled as we all ate our lunch. "You have made Enrique and Sebastiano your partners, so it will not hurt us if you get married."

"I do not want to get married!" I glared at them. "And certainly not to some fool whose interest in me is solely fixed on securing as much money from the Southern Pacific as he can."

Enrique shrugged. "Some of them simply want to be sure the Southern Pacific doesn't go elsewhere. They are afraid you might turn them down."

"I don't see why. I only bought that land because we thought it might be good to expand the vineyards, and then we decided that we didn't want to." I sighed. "I held onto it just to see how much the value might grow."

"It's about to grow pretty high," Sebastiano laughed.

I tried not to snort. The defect in the title involved how the two partners had signed the deed when they had sold the property to the current owner. However, those two former owners had returned to France and were still there. The Southern Pacific had decided that they did not want to go to the trouble of hunting the two partners down, which was why they had rescinded the deal.

There were no guarantees the men from the Southern Pacific would want my property. They hadn't originally. On the other hand, I was forced to concede that the men in the pueblo had some reason for their interest. Admittedly, my business was profitable, but the sale of the land could potentially make me flat out wealthy.

Fortunately, Angelina was already well apprised of the situation with my bit of land when she arrived that afternoon for tea. She, too, was amused, but thought of something else.

"Perhaps you can use this new interest to ask questions that you might otherwise not be able to." She said as we sat in my study.

I considered. "That is possible. But the behavior is so odious. I can barely stomach it, and now that I know why these fellows are so friendly, it is utterly exasperating. They're all acting as if they've hit the mother lode in the marital sweepstakes."

I sighed as Angelina laughed.

"Who cares?" she said. "Maddie, you can be quite flirtatious when you wish to be. And if the fools insist on believing that you cannot see right through their bad intentions, then they deserve to be led on."

"That is neither here nor there." I frowned. "We have more significant and important issues to deal with, namely the care of little Shirley."

"That." Angelina sighed. "My Edgar and I had a good, long talk this morning. He does not mind taking Shirley, but he is worried that we will not get to keep her, and that will break my heart."

"He does have such tender concern for you." I winced, thinking of Anita. "But, alas, he is right. There may be another with a stronger claim."

Angelina let out her breath as she sadly shrugged. She had lost her three babes when they were still fairly young, and while no one would think so from her usually merry demeanor, she felt the loss quite keenly and still grieved.

"That is, of course, true," she said. "And I have had my children and am warmed by their memory. Still, I would rather have what time I can with Shirley and have her taken from me than not have the time at all."

"If you are certain about that..."

Angelina reached over and touched my arm. "Very certain. In fact, I can take her now, if you like."

"Why not?" I got up from the chair at my roll-top desk.

We went over to the barracks and found Shirley sitting in the dining room, looking sad with her thumb in her mouth.

"I cannot get her to stop doing that," Anita sighed, exasperated. "I have removed her thumb so many times, I am almost afraid that I will have to strike her."

Striking children was a practice that I had never held with, another of my dear mother's counsels. She had never seen it do any good, and as I watched the many mothers I treated, I seldom saw any benefit to it, either. Fortunately, when I had discussed the issue with Anita, she had agreed with me, and eventually, as the years passed, corporal punishment became a rare occurrence on the rancho.

Once Shirley saw Angelina, though, the babe ran to her. Angelina picked her up and held her close, whispering to her in Spanish, although I did not hear what she said.

I offered the use of my buggy, but Angelina declined.

"We can walk," she said, then lowered her voice. "It will make the child tired and she'll sleep better later."

I decided that Angelina knew best, then shut the rancho gate after them, and went to see what other chores required attending to.

Shortly after dinner, I was called to Regina's home for an event I had been expecting for several months. One of the young women in her employ had conceived, which happened every now and again. Regina very kindly let such women stay in the house if they needed to, and then either take their work back up, or Regina, and usually me, would find some place for the woman and her child to go.

Adelaide had finally gone into labor. I briefly debated calling Elena to help me, after all, as a physician, she would be called upon to deal with the more iniquitous parts of our world. However, I decided that she was still too young and there would be more than enough time to complete her education in that regard.

Sebastiano drove me to Regina's and waited in the kitchen, talking with some of the men in Regina's employ, who were there to help keep the peace if one or more of Regina's customers became over-excited. I hurried to the room where Adelaide was and found that things were progressing quite nicely. Regina sat with her, as she always did at such events, and the little girl arrived quite promptly and cried lustily.

"She seems very healthy," I told Adelaide, a well-rounded little woman, who smiled through her exhaustion and looked on the now-wrapped babe in delight.

I washed my hands in the room's ewer, then nodded at Regina and followed her to Regina's cramped office.

"Thanks be to God, that went well," Regina chortled as she sat in the chair at the cluttered desk.

"Indeed." I nodded. We had both seen too many times when a birth did not go well. "We must still watch for childbed fever, but I do believe we have room for some optimism."

"For Heaven's sakes, Maddie." Regina rolled her eyes. "We have more than room for optimism. Yes, yes, I know there's always the possibility of something going wrong. But it goes right far more often than not."

I smiled. "True."

Regina looked at me, her smile growing positively evil. "And are you enjoying all the new attention you are receiving?"

I groaned loudly. "It is utterly appalling! I have not the least interest in marrying and if that is not well known in the pueblo, then it most certainly should be by now."

"I would say so." Regina laughed. "But you forget one thing, dearest Maddie. What man have you met who does not believe that he is far more enticing than he truly is?"

I pressed my lips together because the words that were springing to them were from Regina's lexicon, and I do attempt to be a lady in all that I do.

"The miserable brutes," I said instead.

"But you might consider encouraging them," Regina said.

"Oh, no. Not you, too!" I would have paced, but the room was far too tiny for that. "Angelina suggested the same. She said it might afford me an opportunity to ask questions that I might not be able to otherwise."

"Which was exactly my thought, as well," Regina said, her face serious. "We must do something. I know we cannot assume that the man who killed poor Mrs. Dunbar is the same person who killed Mr. Hewitt, but I ask you, what other reason would there be to harm her but that she may have seen the foul man who committed the dastardly deed."

"But she didn't see much of anything," I said.

"If the killer thought she did, would what she actually saw have mattered?"

I folded my arms across my chest, then put my hand on my chin. "I am afraid you're right. It is still possible that there was a second killer. Perhaps he was trying to shoot someone else. Or perhaps it was that demon of a husband of hers."

"I thought she was a widow."

"No. Oh, that's right. We haven't had a chance to talk since we got back." I sighed. "We found the man in the jail in San Buenaventura. He was quite agitated at the time, and we have good reason to believe beat both his wife and his daughter quite cruelly."

Regina threw up her hands. "One of the many reasons why I will never lack for girls. What kind of creatures are we when coming to work in a place like mine is safer and happier than the embrace of hearth and home?"

"I do not know, Regina." I shook my head sadly. "At least, you are kind and do the best you can that way."

"I will not tolerate cruelty from my guests." Regina pulled a handkerchief from her sleeve, sniffed, and dabbed at her eyes. "So many of my girls have known so little kindness. That's why I must show them some."

"I know. And I am grateful for it, as your young women are." I took a deep breath. "But until we women get full control over our lives with the vote, then we will continue to be at the mercy of men such as the despicable Mr. Dunbar."

"And even then, men, being the miserable brutes that they are, will still find a way to keep us in their control." Regina sat up straight. "Which only makes suffrage all the more critical." She finished dabbing her eyes, then looked at me. "We also must consider finding Mr. Hewitt's killer, who is, most likely in my opinion, to be the same fiend who killed Mrs. Dunbar. And if that is the case, then this person has already killed two people and will not stop at killing again."

"That is the essential issue," I said, then shuddered. "I do not know that I'll have the stomach to actually encourage these men. But I won't put them off either, and will use their attempts at wooing me as an opportunity to question them more thoroughly than usual. Will that do?"

Regina reached over and took my hands. "More than, dearest. Now, go, with my blessing, and I shall keep an ear out and point you where I can, within the bounds of the discretion I must keep."

"Have you heard anything?"

"Ah, Mother be praised!" She shook her head. "I almost forgot to ask your opinion of this. That land that the railroad foreswore because of the title defect. It belonged to the Hewitts."

"Did it?" I frowned as I thought this over. "Mrs. Hewitt has not said anything to me about it."

"That's odd."

"Not necessarily. Our new intimacy only happened after the death of her husband, so she would have had little reason to discuss such a private matter with me. And before then, we were preoccupied with issues of his health.

Even now, she might not see the sale as a reason to kill him. It was a finished transaction to all appearances."

"But that there was a defect," Regina said.

"

However, the sale was only canceled within this past week, well after Mr. Hewitt was killed. But wait." I paused as I thought it over. "We know of at least two men who have designs on Mrs. Hewitt, one of whom might actually be in dire need of money."

"Mr. Wills?" Regina looked at the ceiling. "It seems to me that he has, indeed, reformed himself."

"It doesn't mean he has. Or it may be someone else who needs money soon enough that it would give him a reason to kill Mr. Hewitt, then carry off his suddenly wealthy widow."

"The man would still have to wait at least a year for her to come out of mourning, though." Regina's brow creased. "So it would not make sense to hurry up Mr. Hewitt's demise."

"Unless this person was not aware of close Mr. Hewitt was to his demise." I threw up my hands. "But how are we to find out?"

"I will continue listening. The men do gossip so."

"We can but hope." Then I thought of something else. "Do you know what will become of the new infant? Or should I contact the Sisters of Charity?"

"No!" Regina smiled broadly. "There may yet be a happy ending to this one. My man, Mr. Delacruz, has fallen in love with Adelaide, and she with him. So she has decided to marry him and raise the child, which he says he convinced her to do. Now, their only problem is to find a landlord in the pueblo who will overlook his place of employment, as they do not wish to start over elsewhere until the infant gets a little older."

I thought for a moment. "What about a landlady whose need is so dire that she might not mind and so old she might not even notice?"

"You know of a place?" Regina looked surprised.

"I was asked about it just today." I smiled. "Mrs. Gutierrez, who was Mrs. Dunbar's landlady, is quite old and all alone in the world, I understand. And her adobe appears to be in poor repair. But if your Mr. Delacruz and Miss Adelaide would not mind taking her on, it would be a kindness to the old lady."

"It does sound like the ideal arrangement. Addie will be in bed several days yet, but Mr. Delacruz can meet with the lady. Can you arrange the introduction? I will send him over as early as tomorrow afternoon."

"I should be able to."

Regina got up, and we went upstairs to do one final check on Adelaide and the new infant. Then Regina led me to the kitchen, where Sebastiano waited alongside Mr. Delacruz and one other fellow whose name I have long since forgotten. Regina informed Mr. Delacruz of Adelaide's safe delivery and the possible new home for himself and soon-to-be-wife. Mr. Delacruz was profoundly grateful to the point of being fulsome and, taking my exhaustion from the day before as my excuse, I escaped the kitchen.

As it happened, I was still quite exhausted from my travels and when I got home and to bed, I fell asleep quickly, even before I could make my notes on the birth. I did so, however, shortly after breaking my fast the next morning. I had always been fairly scrupulous about making sure my notes on my patients were quickly and accurately record-ed. However, come that January, the state of California had decreed that, by law, anyone attending a birth or a death or performing a marriage, was to get full particulars of the participants, which in the case of births included the names of the parents, sex and color of the child, and place of residence. As I mostly recorded that information in my notes anyway, that did not trouble me. Having to collate the information and file it with the County Registry every quarter was a task I was not looking forward to, and no matter how important and useful the information would prove to be, it continued to be a task that I loathed during all the years that I was required to perform it.

As soon as I was finished with my notes, I decided to head into the pueblo. I was already wearing my indigo walking dress, but instead of the smaller hat that matched, I decided instead to don my straw bonnet with the indigo blue satin ribbon. Had I worn the other hat, I would have needed to carry a parasol to keep even the winter sun off my skin. My fair, white skin was one of my greater vanities, and I took great pains to make sure that the blistering Los Angeles sun would not turn me brown. As I tied the bonnet on, I could not help a sigh, as one of the reasons I did not want to turn brown was that it would not be acceptable in Boston, and I did want to go back home at some point.

I would have preferred riding, as that would have made it harder for men to pay their attentions to me. But given that I needed those attentions to ask the men about Mr. Hewitt's murder, I thought I'd best make it easier for them to do so and walk.

Which I did and had gotten no further than the plaza when the attorney Mr. Melvin scurried up to say hello.

"A fine day, Mrs. Wilcox, isn't it?" he asked, pulling off his hat.

It was, in fact, fairly cloudy, but cool enough to be pleasant.

"Fine enough, thank you," I replied, holding in a sigh.

Mr. Melvin replaced his hat. "And where are you off to this morning?"

"To pay a call on Mrs. Hewitt."

"Ah, yes." Mr. Melvin smiled warmly. "You have courageously chosen to search for her husband's killer, haven't you?"

I watched him carefully. "And what do you know of the affair? I believe you were at the party that night, weren't you?"

"But I was in the hall when it happened. I didn't see anyone leave. Well, beyond Mr. Jessup and Mr. Judson, when they took Mr. Hewitt out."

"Did you see when they returned?"

Mr. Melvin looked briefly at the street as he thought. "Maybe just before? Or was it just after?" He chuckled. "I don't really recall. I'm afraid I was engaged in an exceptionally entertaining conversation with Mr. Glassell at the time."

"I see. Well, thank you for answering my question." I began to walk again. "If you think of anything that will help my search, please contact me."

"Of course, Mrs. Wilcox. I'll be happy to help."

I was exceedingly grateful that the man did not follow me as I continued on my way. Once at Theodora's home, her mother informed me that she had gone to the manufactory to oversee some business. I entered the shop and saw her at the foot of the stairs to her office, speaking with Mr. Ledbetter. He turned to go, and as he did, I saw the oddest thing.

Theodora watched her foreman move away with a look that reflected the baser desires. It was not hard to see why. Mr. Ledbetter was, as I have noted, quite handsome, and even in his ill-fitting suit speckled with sawdust, cut a fine figure. Theodora was still fairly young and in good health, and had been dealing with a husband, one had to assume, had not been able to perform his marital duty for some years.

I would not now mention such a thing, but that it caused me to wonder yet again whether Theodora had, in fact, been the author of her husband's murder. I did not get much time to ponder the matter. Theodora turned and went up the stairs before I could apprise her of my presence.

The manufactory was a large, open room, with a staircase leading to the second floor and the offices there, on one side, and on the wall facing, three bench tables, at which men sat, busily cutting and stitching together leather seat covers or canvas tops. There was a huge door in the back that stood open most of the time. Next to the door, a forge was being worked by two burly blacksmiths, and the air was filled with the ringing of iron against iron as they fashioned undercarriages and wheel rims. A wagon box sat in the middle of the room, with only one of its sides. Three men operated a saw near the door, well away from the forge, while another planed a plank propped up on a couple of barrels next to the bench tables.

Mr. Ledbetter saw me and removed his hat.

"Hello, Mrs. Wilcox. How might I help you today?" he asked.

I smiled even as I sighed. "I am afraid I have a most unpleasant question to ask of you, Mr. Ledbetter. There was a fire the other night at Mr. Medrano's shop. Do you know anything about it?"

Mr. Ledbetter frowned curiously. "I know Mr. Medrano accused Mrs. Hewitt of arranging for it to happen, but Mr. Lomax said it started in the blacksmith's forge. He figured something hot got in with some sawdust, which happens often enough."

"I can imagine."

He began to get angry. "I promise you, Mrs. Wilcox, neither Mrs. Hewitt nor myself had anything to do with that fire and I will fight any fellow that says so!"

I made a note to myself to ask Mr. Lomax about the fire, then excused myself from Mr. Ledbetter to go upstairs.

Poor Theodora admitted me to her office and offered me the sofa near her desk. It was a comfortable room, as much parlor as it was an office, with gay curtains that were generally open to let in the sunshine. They were drawn that morning, however, and Theodora peeked around one to the street below.

"Both Mr. Jessup and Mr. Wills are out there now," she sighed with great bitterness and turned back into the room.

She looked almost peaked as she sank into the dark red chair next to the sofa.

"So much to do," she said, sighing. "And my heart is still so heavy, I can barely breathe, it seems."

"So often it is that way with grief," I said softly. "And I hope not to add to it, but I do have some questions for you."

She waved her hand. "Ask. You must, and it can't be helped."

"Have you filed for the probate on Mr. Hewitt's will?"

"Yes. I did that, oh... Last Thursday, I believe. Mr. Melvin will handle it."

"Has anyone come forward with a debt owed to him?"

Theodora shook her head. "Not as yet. But then, I do not believe the notice has been published in the newspaper yet. Mr. Barter has been quite cross about advertisers not paying their bills."

"He so frequently is," I said.

A wan smile flitted across her face. "Indeed, and it is understandable. Which is why I sent Mr. Ledbetter over there to make sure we had paid for our advertisement, which we had."

"That is all to the better." I looked at her. "And what about life insurance? Mrs. Sutton said that she asked you about a policy on Mr. Hewitt, but that you didn't have one."

"The business was sound enough to keep us," Theodora said. "We didn't need one."

"And yet, Mr. Handley had found such a policy from some years ago, written by Mr. Dawes."

Her eyes lit up. "There's life insurance?"

"Sadly, the policy lapsed shortly after it was written."

Groaning, Theodora slumped back in her chair. "For non-payment, I'm sure. And I did not know about it or it would have been paid for. As you are aware, Thomas made any number of such transactions and often forgot to tell me about them. I could not pay bills that I did not know existed."

"No, you could not." I took a deep breath. "There is also the problem with the title defect on the land the Southern Pacific was going to purchase for the new train depot. I understand that was your land."

"What an aggravation that has been!" Theodora crossed her arms across her chest and glared. "We bought that bit of land years ago, perhaps as long ago as Eighteen-Sixty. I'm not even sure you'd arrived in the pueblo yet. We were thinking of building our manufactory there, then found this plot here in town. But we held onto the land. I thought that it might eventually be worth something. After all, the pueblo was growing even then. I didn't really think about it until the men from the Southern Pacific asked about it. Mr. Kinley did the negotiating for us and won quite a handsome price for it."

I smiled softly. "Dare I ask how much?"

Theodora chuckled. "As if I do not know why you are asking."

But then she told me and while it was not fabulous wealth, it was a goodly amount.

"And you are not bemoaning the loss?" I asked.

"Perhaps a little." Theodora blinked. "But while the money would have been most welcome, considering the loss of my husband, Mr. McKinley assures me that the land will sell and perhaps at an even better price once the depot is built. In the meantime, he is helping me correct the defect as best we can. It is, apparently, not all that uncommon a problem. So many of the Mexicans have not been able to prove ownership of their land because of such lax record keeping. Mr. McKinley says that I might consider hiring

Mr. Brownlow after all this is done, as he is quite a good title attorney and worked with the Land Commission to help the Mexican land owners when we won the state."

I left soon after, my mind full. Mr. Brownlow had begun paying his attentions to me since the previous Sunday. Was it possible that he worked for the Southern Pacific? And even if not, could he have heard about the title defect before anyone else? And apart from attempting to gain from an association with me, did that have anything to do with Mr. Hewitt's death?

Chapter Twelve

As I left the manufactory, an errand boy ran up with a request from Mr. Meyers, another attorney in the pueblo. His wife and children were ailing and would I please come? I was immediately suspicious of the request. Mr. and Mrs. Meyers had lived in the pueblo a good many years and, to the best of my knowledge, preferred one of the other physicians in town. At any rate, they had never requested my services before.

Nonetheless, I went as asked, and found that Mrs. Meyers and her five children merely had nasty colds. Mrs. Meyers, in fact, had already determined such and did not understand why her husband had asked me to visit. I had a very good idea, and if I did not know what was behind the request, I became certain of it when Mr. Meyers showed me to the house's front porch.

First, Mr. Meyers made sure I had my full fee, plus some extra to pay for the lozenges I had left with Mrs. Meyers. Then he made a proposal that was decidedly indecent. In fact, I had to slap him hard to fend him off.

"But... But..." He held his cheek and gaped.

"Mr. Meyers, I am a decent, God-fearing woman!" I snapped. "To make such a suggestion is bad enough. But your wife is inside your house even now. And to take a liberty when I have not in any way suggested that it would be welcome, as indeed, it would not!"

"I— I— I apologize, Mrs. Wilcox."

"Good day, Mr. Meyers!"

I strode off, my face still heated with my ire. It was a most unfortunate time for Mr. Wills to make his attempt to woo me.

"Mrs. Wilcox, we are well met," he exclaimed, pulling off his hat and bowing.

"I am afraid we are not, Mr. Wills." I continued walking.

"Oh." He scrambled to keep up with me. "You seem quite put upon."

"I am afraid so."

"I do not wish to trouble you, but perhaps I can offer some balm to your wound. In the form of a luncheon. At the Bella Union, perhaps?" He looked at me beseechingly, his hat in his hands.

I almost burst into tears, I was so frustrated.

I turned on him. "Mr. Wills, you cannot possibly believe that I am unaware of the situation with the Southern Pacific and the land they wished to purchase. And under that circumstance, how could you believe that I would have an interest in your attentions when you have shown me none prior to this time and suddenly start paying me your attentions now? And that in spite of the appearance that your affections are aimed elsewhere!"

He gulped and looked around. "I do not know, Mrs. Wilcox." He winced. "It is true that I do hold affection for another lady in the pueblo. But I seriously doubt she will have me. She has no reason to." He sighed deeply. "I am a miserable excuse for a man."

The poor thing looked so downcast, I could not help my heart softening despite my pique.

"Not entirely, Mr. Wills," I said, my voice still quite firm. "If you continue to make good on your pledge to avoid gambling, there is no reason not to believe that the lady in question might eventually accept your suit. Therefore, it is up to you to prove yourself worthy, and please remember that she is in mourning for her first husband and will likely be so for at least a year, maybe longer. But that does give you some time to prove good on your pledge."

"You are kindness itself, Mrs. Wilcox." Mr. Wills blinked, then pulled a bright red silk handkerchief from his suit coat's pocket. "I cannot thank you enough." He stuffed the handkerchief back into its pocket, then shifted his marigold-colored vest. "I do hope that when the time comes, you will consider using my services."

I tried not to roll my eyes Heavenward. "I use them often enough as it is. Why would I cease to do so, should I be so fortunate as to have the Southern Pacific come calling? Now, please. I have other calls to make and wish to make them."

I walked off without waiting for his response and headed for the city jail. As I had hoped, Mr. Lomax was in. Alas, even he, the laconic fellow he was, couldn't help chuckling when he saw me.

"Are you going to ply your suit as well?" I growled at him.

He laughed at that. "Pray forgive me, Mrs. Wilcox. But you must admit it's funny seeing those fellows falling all over themselves to get in your good graces."

"Hm." I looked at him. "I am afraid I fail to see the humor in the situation. I have already had to slap one fellow this morning. It is utterly aggravating. I have many more important things to do than fend off a bunch of fools whose only interest in me is to get the Southern Pacific's money. And speaking of such things to do, have you heard about Mr. Medrano accusing Mrs. Hewitt of setting the fire in his shop earlier this week?"

Mr. Lomax nodded. "Problem is, it'll be awfully hard to prove either way, and Mr. Medrano knows it. You know as well as I do how easy it is to forget that a bit of iron is still hot and let it fall where it shouldn't. That sawdust pile was a lot closer to the forge than it should have been. But the other fellows in the manufactory all said that's where they leave it."

"I wonder who knew about that."

"Anybody who'd been in there, I'd expect."

I pondered that briefly. "I suppose that leaves Mrs. Hewitt out of consideration for the deed, as I seriously doubt that she's ever had occasion to visit Mr. Medrano's manufactory."

"If she paid someone to make trouble for the fellow, then perhaps." Mr. Lomax shrugged.

"Which brings us to the question of why would she? She has ample business and, as far as I can tell, does not feel the need to be the only buggy maker in the pueblo."

"Unlike Mr. Medrano."

I shuddered. "I am afraid that sort of greed is something that I simply do not understand."

"Hence your problem with the fellows coming after you."

I did roll my eyes Heavenward at that point. Mr. Lomax chuckled, then turned serious.

"You asked the other night about Mr. Lowman."

"Yes. Have you heard something?"

"I talked to Mr. Mahoney yesterday afternoon. He asked me about keeping Mr. Lowman out of his saloon."

"Which hardly comes as a surprise," I said, thinking of Mr. Lowman's bad odor and worse manners. "But why would Mr. Mahoney want you to prevent Mr. Lowman's entry?"

"It seems the fellow has decided that Mr. Mahoney needs to be a witness to his deal with Mr. Hewitt for some buggies and has been getting more forceful each time he goes in."

"Oh, dear. That sounds frightening, based on what you've told me."

"There isn't much I can do about keeping Mr. Lowman out of there. We just don't have enough police. But I told Mr. Mahoney that as soon as the man comes in, he should call me or one of the other boys."

"Thank you, Mr. Lomax."

"It's the least we can do, although I wish we could do more."

I thought for a moment. "Thank you, Mr. Lomax. I believe I now must pay a call on Mr. Mahoney."

Mr. Lomax nodded, and I left the jail office and made my way to the alley behind Mr. Mahoney's saloon, and found both of his daughters hard at work in the kitchen there.

Alice and Annie were twins and of marriageable age, but both preferred to work for their father, and while I well understood the desire to avoid the marital state, I did find it puzzling that the two young women seemed to, as well. After all, the vast majority of young ladies their age were fully occupied with finding husbands for themselves.

Annie, whose auburn hair had once again come loose from its pins, opened the door to the kitchen that morning. Like her father, she was tall of stature, but was pleasingly rounded. She greeted me and invited me inside, where her sister Alice was occupied at the stove.

"Where's Papa?" Annie asked.

Alice, the very image of her sister, although her hair tended to stay in place, looked down at what she was stirring.

"In his office, I think." She glanced up. "I can't leave this."

"I'll find him," Annie said and led me to the office at the back of the saloon.

The tiny room was cramped enough, and as usual, papers and cases of liquor littered every surface, including the rickety chair that Mr. Mahoney generally offered me. Sighing, Annie scooped up the papers from the seat, then plopped them onto the desk.

"I'll find Papa," she said and suited action to word.

I heard her call at the door to the public area of the saloon and a minute later, Mr. Mahoney hurried into the office. He was in shirtsleeves, but as he frequently received me that way, I paid it no mind.

I held my hand up. "I do not wish to bear any attentions you plan to pay me."

"Not planning on paying you any." Mr. Mahoney gruffly settled himself on the old whiskey crate. "I don't blame you for being fed up to your teeth with it. I tell you, this railroad is going to cause more trouble than it's worth."

My eyes opened wide. "Why do you say that?"

"When the railroad comes, so will the people, and we don't have enough water to support the ones that are already here. You were here for that drought, Sixty-One to Sixty-Four. You know what it was like. And this year, we have not seen a drop in months." He shuddered.

"You may have a point," I replied as I shuddered, as well.

The war years had been incredibly difficult, and so many of our neighbors lost their land and their livelihoods. It was also why Sebastiano, Enrique, and I had considered expanding the vineyards, even though it would have been terribly difficult to water the new vines. We all thought that there might be at least some more grapes, which would mean more wine to sell. In the end, it turned out to be unnecessary, thank God, but I had already purchased the land with what little extra money I'd had.

"Nonetheless," I continued, "I do have a couple of questions for you regarding Mr. Lowman. I have been given to understand that he has been here causing you trouble."

Mr. Mahoney grunted and shook his head. "I do not wish to talk about him, Mrs. Wilcox, because I will be forced to use language that a lady does not need to hear."

"And yet I have heard it so many times before," I said with a chuckle, then became serious. "No matter your good intentions, I do need to know whether the transaction that Mr. Lowman is so insistent about actually happened."

"Who's to say?" Mr. Mahoney frowned. "Knowing that fellow and Mr. Hewitt, they were both probably dead drunk when the deal was struck. And you know what Mr. Hewitt's memory was like. Lowman should have known better than to conduct business without Hewitt's man around."

"So, you have no memory of the event?"

"Even if I did, I wouldn't say so." Mr. Mahoney sniffed. "The last thing I need or want is to be dragged into court as a witness."

"I can certainly understand that, especially against someone as prone to violence as Mr. Lowman." I got up. "I shall have to think on the matter of approaching him, then. Thank you, Mr. Mahoney."

I returned through the kitchen to the alley behind the saloon, but instead of turning toward the closer street, I continued along the alley toward a street further on, as that was actually the shorter route to my rancho.

It is probably true that I was not as concerned about my personal safety when walking about the pueblo as I should have been, hence Olivia's constant worry. That being said, while the men in the pueblo could be, and were, frequently fighting with each other, and more than a few quite probably struck their wives and children with considerable regularity, during the light of day on the streets, the men did not accost the women. One would like to think that it was fine feelings of respect for those of us who were of the so-called weaker sex, and, indeed, for most of the men, I believe it was so. But there were many who, I feared, avoided such behavior for fear of being labeled a coward. After all, only a coward would attack a poor, defenseless woman.

The irony, of course, was that many women in the pueblo, myself more or less included, were perfectly capable of defending ourselves. Mrs. Glassell, in particular, carried a very large pistol in her carpetbag, and not only knew how to use it, but had, and if her reputation as a lady was not harmed by such use it was because no man was going to admit that he'd been outdrawn by a woman.

It was getting on toward noon that day, and even with a weakened winter sun overhead, I felt perfectly safe walking the less-traveled alley. I was alerted first by the whiff of something dreadfully sour overlaid by the odor of a badly kept stable. I had no time to consider before I heard the scrape of boots on packed earth.

I whirled around, pulling aside the cover of my leather satchel. Mr. Lowman backed up for a moment, uncertain about what to do, but his rage shortly took over and he loomed over me.

"What were you talking to Mahoney for?" he demanded, his sour breath almost choking me.

"I do business with the man," I replied, my voice shaking far more than I would have liked.

He shoved me, back first, into the wall of the block we were next to. My bonnet went askew with the bone-jarring slam of my person against the bricks.

"Dagnabbit!" Mr. Lowman swore. "You were talking to Mahoney about my buggies, weren't you?"

I swallowed back my fear. "And I have ascertained that he genuinely does not remember the transaction."

Mr. Lowman screamed something truly vile and bore down on me. I slid my hand into my bag, carefully trying to get to the item that I wanted.

"You and he are conspiring to rob me of my rights!"

"We are not!" I gulped and pulled my pistol out of my bag.

I stuck it in his ribs. His eyes widened at the contact, and he backed up a few paces. I swallowed again, trying to calm the way that my heart was racing so that I might think. I desperately needed to get the man to see reason, but given the state of his rage, I sorely feared that I would not succeed. Shaking inside, I kept the barrel of my gun trained on him.

"Be sensible, Mr. Lowman," I said as calmly as I could. "To what end would Mr. Mahoney and I try to rob you of your rights?"

Mr. Lowman, still breathing heavily, expectorated onto the ground, then winced as he realized that he had done so in front of a lady.

"Eh…" He gulped. "That Hewitt woman is paying you to."

"Why would she not want your custom?" I moved a step forward. He held his position, but looked a little abashed. "She is newly widowed and has three children and her mother to support. She cannot afford to get a reputation in the pueblo for bad dealings. If she is not acknowledging your arrangement with her dearly departed husband, it is because she also cannot afford to build buggies for which she has no contract or receipt for a deposit."

"But I gave him money!"

"How much?"

He swallowed and finally backed up.

I pressed forward, both my hands still on the pistol. "How much, Mr. Lowman?"

His eyes grew wide, and suddenly, his shoulders shifted downward, and he hung his head.

"I do not know," he said softly.

"Because you were in your cups at the time?" I glared at him.

His head shot up. "And what makes you think I was?"

"Mr. Lowman, your reputation for intemperance precedes you." I watched as he hung his head again. "As does Mr. Hewitt's. Most men of business in the pueblo knew not to transact any business with him directly unless Mr. Ledbetter was in attendance. Do you understand now why Mrs. Hewitt regards your claim with such caution?"

"I'm an honorable man," he grumbled.

"No one is saying that you aren't. Mr. Hewitt was very honorable, as well. He simply had a terrible memory, and apparently, you do, too." I pressed forward, my aim still on the man. But this time, he backed up. "Now, I do not see any reason why you cannot begin again with Mrs. Hewitt. I am confident that she will be happy to have your buggies built, and that you will be able to come to fair and just terms. However, for that to happen, you must go to her, hat in hand, with all due respect for her bereaved state." I saw him thinking it over and coming to the wrong conclusion. "Nor can you behave as the bully you have been and expect her to cede to your wishes. You have already tried that and it did not work, and I assure you, will not again."

"Yes, ma'am." Mr. Lowman nodded.

"Now, good day," I said, not releasing my gun.

Slowly, he turned and headed away from me down the alley. I waited for him to turn the corner, then slid my hand into my bag, but kept my grip on the pistol only until I was on the Calle Principal, in full view of any number of people. I noted the odd regard some of the men had for me as they tipped their hats and wished me well, at first, puzzled. Then the lock of my hair fell on my cheek, and I realized that I was rather unusually disheveled. I tried to straighten my bonnet without removing it, and was forced to do so, anyway. After re-tying it on, I made my way back to the rancho.

When I arrived home, late for lunch, Olivia took one look at me and took me to task quite strenuously. I barely heard her, my mind was so full. There was too much to consider, and I could not make sense of any of it. So as soon as I had eaten, I sent Rodolfo with the invitations to Angelina and Regina and asked Magdalena and Olivia to have everything ready in my study for after dinner.

I needed a conference with my two bosom friends and I needed it badly.

Chapter Thirteen

As dinner was cleared, Magdalena assured me that all was in readiness for that evening's conference, with plenty of pan dulces and angelica in my study. However, with a heavy heart, I went to that room for another conference first, this time with Anita.

I had been feeling quite divided among my loyalties. Angelina clearly wanted to keep little Shirley, and she was my bosom friend. However, Anita was a member of my household and equally dear to me, and suffered greatly without a child of her own. I did not, in fact, know how to choose among them, or even if I should. And as I ate dinner, I realized that the best course would be to talk to Anita first to ascertain how strongly she felt about keeping the child.

As it turned out, she did have strong feelings about the babe, but not the ones I thought she had.

"Why does everyone assume that I need someone else's child?" she snapped at me after we had listened to the children's lessons. "I am tired of taking care of everyone else's children as though that will compensate for not being able to bring one of my own into the world. How could that possibly erase my shame? All it does is remind me of my greatest failing as a woman."

"But you are not at fault," I stammered, somewhat surprised.

"It is not my husband's fault!" She paced about the study in her anger.

"Actually, it can be." I sighed. "Anita, who has made you feel so terrible about yourself? Rodolfo?"

She sniffed. "Not my Rodolfo. He is good to me and so very patient." She looked at me, then sat on the sofa and looked blankly at the wall. "It was my mother. She is gone now, but it is her voice I hear every month. She cursed me."

I reached over to her. "Now, Anita, darling, you know that I do not believe in curses and witchcraft."

"There was a man." Anita blinked, and I reached for a fresh handkerchief and gave it to her. "My mother said that I had bewitched him." She dabbed her eyes, then twisted the handkerchief in her fingers. "He was probably just another monster like that man last spring. But my mother blamed me for what he did, and cursed me, that I would never bear a child as punishment for my sin."

"Oh, Anita! I am so sorry you had to bear that."

She glared at me. "You are not going to look down on us as ignorant Mexicans?"

"Heavens, no!" I gasped. "What makes you think we Americans are any less ignorant and harmfully so?" It was my turn to pace. "Poor Mrs. Carson would have her daughter even now had she not given in to her ignorance and made the same base claim your mother did. It doesn't matter whether it's superstition or simply not bothering to think, the result is inevitably a great deal of unnecessary suffering!"

Anita smiled softly through her tears. "Thank you, Maddie." She looked up at me. "I love our children and I love teaching them. I truly do."

"They just cannot make up for the pain you feel or be the answer to why you feel it." I sat down in my chair. "Does this mean you have no objection to Angelina taking little Shirley?"

"None." Anita dabbed at her eyes again. "She loves the babe, and the babe loves her. She wants a child so very badly and will be a good mother."

"You are a good woman, Anita," I said as she stood to go. "Do not believe otherwise, no matter what your mother told you. By now, you have done enough penance, and worse yet, for a wrong done to you."

Anita shrugged. "I will try to remember that, Maddie."

While I had to be grateful that there would be no conflict with Angelina taking the child, the conference with Anita left me quite out of sorts. Nor did my temper improve once Angelina had arrived.

Mr. Sutton drove his wife to the rancho, and they arrived somewhat late. Regina promised to drive Angelina home, as it would be even later when they would likely leave and well after time for anyone to take note of who was riding with Regina. As Angelina brought in her little writing desk, she looked unusually lackluster.

"Dearest, whatever is the matter?" Regina asked as Angelina settled on the sofa in the study.

Worried, I handed Angelina the first glass of angelica. "There must be something terribly wrong. What is it, dear?"

Regina sat next to Angelina as she burst into tears.

"It's Edgar's sister, Vina," Angelina cried. "She and her husband are here from Santa Barbara with their four children to celebrate Christmas with us. They keep telling Edgar that we should not keep little Shirley. That we do not know enough about her parents and that she could be ill-formed in conscience or have some other flaw. That it would be dangerous."

"What?" I gasped. "She is an innocent babe, left all alone by the cruelty of another!"

"I know." Angelina sobbed. "But Edgar is so terrified of losing another child, he cannot help but listen. Worse yet, Vina does not say so, but has made several little hints about Mexican witches and that we are cursed."

"What poppycock!" Regina snarled as she held Angelina.

I snorted, getting up. "A bruja is a healing woman, not a woman who has sold her soul to the devil. What dreadful ignorance! And superstition, I might add."

I sat down next to Angelina and held her, too.

"Why on earth did you invite such a dreadful person to spend Christmas with you?" Regina asked.

"They have never been so cruel before." Angelina sniffed, pulling a handkerchief from her sleeve. "We have never been warm with each other. I thought that was Vina, because Edgar can be quite stoic as well. I did not know that she did not like me, although Edgar says that it's not that, but that she is afraid."

"Hmph!" Regina snorted. "I would say being afraid is too kind an excuse for much of the dreadful nonsense that we see in this world."

"Too true," I sighed. "And here I thought that I would be able to lighten your heart with some news. If there is to be a challenge for the child, it will not come from Anita."

"Anita wanted her?" Angelina looked at me, surprised.

"No. She didn't, and I will not betray her confidence, but it was for reasons that are entirely hers and no reflection on little Shirley."

"I just don't know what I am to do," Angelina said, sniffing.

"I say the first thing we do is find the one responsible for the child being orphaned," Regina snarled. "And in my estimation, the odds are excellent that the man or woman who did the deed also killed Mr. Hewitt."

"You are jumping to a conclusion, Regina," I said. I got up and poured glasses of angelica for her and myself. "We do not have enough information to make that determination."

"But there is no other reason to kill Mrs. Dunbar, but that the killer believed that she saw something." Regina drank her wine quickly and held out the glass again.

"What about her husband?" I asked.

Angelina shook her head. "I don't think so. Why would he have shot her and not taken the child with him? Even if he couldn't have taken the child at the time of the shooting, it would have been easy enough to get her sometime that night. We know he wants to have the child restored to him."

"Hm." I thought about it, then frowned. "The killer left the gun behind." I told them what Mr. Lomax had said to me about the gun he'd recovered. "It was probably accidental. And it was a nice enough piece that I have a hard time believing that Mr. Dunbar had the funds to carry such, let alone not return to get it. But who in the pueblo could own such a nice weapon?"

"Almost anyone," snorted Regina, then thought. "I haven't heard anyone complaining about missing a pistol or other gun."

I frowned as Angelina settled her little wooden desk on her lap and got out her paper, pen, and ink.

"I haven't either," Angelina said after pursing her lips. "That doesn't mean someone isn't."

"And I forgot to ask Mr. Mahoney about it when I spoke with him this morning," I grumbled. "We will all three need to listen to find out if anyone is missing such a weapon, but Mr. Lomax and I have determined that we should not say that we are looking for it, lest we alert the owner."

"An excellent idea," said Regina. "Who else must we consider?"

Angelina picked up one of her papers. "Mrs. Hewitt."

"Oh, dear Heavens," I sighed. "This morning I saw her gazing upon her foreman, Mr. Ledbetter, with the most lascivious look on her face."

"I've heard he cuts quite a fine figure," Regina said with a grin.

"He does," I said, hiding the flush on my face by pouring us each a glass. "I suppose it is possible that she arranged for her husband's death to expedite a liaison with Mr. Led-better. And yet, I have a great deal of trouble believing that. I would like to think that I have gotten better at telling when someone is lying to me."

"Does he seem to reciprocate her attentions?" Angelina asked.

I had reached for a pan dulce, but paused. "Possibly. But I do not think so in the way you intended. I do believe the man is in love with her."

Regina almost spilled her angelica laughing. "How do you mean?"

"The look on his face when he speaks about her," I said. "He seems quite fond of her, and now that I think about it, perhaps more than fond. Which is interesting because today Mr. Wills all but said that he was in love with Mrs. Hewitt, too."

Angelina nibbled on the end of her pen. "Do you think either of them was aware of how close Mr. Hewitt was to meeting his end?"

"If they were," Regina said thoughtfully. "That would certainly suggest that they are not the killers."

I nibbled on the pan dulce. "The worst of it was, Mr. Wills made his confession after attempting to pay his attentions to me." I sighed as Regina laughed and Angelina smiled. "And it was for the reason you both assume. Mr. Wills claimed that the other men put him up to it, but when I made it clear that he should focus his attentions on the woman he actually loved, he still asked if I would be sure to use his services when it would be needed."

"It would appear that Mr. Wills loves money more than he does Mrs. Hewitt." Regina held her glass out in request. "Which I have to say makes more sense than him simply being in love with her, given what you've told us about her temper."

I filled the glass. "He finds her dainty and charming. And I must concede that she keeps careful control of her temper around the men in the pueblo. And Mr. Wills seems to be continuing his pursuit of her, even though the land sale that would have made her fortune has been canceled."

Angelina made a note on her paper. "That does not mean that he did not seek to gain Mrs. Hewitt sooner rather than later."

I thought about that. "Indeed. And earlier, Mr. Wills admitted to me that he owed a gambling debt to Mr. Hewitt. But given Mr. Hewitt's incredibly bad memory, I wonder that Mr. Wills was at all concerned about it. At the same time, Mr. Wills was quite emphatic that he had reformed and that his debt to Mr. Hewitt was the result of a single lapse."

"It's always possible, I suppose." Regina looked at her half-full glass. "He certainly seems to have reformed."

"Who else is paying you attentions, Maddie?" Angelina asked.

"There is Mr. Brownlow," I said, refilling my glass and Angelina's as well. I suddenly frowned. "But he began plying his suit well before the defect was discovered. Nor would he have anything to gain by killing Mr. Hewitt."

"That we know of," said Angelina darkly.

"But he possibly would," Regina said. "He's a title attorney, and he works for the Southern Pacific. He would have not only known about the title defect, he would have known about it before anyone else and has the resources to know whose land was closest to the spot they wanted."

"How utterly aggravating!" I exclaimed. "I do not, in fact, have any interest in these attentions, but it would be nice if they were being paid because of some intrinsic charm or attraction that I actually hold, rather than a bit of land that I happen to own. But what would Mr. Brownlow have stood to gain by killing Mr. Hewitt? He did not have any grievance against the fellow as far as I know. At least, Mr. Judson has not tried to pay his attentions to me, and he certainly had a grievance against Mr. Hewitt."

Angelina gasped. "The election. As I understand it, he blames Mr. Hewitt's pronouncement the night of the party as the reason why he lost."

"Of course he would." Regina snorted, then glared at her glass. It was again empty. "He couldn't possibly countenance the fact that he is enormously unpopular in the pueblo, thanks to his rectitude."

I sighed and refilled Regina's glass. "One would think that would be a virtue in a banker, as Mrs. Judson has pointed out."

"I'm sure it would be," Regina said. "If he did not insist so vehemently that everyone else be held to the same standard he holds for himself."

"And he was in the immediate area when Mr. Hewitt was shot." I got up and began to pace. "I suppose he could have doubled back to the other side of the buggy. Mr. Melvin said this morning that he saw both Mr. Judson and Mr. Jessup come back into the hall, but Mr. Melvin could not say whether they returned before or after the shooting."

Angelina frowned at her paper. "That means that Mr. Jessup could also have shot Mr. Hewitt. But why? He seems to hold Mrs. Hewitt in quite tender regard."

"If that is the reason for the shooting, then either Mr. Wills or Mr. Jessup could have been responsible," I said. "The only difference between the pair's affections is that Mr. Wills seems intent on worshiping from afar. Oh, wait. Mr. Jessup claimed to be in San Buenaventura the night that Mrs. Dunbar was killed, and while we could not prove that he was, we also could not prove that he wasn't."

"That would seem to eliminate him from consideration," Regina said.

Angelina shook her head. "He could have lied about being there."

"He could have, indeed." I sipped, thinking. "He said he left on Friday night's stage. Perhaps I will check the passenger list at the stage office. They should still have it." I reached for a pan dulce, something stirring in my my mind. Alas, I was unable to pin it down. "As for people who have grievances against Mr. Hewitt, both Mr. Medrano and Mr. Lowman do, and we know that Mr. Medrano was close by at the time of the shooting. He claimed that he was visiting his mother. She agreed that he was, but that he had gone there because he was drunk and wanted to sleep there for some reason."

"Is Mr. Medrano married?" Angelina asked.

"Not to the best of my knowledge," Regina said. "His attention seems solely fixed on bettering his fortunes, and preferably at the loss of someone else."

"He is quite the odious fellow." I poured myself a glass of angelica and glared at it.

Angelina looked up from her papers. "What about Mrs. Glassell?"

"She refuses to speak to me," I said. "Which is quite odd, indeed. In the past, when I have been hunting for a killer, she has been quite eager to share all the terrible things she's heard about her neighbors. Yet I cannot imagine she had a good reason to shoot Mr. Hewitt."

"Perhaps she does." Angelina said. "Have you heard that she is rallying the women of the pueblo for a temperance revival next month?"

Regina laughed. "As though that movement could ever get a foothold here."

"Given the large number of dissolute husbands in the pueblo, it well could," I said, then looked at Angelina. "But while I can see that Mrs. Glassell would intensely dislike Mr. Hewitt, it seems more likely to me that he would be the reason why she wants the temperance revival, not why she would kill him."

"Wait," said Regina. "Wasn't the fete where he disgraced himself her party? Could he have disgraced himself one too many times in her eyes, not to mention relieving poor Mrs. Hewitt of her trial?"

"I suppose that's possible." I thought about it. "I shall have to try to see her again. Angelina, who else should we consider?"

"Mr. Handley," Angelina said, then sipped from her glass. "And I had a thought about him. What if he lied to us about the insurance policy? Perhaps there was a policy after all and he does not want anyone to know about it so that he can get the money from it for himself. That would be a reason to kill Mr. Hewitt."

I shook my head. "But Mrs. Hewitt did not know about the policy and it would make no sense to pretend other-wise, as she was the one to benefit from it. And we know there was a lapsed policy."

"Unless..." Regina sat up straight, her eyes glittering. "Mr. Handley made the policy, but made himself the ben-eficiary and kept up the payments for Mr. Hewitt while waiting to kill him. It's quite possible the man holds life insurance policies on several men in the pueblo and intends to slowly, one by one, kill them, then collect the money."

"What a dastardly plot!" I gasped. "And yet, it seems utterly plausible. But how would he get away with it? Surely the insurance company would wonder why so many of his policies were being paid, especially, as Mr. Handley has suggested, part of his job is to avoid paying on such claims."

"Maybe he only needs one or two," said Angelina, scribbling away. "The question is, how do we find out?"

"That will be my job," Regina said. "I know just how to do it."

I looked at Angelina. "Didn't you say that you were going to find what you could about Mr. Charles Hewitt?"

"There was nothing to find." Angelina shrugged. "He's a drunk, like his brother, and he's already left the pueblo. No one knows for where."

"If he's a drunk, then it is not likely that he would have been able to shoot either Mr. Hewitt or Mrs. Dunbar," I said. "When did he leave?"

Angelina frowned. "Sometime before Mrs. Dunbar got shot. I know because I was told that he was gone before that event occurred."

"Then at least we can strike him from our list of possible killers," Regina said, wiping the crumbs from a pan dulce off her jabot.

"But we do have another possible reason for the killing," I said slowly. "The sale of the Hewitt land to the Southern Pacific."

"The sale was canceled," Angelina said. "And after Mr. Hewitt died."

"Precisely," Regina said. "Maddie and I were wondering if someone wanted to carry off a wealthy wife thanks to that sale, and made her a widow to do so."

"That would mean either Mr. Wills or Mr. Jessup," Angelina said, looking at her papers. "Wait. What if Mr. Brownlow wasn't the only one who knew about the title defect? Maybe someone else found out about it and became enraged and shot Mr. Hewitt."

"Who could have been hurt by that?" I asked. "Mrs. Hewitt was because her land was not sold as it should have been. But she told me that Mr. McKinley said it will be worth even more once the depot is built, and there will be plenty of time to clear up the defect."

Angelina held out her glass. "And having her husband shot when he was about to die anyway would not better that situation. Nor would it make for good revenge if she was angry about it."

"I wonder if Mr. Wiley would have been hurt," I said, thoughtfully. "He certainly has been paying his attentions to me as if he expects to gain by it. But that means the defect has helped him, not hurt him."

"Mr. Brownlow." Angelina picked up a pan dulce, glared at it, then put it back down. "Finding that defect so late in the process could have hurt his job with the railroad."

"I seriously doubt that," Regina said. "Defects like that are why you hire a title attorney and they can turn up at any point in the process."

I frowned. "I believe that is true. Unless Mr. Brownlow had some other gain that he hoped for as a result of a successful sale to the Hewitts. But it would have to have been a significant one to make him angry enough to shoot someone in cold blood. Although, he has been paying his attentions to me even though I have warned him that he has little chance of succeeding in his suit, and as Regina noted, he could have known well ahead of anyone else that my bit of land might be wanted." I groaned in annoyance.

Regina chuckled. "Maddie, I cannot understand why you are not taking great pleasure in leading the poor fools on in their pursuit."

"Because I do not care to be the object of indecent proposals!" I glared at her. "Even the married men are coming around. Mr. Meyers made just such a proposal this morning out front of his house with his wife inside."

"I think I may know the reason for that." Regina sighed. "Last night, several of the men were making jokes about the joys of a lusty widow and have decided that you are such."

"What?" I felt the blood drain from my face. "What about my reputation?" I stalked the room. "Oh, if that— That—"

"Trust me, he hasn't," Regina said as Angelina's eyebrows rose. "I have made very sure of it. And warned him again last night if he even so much as thought about doing so. Your little secret is safe."

"Maddie," Angelina suddenly laughed. I would have been glad of it had the turn our conversation had taken were anything than what it was. "Have you...?"

"There might have been... an understanding." I flushed deeply. "But I have been nothing but discrete."

"She has been," Regina said with a smile. "Perfectly discrete. Nonetheless, there are those among the so-called gentlemen of the pueblo who, for no good reason, have decided that it would not only be easier to turn Maddie from the path of the righteous than they thought, but more amusing, too."

I sank into my desk chair. "Oh, dear Heavens! What am I to do?"

"Absolutely nothing, dearest." Regina reached over and patted my hand. "It is only their foolish pride speaking."

"I had to slap Mr. Meyers today."

"And you may have to slap a few more." Regina rose majestically. "But do try to enjoy it."

Chapter Fourteen

I finally got to read the letter from Carrie while breaking my fast the next morning. Marisol had done a superb job of brushing out and setting to right my walking suit, so I again donned it and settled in with soup, fresh-baked biscuits and coffee, to read.

It was full of the usual news. My father's complaints about his health were ongoing, but nothing seemed to be terribly wrong with him. Carrie and I both agreed that despite his travails, he was likely to outlive all of us. Our brother was being his usual pompous self. Our sister, Abby, who was expecting her second child, seemed to be doing very well.

Then there was Carrie's arrest and consequent examination. Carrie was even more of a suffragist than I was, and had even gone so far as to vote illegally in a local election. Carrie, fortunately, had married happily and her husband, Ambrose Stanton, not only agreed with her cause, he joined her in it.

"At the end of it all," Carrie wrote. "The judge admonished we sisters to return to our homes and obey our husbands, as good wives should. Several of the husbands stood and cheered, but Ambrose rose and shouted over them, 'Then my wife will vote again and again, as that is my wish as her husband!'"

I laughed heartily, but at the same time, my heart ached to see her, to be home in Boston, with snow, and the embrace of my dear sisters. It seemed a blessing when I was called to care for a young woman with pneumonia. After all, I would not have time to brood over being away from home. The patient's fever was not terribly high, and her lungs did not sound overly congested, although her cough was very nasty. There wasn't much to be done besides preparing a mustard plaster and prescribing rest and lots of beef tea.

And, alas, that left me feeling even more out of sorts than I had been. There was so little we could do about such diseases, and even now there is not much to be done about pneumonia, except wait and hope. So, it was not to Mr. Wiley's benefit when he found me crossing the pueblo as I headed toward the stage office to find out if Mr. Jessup had, indeed, purchased a ticket.

"Mrs. Wilcox, what a pleasure it is to see you this morning," he crowed.

I turned on him. "Oh, for Heaven's sake! Why are you pursuing me this way? You, of all men, cannot possibly believe you will achieve anything by courting me. I know full well that you do not want me as a wife, and you know full well that I do not want and will not take a husband."

"Well..." He stepped back and sighed. "The other fellows put me up to it. They are hoping to get a cut of the proceeds if you agree to let them help you with the negotiations on the sale to the Southern Pacific. They seem to believe that I have the best chance of convincing you to let them help."

"Why?" My blood suddenly drained from my face. "You did not say—"

"I did not!" He held his hands up as a look of sheer panic took over his face. "I said nothing. It must be because we do business and are known to be friends. Perfectly circumspect friends." He swallowed. "I promise you, Maddie. I am utterly terrified of what Mrs. Medina would do to me if I said anything."

"You'd best be more afraid of me."

"No." Mr. Wiley stood resolute, then spoke gently. "I do not want to be afraid of you. For all our little understanding was brief, I do look on it fondly."

"We are not well-suited to each other," I said, tears coming to my eyes.

He sighed. "No, not well-suited. But had we married, I like to think that we could have made a companionable marriage."

I shook my head. "Possibly. At least you would have been kind." I looked at him again. "What was your opinion of Mr. Hewitt?"

Mr. Wiley looked puzzled. "I'm not sure. I didn't really think about him one way or another. I mostly dealt with Mr. Ledbetter, as it was… Shall we say, more likely that the terms of an agreement would be fulfilled."

"It would have been."

"Why do you ask?"

I shrugged. "He was murdered and it would help to know who had a grievance against him."

"Well, yes." Mr. Wiley's brow creased as he thought, then shook his head. "He was a dissolute, but an agreeable fellow overall." He looked at me. "Pray forgive me, Maddie, for presuming upon the bounds of our friendship, but there is good reason to believe that you will be soon visited by the agents of the Southern Pacific. You are an incredibly astute woman of business, and if there were to be only one agent and from anybody but the Southern Pacific, I would grant you Godspeed and sit back and watch with great relish."

"Indeed. They are not known for their gentlemanly behavior." I sighed.

"Even with Mr. Ledbetter at the head of the last negotiation, we had a full team of agents working together." Mr. Wiley looked plaintive. "It is absolutely critical that they build that depot here in Los Angeles. It is their preference and we can use that to our advantage, especially since they have bought the Banning line. However, they are not bound by anything to stay here and may yet decide it will be easier for them to go to San Diego or San Bernardino. Or build a whole new town."

"I am well aware of that." I smiled. "You are probably right about having a team of negotiators, so I will give your concern my greatest consideration. And..." I paused, then took a deep breath. "John, if we are to remain friends, then we must be honest with each other and avoid these ridiculous theatricals."

Mr. Wiley smiled and offered a short bow. "It will be my greatest pleasure to do so, Mrs. Wilcox."

He tipped his hat and went on his way. I was about to go on to the stage office when something else occurred to me. I had yet to speak to Mrs. Downey about whether or not her husband had been subjected to any threats and to tell her about Mrs. Dunbar having been followed. So, I changed course and went there first.

Mrs. Downey was in and happy to see me. We settled in her front parlor and were served pan dulces and tea.

"Oh, Mrs. Wilcox, I am so glad you came," Mrs. Downey said once she had poured. "I meant to send you a message, but with all there is to be done before Christmas, I completely forgot. I did ask the governor about any threats he had received, and he said that it has been blissfully quiet in that regard."

"I am not surprised," I said, taking a sip of tea. "However this might surprise you. Someone was following Mrs. Dunbar around in the days before her death."

"Good Heavens! Who?"

"That is what we do not know." I nibbled on a pan dulce. "I was hoping that you or one of your household might have seen something and not realized that was what they saw."

"I have seen nothing." Mrs. Downey shook her head. "How is the little girl?"

"Being well-cared for," I said, then looked at Mrs. Downey. "Mrs. Sutton has her. We would prefer it if you did not speak of it, however. It turns out that Mrs. Dunbar was, in fact, still married. Unfortunately, to an exceptional brute, so you can imagine why she told you that she was a widow. The man complained quite violently that he wanted his child, but did so from a jail cell into which he had deservedly been put. And immediately before she died, Mrs. Dunbar made me promise not to give little Shirley to him."

"Oh. Well, of course you must honor that." Mrs. Downey frowned. "And you are certain he would harm the babe?"

I nodded. "According to his former landlady, he already had, along with her mother, on multiple occasions. And the sheriff in San Buenaventura even agreed it would be ill-considered for him to keep the child."

That made Mrs. Downey sit back in shock. After all, a man's wife and children were practically his possessions for him to do with as he pleased. For another man to withhold the child, that meant that the father was an exceptionally evil man, indeed.

"My word," she said finally. "I can well imagine you want the child hidden. But why hasn't her father already come?"

"We do not know. We fear he may have been the one who killed his wife, but as no one seems to have seen anything, we cannot say with any certainty. Otherwise, the killer was the same person who killed Mr. Hewitt, and took Mrs. Dunbar's life because he feared that she had actually seen something."

"How terrible, indeed." Mrs. Downey shuddered. "I shall not say anything about the child's whereabouts." She paused, then took a sip of her tea. "And how are you otherwise?" She couldn't help smiling.

And I couldn't help but roll my eyes Heavenward. "You can imagine. It has been utterly ridiculous. Am I to hear that your husband will be plying me with a suit?"

Mrs. Downey laughed. "No. He is more honorable than that. But he did ask me to tell you that he will be happy to help with such negotiations as you find yourself in. I told him that you are perfectly capable of negotiating a land sale."

"Under normal circumstances, I would agree," I replied. "But we are talking about the Southern Pacific. We shall see."

I quickly finished my pan dulce and tea and bade Mrs. Downey a good day.

I returned to the center of the pueblo and decided to call on Mr. Mahoney before I went to the stage office. Mr. Mahoney was in the alley when I approached.

"Good day, Mrs. Wilcox," he said as I walked up.

"I forgot to ask you something yesterday," I told him. "Have you heard any talk about a missing gun? A six-shooter specifically."

"None. Should I ask about it?"

"No!" I gasped and adjusted my bonnet. "Please promise that you will not, or let anyone know that I asked about it. It is critical that we do not alert the wrong person."

"My word on it, then. I'll not say anything."

"But do tell me if anyone does and note who that person is."

"Happily."

"Thank you, Mr. Mahoney, and good day."

I left the alley closer to the back of the saloon. But when I got to the street, Mr. Brownlow stepped up.

"Ah. Mrs. Wilcox. I am so happy to see you." He tipped his hat and smiled expansively.

"I am afraid I am on an urgent errand, Mr. Brownlow," I said, not stopping.

He caught me up. "I shall not detain you, then. Might I call on you Sunday afternoon?"

"I suppose." I suddenly stopped walking. "Mr. Brownlow, you are a title attorney, correct?"

"Yes." He smiled and puffed out his chest.

"Are you under sole contract with the Southern Pacific, or are you able to take on another client?"

He blinked. "I work for them independently. Why?"

"As I'm sure you know, I have a piece of land next to the plot originally designated for the new train station depot. Would it be possible for you to verify that my title is clear and without defect?"

"I probably should anyway, Mrs. Wilcox." He smiled again, this time a little puzzled. "That you should ask is quite perspicacious of you."

I couldn't help a glare. "With all the noise in the pueblo about the last one? Why wouldn't I double check?" I smiled quickly. "And how much will it cost to do so?"

He put his hand on his chest. "It will be my pleasure."

"And it will be my pleasure to pay you. Please see to it that I am invoiced." I looked down the street only to see Jaime riding up side saddle on Daisy. "Oh, dear. That can mean only one thing. I must be on my way."

Jaime pulled up as Mr. Brownlow walked on.

"What is going on?" I asked.

"Another runaway horse on the north side of town." Jaime dismounted and handed me Daisy's reins. "Knocked over many, many people. At least two died. Dr. Skillen asked that you go straight to the hospital."

The lad helped me mount as best he could, being still fairly short. I kicked Daisy into a run and made it to the hospital in short order. Elena had already arrived. We spent the rest of the afternoon and into the evening setting bones, wrapping head bandages and one rather tricky surgery to attempt to repair a shattered foot, but ultimately I had to amputate it.

It was well after eight o'clock when I finally got back to the rancho. Olivia had held my dinner, a lovely rabbit stew. For all she would scold when I was late for a meal, she was very kind and sympathetic when my work did not end well. I wrote my notes, then went to a restless sleep.

The next morning, dressed in my red poplin work dress, I was about to go to the stage office when my intention was yet again thwarted. However, it was not so much being thwarted that worried me, but the reason why. Rodolfo had already saddled Daisy upon my request. It being Saturday, it seemed highly likely that I would be needed in a variety of places, culminating in my residence at the hospital.

I hurried out to the farm on the distant edge of the northeastern part of the pueblo. The adobe was rather run down, but in much better shape than it had been, and the farm surrounding it looked far more prosperous than it had the previous spring. I could not help but smile. The arrangement that had been devised the previous early summer seemed to be working out exceedingly well.

Mr. Lomax had a most curious history. He was a Mormon when he came to Los Angeles with his two wives, Ruth and Sabrina. For all he was laconic, he was quite sentimental about both women and especially their children. He had only surrendered Mrs. Sabrina to a Mr. Efrem Smith the summer before, when Mr. Smith purchased a large plot of land adjoining Mr. Lomax's place. That way, Mr. Lomax still could be close to the children he'd had with Mrs. Sabrina and keep Mrs. Ruth and her children as well. That Mr. Lomax seemed to have a greater interest in his work as a policeman than a farmer did not entirely surprise me. That Mr. Smith was quite happy to make up for Mr. Lomax's deficiencies as a farmer did. Nonetheless, I was pleased.

Mr. Lomax was in bed in the room he shared with Mrs. Ruth Lomax (Mrs. Sabrina now being Mrs. Smith). Mrs. Lomax had always been rather round of shape, with dark hair. But that at that time, she was considerably rounder as she was expecting a new infant that spring.

"It's nothing serious," Mr. Lomax grumbled.

Mrs. Lomax shook her head and glared at her husband. "It could be if there is any contagion."

The cut on Mr. Lomax's arm was long, but not deep.

"Mrs. Lomax is quite right," I told her husband. "And she was right to call me. You will not be able to provide for her and all of your children if you lose an arm to gangrene."

Mr. Lomax grunted. "I'll be fine. It's just a scratch."

Mrs. Lomax and I looked at each other and shook our heads.

"Even just a scratch can be dangerous," I admonished him, reaching into my bag.

Although I had but a few ounces left of carbolic acid, I decided that Mr. Lomax's arm warranted one or two.

"And how did this happen?" I asked, dosing the cut and debating whether I should stitch it closed.

"The usual," he grumbled. "Stupid drunks."

I smiled, even though his language was unusually frank for him. One of the greater blessings of Mr. Lomax was that he seldom used language unfit for ladies.

"Would you kindly elucidate?" I asked.

Mrs. Lomax threw up her hands in frustration. "We are speaking to my husband, are we not?"

Mr. Lomax grunted. "I was called to Mr. Mahoney's saloon late last night. Mr. Mahoney was worried that Mr.

Jessup might cause some trouble. He was definitely not well. Mr. Jessup, I mean."

As in, Mr. Jessup was the worse for drink.

"I was unaware that he had a problem that way," I said.

"He doesn't. But he was bemoaning and crying over Mrs. Hewitt, no less." Mr. Lomax looked at me.

I frowned and nodded at his arm. "Was he responsible for this?"

Mr. Lomax shook his head. "That was two other fellows who fell to right after I arrived and determined that Jessup was more likely to fall asleep in his whiskey than not. One of the fellows had a knife and, well, you can see what happened."

I looked the cut over again. It had long since stopped bleeding.

"I see," I said. "It does not look like this will need sutures. A good, solid bandage will suffice. But you must stay alert to the first signs of contagion."

I went on to enumerate such signs to both Mrs. and Mr. Lomax. I did not doubt that Mr. Lomax, being a man, would ignore such signs if not for his wife. But he was a tender and kind husband, which meant that I would be sent for if she was worried, even if he was not.

I left soon after to go on my original errand, i.e. the stage office, and actually arrived there in good time, as opposed to being distracted by some other, greater need. I tied up Daisy outside the office and went inside the wooden building.

I was quite encouraged by what I found there. Mr. Jessup's name was on the list of passengers for the Friday before Mrs. Dunbar's death, which meant that he was, indeed, in San Buenaventura when the fatal shots had been fired, and thus, could not have fired them. I cannot say that I had any particular fondness for Mr. Jessup, but I was relieved. Given the large number of people who could have killed Mr. Hewitt and Mrs. Dunbar, having one less was a very good thing to my mind.

Regrettably, my elation at being able to eliminate one of our potential killers from our list was relatively short-lived. I had just left the stage office when Mr. Navarro approached.

"I am glad to see you here," he told me, as I walked to where I had left Daisy tied up. "I have some information for you that you might want to consider regarding a certain gentleman who has been vying for your hand of late."

"Mr. Navarro, while I appreciate your concern, you must be aware that there is more than one gentleman, however loosely I use the term, vying for my hand at the moment."

His so very charming eyes lit up as he chuckled. "Indeed, there is." He grew serious. "My concern, however, is regarding Mr. Brownlow." Mr. Navarro looked around at the street. "He worked for the state Land Commission before he took on tasks for the Southern Pacific."

I paused before untying the horse. "The commission that was supposed to make sure the Mexican land grants were honored under the Treaty of Hidalgo." I had little reason to believe that was what had happened, and Mr. Navarro's snort of disdain supported that belief.

"The commission did as much to disprove the land holdings as they did to uphold them," the young man said. "I am blessed that my family kept very careful records and had surveyed their property accurately."

"So, in other words, you believe Mr. Brownlow to be something of a traitor."

Mr. Navarro winced. "Perhaps not a traitor, and certainly not to the United States. But less than honest? I must question his sincerity, since the Land Commission did as much as it could to disprove any Mexican holdings."

"Indeed." I frowned. "You are absolutely correct, Mr. Navarro."

I was about to say more when Mr. Navarro knocked me to the ground as a pair of shots rang out. A moment later, Mr. Navarro was on his feet, his pistol drawn, and he ran, presumably in the direction from which the shots had come. Daisy neighed and stamped, but did not rear or otherwise spook. She was a very calm horse.

I slowly got to my knees as Mr. Judson and Mr. Brownlow both appeared and insisted on helping me to my feet.

"It's indecent!" Mr. Judson sputtered. "Are you hurt, Mrs. Wilcox?"

"Not in the least." My bonnet had fallen off my head, and I dusted off my dress.

"Are you sure?" Mr. Brownlow asked anxiously. "It looked as though that policeman landed quite hard on you."

"Perhaps, but he probably saved my life in doing so." I fumbled with the bonnet's ribbons, then looked about on the ground. "Are all my things here?"

My leather satchel remained closed, so I surmised that nothing had fallen out. Daisy snorted and stamped a little, though.

"Saved your life?" Mr. Brownlow gasped.

"She was shot at!" Mr. Judson sputtered. "It's indecent, I tell you. Perfectly upright people not being able to go about their business in broad daylight for fear of gunfire. I will have to write a communication to the newspaper. And speak to the Common Council about this."

Mr. Navarro chose that moment to come trotting up, shaking his head.

"What happened?" I asked as Mr. Judson continued fulminating.

"I saw the sun on the gun barrel." Mr. Navarro looked somewhat abashed. "That's why I knocked you down. I apologize."

"I am glad you did," I said.

"What made you so certain that the gun was about to start shooting?" Mr. Brownlow demanded of Mr. Navarro.

Mr. Navarro sighed and looked at me. "It was aimed right at Mrs. Wilcox."

Chapter Fifteen

Sadly, Mr. Navarro had not seen who had done the shooting. He was fairly sure the shots had come from a nearby alleyway, but had been too occupied with protecting me to have seen more. For that, I had to be grateful. Nonetheless, it was aggravating.

I went next to the funeral parlor and conferred with Angelina in her little study. We both agreed that we must have discovered something the malefactor feared, but we were both at a loss as to what.

"How is Shirley?" I asked.

Angrily, Angelina pressed her lips together. "Billy, my nephew, keeps saying that Shirley bites him, but I see no sign of it on him. However, I did find one odd bruise on Shirley. When Vina insisted that Shirley was doing the biting, I hired a nurse to take care of the children, and see to it that they are bathed and fed."

"And to be a witness should it be needed?"

Angelina snorted. "Hopefully, the nurse will be able to prevent any trouble." She sighed and blinked her tears. "Billy screams constantly. He is only five, but every little thing makes him furious. Shirley, on the other hand, never cries. She barely lets out a whimper, but she is terrified of Billy. I am at my wits' end, I tell you."

I put my hand on her arm. "I do not know what to tell you, but if you need a respite, please bring Shirley and yourself to the rancho at any time."

"Thank you, Maddie." She groaned as screaming erupted upstairs. "I'd best go. Can you talk to Regina, please?"

"I will and I can see myself out."

Angelina nodded gratefully and ran further into the house to the stairs.

I next rode to Regina's house and checked on the new mother and her child. Adelaide was doing very well, and the baby girl was eating lustily and was exceptionally healthy. Adelaide told me that Mr. Delacruz had secured lodging for himself, his new wife and their baby with Mrs. Gutierrez.

"He will soon marry me in actuality, as well, so we will not have to pretend to be for very long," Adelaide said happily.

I was pleased, and said so, then went to confer with Regina, who was strangely idle.

"There is an important meeting at the train station depot," she told me. "All the men who have freight on board the Orizaba are there, including several who would otherwise be here."

"No!" I gasped. "I need to be at that meeting. I have freight on that boat, too, and sorely need it."

I ran for the door.

"Best get your invoice then," Regina called after me. "I think they mean to pay the deposit."

I ran Daisy back to the rancho to fetch the necessary paper, then hurried to the old train depot. As Regina had said, the men had agreed to pay the despised deposit, and they could hardly not do so, as the steamship company's agent refused to listen to reason. There was some talk of a lawsuit, but in the meantime, we would pay as many of the men had as urgent a need of their goods as I did.

Unfortunately, even as I turned over my invoice to the agent, I was informed that my goods would not arrive until late that Monday, or even early Tuesday. My aggravation only increased, and I took my time counting out the small coins I had brought. It was perhaps petty of me, but I was not the only one to do so.

That Saturday night was chaotic, as usual, but there were more cuts than broken bones and only one knife fight to clean up after. We ran completely out of carbolic acid, and I resorted to some heavily distilled liquor to sterilize everything, hoping that it would work. I managed to keep enough ether, but ran out of morphine and had to resort to laudanum for later. Elena and I didn't see our beds until after three o'clock in the morning.

I made it to Sunday services and had to wonder why I bothered as Reverend Elmwood preached the same sermon he did every year at that time, and it had not improved in the repetition. Sunday dinner at the rancho was exceedingly pleasant, but as we finished eating, my stomach slowly grew more sour.

I was not looking forward to Mr. Brownlow's visit, but he arrived just as the small clock in my study chimed the hour of one. I received him in the front parlor of the adobe, served tea and pan dulces, then sat on a chair as far away from where he sat on the sofa as possible and still be reasonably friendly.

After complimenting me on the excellence of the sweet breads, Mr. Brownlow sat back on the sofa.

"How are your girls?" I asked, looking for some safe topic to bring up before asking after what I really wanted to know.

"So kind of you to ask after them." He smiled proudly. "All very well and healthy. My oldest will be examined on Tuesday with the rest of her class. Will you be there?"

"No, I am afraid not." I smiled but did not elaborate.

He paused, then smiled again. "I must say, Mrs. Wilcox, I have been told by many that you are a most astute woman of business, and I am quite happy to find that they were right."

"I am glad that my reputation that way precedes me," I replied quietly.

"It was most astute of you to have me check on the title to that land near the Huertas."

"How so?" I asked. "Is everything as it should be?"

"Perfectly so!"

I sipped some tea. "I am not surprised. I do not tend to let those sorts of details escape me. Still, I appreciate your checking. How much do I owe you?"

"Please, Mrs. Wilcox." Mr. Brownlow shook his head. "I cannot take your money, especially since I should be obligated to verify the title at some point soon."

"I hope the issue with the other title did not cause you problems with the Southern Pacific."

Mr. Brownlow chuckled. "Indeed not. That sort of problem is precisely why they engaged me in the first place. Sloppy record keeping. It has been quite the problem in this state, I assure you."

"But quite convenient when you wish to acquire something at the least cost." I hid my smile behind a sip of tea.

I had feared that he would take offense at my implication, but he merely chortled again.

"You are referring, of course, to my work with the Land Commission. I know that some looked upon it that way, but I can promise you, Mrs. Wilcox, I wanted those families to keep as much of their land as they could. And saw to it that they did."

"I'm sure you did, sir," I said. "But about the title on the Hewitt land, I cannot help but wonder who else it hurt besides poor Mrs. Hewitt."

"I can't imagine it hurt anybody else. Unless someone was hoping to win Mrs. Hewitt's heart and her wealth with it." He sighed. "One hates to admit it, but there are fellows out there who are quite happy to take advantage of a young widow, especially a pretty one. You'd best be warned."

It was my turn to chortle. "Mr. Brownlow, I thank you for your concern. But I have been a widow for almost thirteen years now, and as such, am not unschooled in the ways of greedy men. My head has yet to be turned. Which is why I wonder at your persistence when I have already told you that my mind is made up not to wed again."

"What?" Mr. Brownlow looked shocked, then laughed again. "No. No. You have no wealth that interests me, and given the community property laws in the state and your partnership with the Ortiz brothers, I would not reap much benefit from your interests. No. I am merely in need of a wife and you seem uncommonly sensible. I find that often wanting in a woman."

"I see. Well, again, I cannot encourage you, and will not."

He sat up. "No matter. You will find that I thrive in challenging situations. And we may as well be friends, as I suspect we will be doing some business together soon enough."

He left shortly after that. I could not help but reflect that if he thrived on challenge, he was going to be in the very pink of health in his suit for me.

I checked the clock in the living room, and it was not that late, so I had Daisy saddled while I changed to my green riding habit, thinking that I really should get another one made, then went to the hospital to check on patients.

The next morning, Theodora asked me to lunch at her manufactory office. Mr. Lowman was coming by to discuss getting the buggies he wanted built and she wanted a witness present that she could trust in addition to Mr. Ledbetter. So, wearing my riding habit, I visited a few of my patients, including the young woman whose foot I'd had to amputate the week before. The poor lass was grateful to be alive, but devastated by the loss. She was also healing well, and I reassured her that she would find a way to manage and be useful.

Lunch was ready in the office at the manufactory at a small table that had been placed in the center of the office and that was set for four people. Mr. Ledbetter showed me up to the room, then left to await Mr. Lowman. Theodora was nervous, but the more fiery part of her nature remained in close reserve.

Mr. Lowman arrived but moments later, and both Theodora and I raised our eyebrows at the incredible change that had taken place. He even held his hat in his hands. But more than that, his suit was new, his hair freshly pomaded and combed down. His beard had been perfectly trimmed, with not a whisker out of place. Even his breath was newly sweetened.

Theodora and I shot glances at each other. Then she smiled.

"Please come in, Mr. Lowman, and have a seat," Theodora said. "Let us eat and then I am sure we can come to terms that we will both find profitable."

"Thank you, Mrs. Hewitt," Mr. Lowman said. "But first, I must offer you an apology for my earlier behavior. It was most unkind, especially in light of your recent bereavement."

Theodora smiled. "Then I will accept your apology and we need speak no more of it. Mr. Ledbetter, will you join us?"

We sat down to an excellent lamb stew and discussed a great many things, including the perfidy of the Pacific Steamship Company, how Theodora's daughters might fare with their exams, and the coming masquerade party at the new skating rink on the night after Christmas.

As we finished, Theodora began the negotiation by explaining her price and what that included. She and Mr. Lowman dickered for some time, but in the end, they both agreed that since there had been a misunderstanding, Theodora would accept a somewhat smaller than usual deposit on the buggies and would have said buggies constructed more quickly than normal. Mr. Lowman agreed to pay the full price for them. Mr. Ledbetter set everything down on paper and both Theodora and Mr. Lowman signed the sheets. Mr. Lowman paid the deposit and left.

I left soon after and found Mr. Lowman on the street waiting for me.

"I am impressed, Mr. Lowman," I told him as I walked back toward the rancho. "You seem to have taken my words to heart."

"Well, you did have a gun pointed at me." He grinned, then made a face. "And you were right. You get so used to people trying to skin you that sometimes you forget that not everybody is." He sighed. "I do have a temper. My mother always said I was as ornery as a mule with a burr under its saddle on a bad day. That doesn't always work when you're trying to do business."

"But being appropriately penitent when necessary does, obviously." I smiled at him.

He glanced back at the manufactory. "You think she'd mind if, when she comes out of mourning, I pay her my attentions?"

"You don't seem that smitten."

"She is a spitfire and I like that." Mr. Lowman shrugged. "And nice looking, too. But, truth be told, having that manufactory would be a good thing for me."

"Hmm." I sighed, then looked at him. "Well, I cannot and will not tell Mrs. Hewitt what to do. But if your objective in courting her is acquiring her business, I would approach her with a great deal of caution, as she is likely to see right through you."

Mr. Lowman laughed. "I expect she would. She's a spitfire, all right."

He moved off toward his livery stable. I was about to go back to the center of the pueblo when Mr. Ledbetter called softly to me. I went back to the door where he stood.

"Is everything well, Mr. Ledbetter?"

"Yes." He sighed and smiled. "Everything went better than I thought it would. I just wanted to say thank you,

Mrs. Wilcox. You've been a real rock for Mrs. Hewitt, and she truly appreciates it, as do I."

I looked at him. "You seem quite fond of her."

"I am at that, ma'am." Mr. Ledbetter shifted uncomfortably.

"Actually, more than fond, I would say." I smiled at him. "Mr. Ledbetter, are you in love with Mrs. Hewitt?"

"It's not going to do me any good," he said sadly. "I do not dare declare myself, even after she comes out of mourning, and truth be told, that's even assuming she does. She truly loved Mr. Hewitt."

"But why not declare yourself?"

He looked shocked. "She is my employer, ma'am. You know full well it would devastate her social standing in the pueblo. Not to mention that there are enough folks in the pueblo already saying that I want to take over the manufactory."

"And you don't?"

He shook his head. "Actually, I'd just as soon she sold the place. That way, we could leave, and I could declare myself, and we could start over someplace else. But I don't think she's going to do that. She has too many ties to this place, and the girls are settled here. That's important, too, you know."

"Indeed, it is." I thought of something else. "I'm not saying you have done anything, but, Mr. Ledbetter, where were you when Mr. Hewitt was shot? Perhaps it would be best to know so that we can answer any untoward insinuations."

"I'd gone to get an extra carriage robe for Mr. Hewitt," Mr. Ledbetter said. "I'd pulled the buggy around to the front of the hall as soon as I heard about him... Well, you know." He shuddered at the thought of the humiliation Mr. Hewitt had caused. "He'd been doing so poorly, I thought he might be needing the extra robe. I was down the street when I heard the shots fired."

I nodded. "Thank you, Mr. Ledbetter."

"Thank you, ma'am." He tipped his hat, then looked back into the shop. "I'd best be getting back."

"As I must," I said. "Good day."

I hurried back to the rancho to find that Regina was there waiting for me and she was not entirely happy.

"You neglected to tell me on Saturday that you had been shot at that morning," she said, pacing the front parlor.

"Oh, dear. I meant to. But when you told me about that meeting, I had to leave right away and the shooting slipped my mind."

"Slipped your mind? Maddie, dearest, you are becoming far too accustomed to people shooting at you."

My stomach twisted with guilt, as I was once again endangering people I cared about while searching out someone I did not necessarily have any business searching out.

"Oh, dear. I hope not." I swallowed and moved toward the adobe's small indoor kitchen to cover my worry. "Would you like some tea?"

"Tea?" Regina groaned. "If you add some angelica, I might."

"It's too early in the day for our usual conference libations."

"True." She sighed. "But what about Saturday?"

I told her what had happened after asking for some tea from Olivia, who was working on dinner.

"I think someone was getting worried that you've found something out," Regina said, settling onto the sofa.

"Which is what Angelina said." I made a face, then took the tea tray from Olivia. "It makes no difference. We haven't found much of anything. I have discovered that Mr. Lowman has his eyes on the buggy manufactory, and will happily court Mrs. Hewitt to get it. Not to mention that Mr. Ledbetter is in love with her and suffering in silence over it."

"Oh, glory be." Regina took the teacup I offered her and sighed over its contents. "The worst of it is the intelligence that I have for you. In short, you'd best be looking for gunmen around every corner."

"I already do," I sighed. "Did you find out anything from Mr. Handley yet?"

"Yes. I presented the plot as part of a parlor game last night, and Mr. Handley reminded us that he does not write life insurance. But one fellow thought that the plot was such a fine and interesting idea that someone should. To which Mr. Handley said that he knew someone who had done so. In fact, it is actually quite easy to defraud an insurance company, as they are dependent on the honesty of their agents to verify the legitimacy of claims. However, Mr. Handley said that paying the premiums would be an awfully expensive way to go about making some money. In addition, the insurance companies would be looking very closely if an agent put through more than one such claim in a relatively short time. In fact, that is how some of these dishonest fellows get caught."

"Wouldn't the draft be made out to the beneficiary?"

"And no one has ever deposited a draft made out to someone else in their own account?" Regina shook her head.

"But here is the meat of what I have to say. Another fellow saw right through what I was asking and remarked that you often times cared for my girls and wondered what I was telling you."

"But, Regina, you are more than discrete."

"Which I was able to remind all of them." She sighed. "I cannot say who, but more than one of the men last night are on Angelina's list. I did say that while I am happy to hide most sins, I cannot hide the sin of murder, and the men agreed that one couldn't. But I feel very worried that one of those men is quite eager to see you stopped in your search, and even if there were no need for discretion, I couldn't say who, because I have no idea which one." She leaned forward and took my hands. "Maddie, please be careful. Promise me, you will."

"I have every intention of exercising caution. Alas, I cannot mew myself up in my adobe and expect to find out much."

"True. But try not to go out alone. Please!"

"I'll do what I can."

Regina left soon after. I could not fault her. Angelina and I were the only bosom friends she had, and she constantly worried that I would leave the pueblo, abandoning her to loneliness.

Chapter Sixteen

If one is going to accept the thesis that all's well that ends well, then in retrospect, the next day's events were not nearly as devastating as they could have been, and in fact, were actually quite helpful. And I do not mean regarding the various injuries that were sustained. However, also in retrospect, I probably should not have done what I did.

It seemed a simple enough idea to make sure that I had several members of my household with me as I went into the pueblo that day. Often it had helped to prevent an attack upon my person. Besides, with Christmas a week away, we all needed to do some shopping to purchase presents for the others in the household, especially the children.

So that morning, upon receiving word that my medical supplies were finally in Los Angeles, I invited Magdalena and Olivia to come with me. We would go to lunch at the Pico House hotel, where Olivia's oldest, Ramon, worked as one of the managers of the restaurant, then visit some of the shops. I would fetch my supplies, and we would go home after a lovely afternoon. Olivia did not hold with restaurants, being justifiably proud of her own abilities in the kitchen. The one exception was, of course, the Pico

House, because Ramon would treat her like a queen while she reveled in maternal pride for her important son.

Sebastiano drove my buggy, of which I was quite proud. It was a very fine one, with lovely high-backed padded leather seats in two rows, and a top that could be folded back, which we had that day. Magdalena and I sat in the back seat, with Olivia and Sebastiano in the front. Rodolfo had hitched the buggy to Daisy, and we drove off, a gay party, indeed. Ramon was at the hotel restaurant when we arrived. He immediately seated us at one of the best tables, then informed us that we would be his guests for lunch and that we were to order whatever we wanted. Olivia beamed.

After lunch, feeling very well fed and feted, we made our way down the Calle Principal to the many shops there. Soon our arms were filled with packages and Sebastiano took several of them and left to fetch the buggy so that we would have someplace to put our treasures. I forget which shop Olivia and Magdalena had gone into. I had seen some toys at another and went in to see if I could find a doll or such for Shirley. I found quite a nice one with soft blonde hair curling becomingly around the porcelain face, which I bought and had wrapped.

As I returned to the street with my purchase, Sebastiano pulled Daisy and the buggy up alongside the front of the stores. Mr. Brownlow hurried up as well.

"Mrs. Wilcox, good day to you," Mr. Brownlow said, reaching for one of my packages. "Here. Let me help you."

"Mr. Ortiz is right here," I said, seeing Sebastiano get down from the seat on the street side of the buggy.

"It will be my pleasure." Mr. Brownlow put the package onto the buggy's seat, then helped me in.

Screaming in terror, Daisy suddenly reared, and Mr. Brownlow tumbled back. I did not have time to wonder what had caused her terror, for the next thing I knew, Daisy ran full out down the street, the front seat empty, the reins dangling between the traces. I grabbed onto the buggy seat and looked around, my heart pounding. I wondered if I could get to the front and possibly call Daisy to a halt. The buggy lurched, and I nearly fell off the seat. I tried again to climb over the back of the front seat, but tripped on my skirt. The buggy lurched again, and I toppled onto the floor.

I have since learned that this is probably what saved my life. A moment later, Daisy screamed again, and the buggy slammed to a stop and fell over. I slammed first into the front seat, then skidded onto the dry dirt road.

Daisy snorted and neighed in pain, but I could not see her from where I lay, every bone in my body jarred and aching. I was dizzy, as well, and wondered if I had injured my head. Hooves pounded on the road as Mr. Navarro, Mr. Jessup, and one other fellow galloped up.

"Mrs. Wilcox." Mr. Navarro bent down, having leaped off his horse. "Are you hurt?"

"Some," I said, trying to get up. I blinked my eyes, and the dizziness faded.

Mr. Jessup cursed. "Broke both her legs. Too bad. That was a nice horse."

"What?" I yelped.

There was a single gunshot, and Daisy's pained neighing was silenced.

"No!" I screamed and burst into tears.

Mr. Navarro helped me to a seated position, and along with Mr. Jessup, helped me to my feet. I thanked God that nothing seemed to be broken, even as I still wept. Another buggy had been found, and I was driven back to the Calle Primavera by Mr. Medrano, who had also been on the street when Daisy ran away.

"Where is Sebastiano?" I asked.

Mr. Medrano pointed, and I saw Olivia sitting in the street with her husband's head on her lap.

"Oh, no!" I gasped. The fear and feelings of guilt descended upon my heart in a crushing instant.

"He's alive, Mrs. Wilcox," Mr. Medrano said. "He should be thankful he has such a hard head."

Sebastiano was conscious when they brought him to Mr. Medrano's buggy, although his face was an ashen gray.

"You are hurt?" he asked, looking at me.

"It would seem not seriously, although I ache enough." I reached over. "We'd best see if your skull is fractured."

Olivia slapped my hands back. "You will do nothing! You are hurt, too. Elena can take care of both of you, or I will call Doctor Rusk."

I did not doubt that she would summon my least favorite rival in the pueblo. Full of self-importance and utterly lacking in either knowledge or sympathy, he was easily the worst doctor in the pueblo at the time.

Marisol came running out of the adobe when we pulled up. Elena was close on her heels. We put Sebastiano in the small bedroom in my adobe that we reserved as a sickroom. Olivia and Elena tended to him while Marisol and Magdalena helped me to bed.

My beautiful green riding habit was in shreds. My horse was dead. My partner was possibly on his deathbed, and worse yet, it was quite probable that my search for Mr.

Hewitt's killer had put him there. I couldn't help it. I wept copiously.

Wang Fu also showed up promptly. He spent several minutes in conference with Elena while I begged Magdalena to tell me how Sebastiano was. Wang Fu went to see to Sebastiano, and Elena slipped into my room.

"Well?" I demanded.

"I am here to examine you," she said.

"What about your father?"

She smiled. "I think he will be fine."

"Did you check his eyes?"

"I checked his eyes. They are reacting normally. He does not have any depressions in his skull, although he is growing quite the goose egg near the back of his left ear." She folded her arms and glared at me. "Now, what about you? Where do you hurt?"

I sighed. "Everywhere, it seems." I twisted my head. "But it's mostly my neck and shoulders. I do not believe I have any fractures."

"I will determine that," she said with surprising firmness. She really was getting to be quite a good doctor.

After several minutes, Elena concurred that I mostly suffered from aches, scrapes, and bruises. She set about bandaging me, then insisted that I stay in bed for the next two or more days. Wang Fu came into the room, told me that Sebastiano's head injury was relatively minor, then got out his needles. It was an odd cure, and did not heal immediately. But it did eventually help with my pain. Indeed, I wish I could find another such doctor now, but thanks to the Chinese Exclusion Act of the 1880s, those Chinese who can perform their needle cure are now quite hard to find.

Olivia brought me soup for my supper that night. I accepted the bowl sitting up in my bed.

"Are you angry with me?" I asked, dreading her answer.

"Why would I be angry with you?" she growled.

"Because someone wants to kill me again." I looked at her much like a small, naughty child looks at her mother. "And almost killed your husband as well."

"You do not take care of yourself." She sighed loudly. "But it is like you say. These terrible people, they keep killing and must be caught somehow. You tried to do the right thing today by bringing us with you, and that man still tried to kill you. Mrs. Dunbar did not see anything, you said, and yet that monster killed her." She closed her eyes, then shook her head. "Maddie, mija..."

I choked. Mija means daughter or loved one. For Olivia to use that most intimate of terms... It was so very touching.

She frowned. "I cannot help but worry about you. What you do is dangerous. Yet, who else will? You found that monster preying on our girls last summer. You have found other killers and stopped them." The furrows in her brow deepened even further, as if that were possible. "We must stop this evil man. Tomorrow, when you are feeling better, we will invite your friends, Mrs. Medina and Mrs. Sutton. We will have a council of war. We will find this man."

"It could be a woman," I said, weakly.

Olivia snorted. "It could be. That part does not matter. What does is finding this fiend and putting a stop to his murderous intentions. Or hers."

"Olivia, I did not wish anyone in this household to come to harm."

"Of course you didn't!" Olivia snorted. "I know you have never intended that, or even harm to yourself. But we cannot always prevent that. I know that now. You rest. We will find this terrible person tomorrow."

I soon finished my soup and tried to rest. It was not to be. The pain I still had in my body did not help. However, it was the worry in my mind that kept me awake during that long night.

The tributes began arriving soon after the sun rose the next morning. Flowers, sweets, all sorts of ridiculous things. Mr. Meyers sent sugared violets, which I happen to like quite well. Mr. Handley made sure I had a huge bouquet of roses, which were just starting their winter bloom. Mr. Carson sent a book, Tales of an Indian Girl, by C. Elmer, which I already owned and he should have known since he'd, personally, sold it to me the previous fall. Fresh oysters were delivered, along with crystalized fruits and even a box of chocolates adorned with marigolds from Mr. Glassell. Bottles of French cordial, gifts of brandy and even wine made their way into my adobe.

Olivia let me sit in the front parlor that morning, although she bundled me up quite tightly under two different quilts. I looked at all the gifts in wonderment. There were a few sincere ones. Mrs. Samples had sent a lovely pillow for my comfort stuffed with wool from their family's sheep. Mrs. Lomax and Mrs. Smith sent a quilt that they had made together.

But many of the gifts being offered for my aid and comfort were obvious ploys to sweeten my temper.

"Good Heavens!" I groaned, looking at one such gift, a small cask of claret. "This is one of our wines. They did not even trouble to remove our winery's mark from the cask."

Olivia laughed and handed me a bowl of soup. "Eat this. It is beef tea to build strength and plenty of corn for your stomach."

"Thank you, Olivia." I smiled at her and took a sip. "How is Sebastiano this morning?"

"His head aches and he complains loudly. Elena says that is a good sign."

I chuckled. "It is."

"I will bring him out here this afternoon, when Mrs. Medina and Mrs. Sutton arrive." Olivia's eyes flashed darkly. "He has some news for us."

It was not good news, however, it was nothing that surprised me. Indeed, I had already guessed at what it might be. But I put that aside to finish my soup and inquire after the packages that had been in the buggy. They were mostly intact, having been strapped into the boot at the back of the conveyance. One package, however, had been completely smashed. It was the doll for Shirley. Linda, Enrique and Magdalena's eldest, brought it to me. The lovely blond curls were a tangled mess, and the face was smashed.

"How terrible," I whispered.

Linda, always shy and quiet, nodded, gave me a quick embrace, then hurried away.

Regina and Angelina arrived shortly after we'd eaten lunch. Angelina's mood was quite sour, even though she had brought Shirley with her. Anita happily took the babe to play with the others. Shirley went quietly and even offered Anita a shy smile.

Angelina gasped. "I am amazed. She will not go to Vina and clings to me unless I hand her over to the nursemaid."

"Oh, dear." I frowned, as I had seen similar from young children, but could not quite recollect what it meant. "I am glad, at least, that she finds some respite in this place."

Olivia and Elena brought Sebastiano in, growling and complaining, then settled him into one of the more comfortable chairs.

"I am not an infant!" he snarled as Olivia tucked yet another quilt around him.

"No, Papa, not at all," Elena said soothingly as she checked his eyes. "But you are injured and we want to see you back to your usual strong self as soon as possible. See? Even Maddie is resting and doing as she is told."

I was not, in fact, doing exactly as I had been told, having gotten up on my own more than once to stretch out my aching limbs. But I was not going to say so to Elena or Olivia.

Olivia disappeared and returned with a tray filled with a large teapot and several cups. Maria followed, carrying a large platter of pan dulces and biscuits. Maria set the tray down on a nearby chest while Olivia poured and served tea. Maria quickly left the room. Olivia pulled up one of the extra chairs Enrique had brought in and settled into it. Regina's and Angelina's eyebrows rose.

"I have every reason to be here," Olivia announced defiantly. "We must find this monster."

"I heartily concur, Mrs. Ortiz," Regina said with a smile. "But generally you would rather Mrs. Wilcox did not do the searching, let alone wish to participate in the search yourself."

"It does not matter." Olivia held herself up straight as an unwilling but fond grin crept across Sebastiano's face. "There is a very bad man about who hurt my husband and my friend. I will do everything I can to find him and bring him to justice! Now. Señor Ortiz has something to tell us."

Sebastiano cleared his throat. "It is how we know that this was no chance event. The horse, Daisy, was spooked intentionally. First, I was hit on the head quite hard, and then I heard the sound of a rattlesnake. That is when Daisy reared."

"A rattlesnake?" Angelina asked. "But that could be chance."

It did not happen often, but the venomous creatures did occasionally find their way into the main part of the pueblo.

"Not this time of year," Sebastiano said. "They are hibernating and, even then, almost always avoid where people are gathered. When they do come into that part of the pueblo, it is late at night and when the mice have gotten very numerous. We've had almost no mice this year. So someone must have gotten a snake's rattle. It would be easy to hide. Then he shook it next to Daisy, and if he was close enough to me to hit me, then he was close enough to spook the horse."

"I did not know about the snake rattle," I said. "But I had surmised that someone had intentionally spooked Daisy. She is—" I choked suddenly. "Was a very calm horse. She'd neigh and stamp if she was afraid, but would not rear and barely moved last Saturday when I was shot at. And she was quite near me at the time."

"And you did not see who hit you?" Angelina asked Sebastiano, as she pulled papers from her little writing desk that she had brought and settled on her lap, as always.

"I was hit from behind."

I sighed in relief. "I was so sure that you had been caught by one of Daisy's hooves."

"I did not even lose consciousness," Sebastiano said. "Even if I was knocked to the ground."

"Which does not make your head injury any less serious," I said. "But that is good to know."

Regina looked pensive. "Well. Someone has most certainly decided that Maddie poses a threat to his discovery. The question is who."

"And what are we going to do about it?" Olivia added. She frowned again, thinking. She gasped as she looked at all the tributes that had been piled on the back wall of the parlor. "Perhaps we should check and see if all these gifts do not harbor something deadly. If something does, we see who brought it!"

Angelina, Regina, and I all looked at each other.

"A most excellent idea, Olivia," I said.

"But if something is poisoned, how will we know?" Angelina asked. "We can't taste it."

I sighed, thinking of the sugared violets.

"Rats," Olivia said as if the idea were manifestly obvious. "They will eat anything, and if a rat dies, who cares?"

"Presumably the rat's relatives," Regina said with a chuckle. "But no one else, I am sure. And, Heaven knows, we all want to be rid of the pests."

And so we all fell to. Olivia sent Jaime, his younger sister Lupe, and Ignacio Mendoza, to find and capture some rats, something the children were quite eager to do and managed with astounding and worrisome success. Angelina helped me sort the tributes and made note of each one that I received. Sebastiano carefully poked through all the bundles of flowers, but nothing dangerous lurked among the blooms except a few rose thorns. He soon tired, however, and Elena and Enrique came to put him back to bed.

Regina had gotten Angelina's most recent list of potential killers and we talked it over with Olivia, who had seen Mrs. Glassell come out of the shop where I had bought the doll shortly before I did.

"How is it that I did not see her there?" I asked, my brow creasing as I tried to remember. "It is not a large shop at all, although there is one tall shelf near the side that someone could hide behind."

"But why would she hide from you?" Angelina asked. "That does not make sense at all."

"That it does not," I agreed. "Unless she killed Mr. Hewitt in anger at spoiling her fine party, and otherwise being a trial to his wife. And we know that she was on the street when Mrs. Dunbar was shot. Mrs. Glassell also carries a large gun, although where she would have kept it that night of the party and being in evening dress, I cannot say." I paused as I thought of something. "She also had her carriage robe, and her buggy was right there, so if that was where she'd hidden her gun, it would have been easy to fetch it and the robe, and then shoot Mr. Hewitt. I believe her carriage man, Mr. Gluck, was nearby, but not immediately so. However, I have no idea if he was in the vicinity when Mrs. Dunbar was shot."

"Our cousin Mirella works for the Glassell family." Olivia's brow creased. "I can easily find an excuse to talk to her and find out what I can. Oh. And there is Mr. Brownlow."

"That's right," I said. "He helped me into the buggy, then fell back as Daisy reared."

"He has also been walking by the rancho gate every few hours since we brought you back here," Olivia said. "I thought you told him that you cannot encourage him."

"I did," I grumbled. "It would seem that he appreciates the challenge, and as we will probably be doing some business in the very near future, I can hardly snub him."

Regina frowned. "However, he seems to have the least reason to want to kill Mr. Hewitt, and none to kill Mrs. Dunbar."

"Which is, of course, assuming he was telling the truth when he told me that it was not unusual to find a title defect so late in the process." I thought over what he had said and how he had said it. "He told me that it was the reason men like him are generally engaged. He did not seem as though he was lying. If anything, he was quite congenial about being asked instead of taking umbrage, which he might have even if he were quite innocent."

"But if he was congenial, then it is not likely he had a reason to take umbrage," Angelina said, then she made a note on one of her papers. "Who else was in the immediate neighborhood?"

Olivia frowned. "A rather short, fat man without a beard. He also had on a bright orange vest under his suit coat."

Both Regina and I spoke together, albeit quite accidentally. "Mr. Wills."

"Oh, the notary," Angelina said.

"I think he may have walked across the street toward the buggy when Sebastiano pulled up," Olivia continued.

"Isn't his office in the block where that shop was?" Regina asked.

"Yes, I do believe it is," I said. "And I do not recall if he was among the crowd that was there when Mr. Medrano brought me to Sebastiano."

"Mr. Medrano was there?" Angelina asked.

"Yes," I said. "He drove up to where my buggy had been stopped and brought me back to where Sebastiano was, then drove us all back to the rancho."

"That is interesting," Angelina said. "Especially since we know he wanted to put Mr. Hewitt out of business and was nearby at the social hall when Mr. Hewitt was killed. Do we know where he was when Mrs. Dunbar was killed?"

"We do not," said Regina. "He was not at my establishment. In fact, he seldom is."

"Then I shall have to find out where he was when I can," I said.

"Was anybody else there?" Angelina asked.

"Mr. Navarro had to have been reasonably close at hand," I said slowly. "As was Mr. Jessup. They and some other fellow whose name I do not know. They were trying to catch us when Daisy tumbled. Mr. Jessup… He's the one who ended Daisy's suffering."

"Oh, Maddie," Regina sighed as she put her hand on my arm. "You know she couldn't have lived like that."

"I know." I reached for my handkerchief. I sniffed. "In any case, we know that Mr. Jessup was in San Buenaventura when Mrs. Dunbar was shot. On the other hand, he does have a reason to have killed Mr. Hewitt in that he was, apparently, in love with Mrs. Hewitt."

"As was Mr. Wills," Angelina said. She snorted and let out a word that shocked all of us except Regina, who, even though Angelina had spoken in Spanish, still understood the word, did not care and often used worse herself.

"There are too many people to consider. And no proof that any of them could be the killer."

"Has anyone heard about someone missing a large six-shooter?" I asked, then explained to Olivia and Sebastiano about the gun Mr. Lomax had found.

They shook their heads, and I admonished them not to say that we were looking for one, to which they agreed.

"What about Mr. Ledbetter?" Regina said suddenly. "My gentlemen were joking that he seems to have designs on acquiring the buggy manufactory by wooing Mrs. Hewitt."

I sighed. "That does seem to be the ongoing rumor. There may be a hint of truth in it. He does appear to have a deep love for her and said as much on Monday. However, not unlike Mr. Wills, he seems to be focused on suffering in silence, as he does not believe that his suit will be received well. Nor does he really want the manufactory. In fact, he said that he wished Mrs. Hewitt would sell it so that they could go elsewhere, he could declare his love without harming her social standing, and then the two could start over."

Regina sighed, then looked us over. "Is there anything else to consider?" She waited as we all shook our heads. "Then it seems to me that we have enough work to keep us busy until the Last Trumpet calls us. We'd best have at it."

Chapter Seventeen

There was not much I could do the next day as Elena had decreed that I still needed to rest and recover from my injuries, and if her father could stay down, so could I. I soon came to suspect that Elena was playing me against her father in an attempt to keep both of us doing what, in truth, we needed to do, that is, rest.

Still, she and Olivia agreed to let me receive a delegation from the men of business in the pueblo, which I was happy to do, being quite bored with my enforced inactivity. At least, the children had enjoyed bringing in the rats they had captured and letting them taste all the treats that had been brought to me. I was quite elated when the vermin survived the sugared violets and, regrettably, I over-indulged in them.

By eight o'clock that night, however, I was properly attired in my ochre visiting dress, having heard the children's lessons, and waited in the largest chair in my front parlor. A small stove held a burning fire as the air had turned very cold. The chairs from the previous day's conference had been arranged around my chair. A large pitcher of angelica waited on the nearby chest along with several glasses and a platter of pan dulces and biscuits. I had my glass poured and sitting next to me on the whatnot table next to the chair. Enrique saw to admitting the men and waited next to the door while we talked.

The delegation was led by Mr. Wiley and Mr. McKinley, and also included Mr. Judson, Mr. Wills, Mr. Carson, and Mr. Meyers. I had never liked Mr. McKinley, who was a dark-haired fellow with a temper. But he was a good land agent and had already negotiated with the Southern Pacific over the land that Mrs. Hewitt owned. Therefore, it would be worth my while to at least hear him out.

I invited the men to pour themselves some angelica and help themselves to the pan dulces and biscuits. They all poured, but only Mr. Carson and Mr. Wills took something to eat. As they settled themselves on the couch and chairs, Mr. McKinley glanced at Mr. Wiley, then smiled at me.

"Mrs. Wilcox," Mr. McKinley said. "As I am sure you are aware, the Southern Pacific Railroad company has taken an interest in a plot of land that you own that is next to the Huertas de las Molinas."

I do not recall if there were actually any mills at the location of the lands in question, but that was what the area was popularly called, even if many of the huertas, or orchards, were no longer tended.

I chuckled. "How could I not be, given how many lovely tributes I received yesterday, some from you gentlemen."

Mr. Wiley winked at me. He alone had not sent anything, but had visited briefly the evening before, and it had been quite a friendly and modest visit. The other men glanced at each other and shifted.

"And I do thank you for them," I continued. "It was quite kind of you to offer such aid and comfort."

"It was our pleasure," Mr. Wills said quickly.

"Nonetheless," Mr. McKinley cut in. "We are set to meet with the representatives of the railroad tomorrow morning and we are dealing with a most delicate situation here."

"As in the rail depot is utterly necessary to the growth of our fair pueblo and the men of the Southern Pacific are not known for their fair dealing." I sipped some angelica. "Is that not it?"

Mr. Judson cleared his throat. "There is considerable concern that the fellows from the railroad will be quite happy to take gross advantage of a young widow."

I held in my annoyance at the obvious flattery. Granted, I was not terribly old, but being in my thirties at the time, I was not that young, either.

"Of that I have no doubt," I said and shrugged. "Is there any reason why we shouldn't let them believe that is exactly what they are dealing with?"

The men shifted and looked at each other.

"But, madam," Mr. Judson stammered.

"Please, Mr. Judson." I took another sip of my angelica. "There is not a man among you here who does not know that I am anything but a poor, senseless and helpless widow. Still, even with my considerable acumen in the realm of business, I am not so foolish as to believe that I am entirely up to a negotiation with the Southern Pacific on my own. So, I am willing to accept help, even though I almost trust the Southern Pacific more than some of you." I looked straight at Mr. McKinley and Mr. Meyers. "I think, however, if we allow the Southern Pacific to believe that I am, shall we say, less sensible, then that might give us a slight advantage when they find that I am anything but. And if they have already heard that I am more than sensible, then we have nothing to lose."

Mr. Wiley chuckled. Mr. McKinley promptly tried to get me to accept a price that was considerably lower than what Mrs. Hewitt said she'd agreed to, and I had a good idea of why. I named my price, which was considerably more.

Mr. McKinley sat back and swallowed. "Eh, are you sure?"

"Afraid you're not going to get a very good cut, Mr. McKinley?" I asked. "I know how much the Hewitts were to receive and that I am offering more acreage."

Mr. Meyers and Mr. Carson sputtered, and Mr. Judson sighed heavily.

I looked at them and raised my eyebrows. "You did not think that I would have taken the time to find these things out? I have also verified that my title to the land is perfectly clear. At least it is, according to Mr. Brownlow, whose own interests would not be served by telling me otherwise. Now, the land is certainly worth it, and the railroad people not only know that, they are at a slight disadvantage in that they have already invested heavily in our pueblo by the purchase of the Banning line."

Mr. Carson sputtered, but Mr. Judson silenced him.

"Mrs. Wilcox," Mr. Meyers said. "We are also at a slight disadvantage in that the Southern Pacific can go where it wills."

"I am well aware of that, Mr. Meyers." I sipped, then smiled. "That is why I am not asking for more. But I am not willing to accept less than my due because of yours and others' greed. Are we clear? I do not dispute offering you some part of the proceeds in consideration of your efforts to make a good negotiation. But I will not sell unless I know the full amount that is to be paid, and what portion of that I am to receive. And it had better be at least ninety percent of that full amount. Ten percent as a commission is more than generous as it is." I smiled as the men shifted and looked at each other. "Now, I do believe that we need to decide who will represent this poor senseless widow in these negotiations. Mr. McKinley, I am willing to give you a certain preference, in that you have already worked with these fellows. However, I would like to see Mr. Wiley and Mr. Judson participate, as well. I can trust them."

The men stepped out to the front of the adobe to have their conference, but in the end, they agreed to my terms, with Mr. Wiley agreeing to fetch me the next morning for the meeting with the Southern Pacific. They departed quickly, although Mr. Wiley lagged behind.

"My darling Mrs. Wilcox," he said, laughing heartily and taking my hands as we stood next to the door. "Once again, you have reminded me of why I am so glad that we did not make our little association a more permanent one. We are, indeed, ill-suited for each other, and yet..." He sighed happily. "You were magnificent tonight, madam."

"We shall see." I sighed. "I truly wish that I did not have to spend time on this right now."

"Your search for Mr. Hewitt's killer."

"And Mrs. Dunbar's, but yes."

"Regrettably, I have nothing to offer you in terms of information." He chuckled. "At least you do not suspect me of the deed."

I smiled. "Not at the moment."

He laughed full out, gently kissed my hands, then left the adobe, his breath fogging in the night air.

The meeting the next morning took place at the United States Hotel. I again wore my ochre visiting dress, but carried a parasol trimmed in black lace along with it. Mr. Wiley arrived at the rancho in a buggy he had rented from Mr. Lowman's livery stable. Enrique shook his head, but helped me into it, and off we went.

I do not recollect the names of the three agents for the Southern Pacific and have no idea why I did not make note of them. However, they tried to ply me with compliments, which I accepted politely, then tried to offer me even less that Mr. McKinley had suggested the night before. They were rather astounded when I pointed out that, based on what they had agreed to give the Hewitts and what I actually had, their offer was almost insulting. Mr. McKinley insisted on being reasonable and we got significantly more than I had hoped for, even after I would surrender the ten percent to Mr. McKinley, Mr. Wiley, and Mr. Judson.

We were all surprised that it did not take that long to transact, which probably meant that the men from the railroad were more anxious to get the land than we'd thought and we probably could have asked for more. But I could see no point in being greedy and was quite happy to receive the generous amount that I did.

Mr. Brownlow had also been in attendance at the meeting, and had reassured the railroad men that the title to my land was, indeed, clear. He joined Mr. McKinley, Mr. Wiley, Mr. Judson, and me at a lunch at the hotel to celebrate.

"Mrs. Wilcox, you are quite unaccountable," Mr. Brownlow said jubilantly.

"She is at that," snorted Mr. McKinley. "Still, we have nought to complain about. The terms are in writing and the deal is done."

"And the amount you three are splitting is quite generous," I said. "We have done well today."

However, as I left the hotel to head back to the rancho, Mr. Brownlow followed me.

"Mrs. Wilcox," he called. "Might I have a word with you?"

"Only a word or two, Mr. Brownlow," I replied, still walking. "I do have other obligations to which I must attend."

"I... Eh..." He looked befuddled for a moment, then smiled and matched my pace. "I am confounded by you, madam. Your mind is so masculine and yet you remain wonderfully feminine."

I stopped and glared at him. "What can I do to discourage you, sir?"

"Nothing, I'm afraid. Absolutely nothing." He laughed and walked off.

I sighed. I did have other obligations, but I was suddenly unsure of which to fulfill next. Regina's comment regarding the rumors about Mr. Ledbetter came to my mind, and I decided to pay a call on Theodora.

She was at home rather than the manufactory office, and once I knocked, I was shown into the front parlor.

"How are you?" I asked her as she came into the room.

"Well enough." She waved me to a seat on the sofa, then settled sadly into the nearby chair. "I am afraid I am having one of my more difficult days. My heart simply feels too heavy to bear at times."

"You poor thing," I said.

She looked up at me. "I heard you had a meeting with the Southern Pacific this morning."

"I did, indeed."

I went on to describe the negotiation, which made her smile.

"I am glad to see that you have prospered," she said, quite genuinely. "I will grant you that I am still very annoyed by that title defect. It was the result of yet another of Thomas' failings. He was never very good at business even when he was sober. Which is why I do not hold your good fortune against you."

"I will be happy to share the proceeds with you," I said.

"No, no." She looked up at me and smiled wanly. "You are kind to offer. But no. It is something else. I do not know why yet another reminder of his deficiencies should make me miss him so, but it does."

"Who is to say when it comes to matters of the heart?" I smiled at her, then took a deep breath. "Speaking of such, I am not sure if you are aware of it, but you have another admirer, this one rather close to you."

She closed her eyes. "Mr. Ledbetter."

"He does seem to have rather deep and sincere feelings for you."

"I am, I'm afraid, fully aware of that." She shuddered. "It's actually rather hard to miss. I do not wish to encourage him and he is very handsome and quite pleasant to look at. But at the same time, he is not very interesting, nor does he have more than a rudimentary acumen for business."

"Do you think he could have...?"

"Killed Thomas? No." Theodora almost laughed. "He was utterly loyal to my dear husband, which is part of the problem. His feelings do make things quite awkward. But his loyalty is complete and I am fully dependent on him to represent me with men who will have no dealings with a woman. I tell you, Maddie, it is so unjust, but what else are we poor women to do?"

"My goal is to secure the vote for women. However, it has been suggested to me that such action will only go so far in getting us out from under the control of men."

"I fear that may be so, as well." She sighed. "But it would be something. And at least you got some gain over those fools today. I salute you."

I laughed, then sighed. "I do have some other business that I should probably transact with you today. I do not know if you heard about the misfortune I came to this past Tuesday."

"Oh. The runaway." Theodora shuddered. "You poor thing. I was shocked. Your Daisy was such a calm horse. I heard that she caught her hoof in a hole in the road."

"To be honest, I did not know that. Only that we had to destroy her, and I did love that horse." I sighed deeply.

"It must have been a terrifying ride."

"It was, but while I am still feeling the resulting aches and pains, I was not seriously hurt, thank God. Nor was Sebastiano."

"But you will need a new buggy now."

"Yes, I'm afraid. I do not know how quickly you can build a new one for me, especially with Mr. Lowman's order."

She shrugged. "I can arrange it. In the meantime, I will loan you mine." Her sigh was most profound. "I shall not be using it for the foreseeable future. I am in mourning and am glad of the excuse not to go anywhere."

I protested, but she insisted. We both dickered for a few minutes longer. I made note of our terms, and smiling, so did she. Then shortly after, I bid her good day and left.

From there I went to Mr. Medrano's manufactory and found him on the workshop floor. He escorted me to the outside door, then stepped outside to speak with me.

"And how are you today, Mrs. Wilcox?" he asked, his smile as insincere as ever.

"Quite well." I smiled somewhat more warmly. "I do need to come to a better understanding of something. Two Saturdays past, on the seventh, a Mrs. Dunbar was shot and killed, leaving behind a small girl. You heard about the event, did you not?"

"Oh, yes. It was a terrible, terrible thing." He affected a look of righteous indignation and failed.

"I have heard some unbecoming rumors." I held up my hand. "I do not believe them, but that I might refute them, can you please tell me where you were that evening, early on?"

He gaped. "I did not do it!"

"I am not saying you did. But when someone else does—"

"Who is saying that I did?" His eyes blazed, and he stepped closer to me than I liked.

"Just base rumors, sir," I said quickly. "I hardly like giving them credence. Still, it would be easier to tell the rumormongers that I heard from your own lips that you were nowhere near that part of the pueblo at the time the shooting occurred."

"You think I killed her," he snapped. "I did not! Anyone who says so is a vile and base liar. I had no reason to. No one did!"

"That certainly appears to be the case," I said.

"Get out of here! I do not need your accusations."

"Of course." And I scurried away.

I must be honest. I have no idea why I lingered a few minutes longer in the immediate vicinity. Perhaps I was trying to catch my breath. Nonetheless, I stayed long enough to see Mr. Medrano leave his manufactory and stalk off down the street. There was naught to do but follow him, so I did. He led me straight to a saloon that I knew well. It was owned by a Mr. Uribe, who was seldom in residence. But his saloonkeeper, Mr. Sedonez, and I had a fairly comfortable acquaintance as Mr. Uribe bought a considerable amount of my wines and angelica.

I entered through the back into the storeroom filled with crates and casks. A soft call at the door, and Mr. Sedonez appeared quickly. He had full white hair and whiskers, but was well-built and his face was unlined. He couldn't have been a young man, but he had the bearing of one.

"Mrs. Wilcox." He smiled. "It is always a pleasure to see you."

"I do hope so," I said. I tried not to wince and failed. "I need to ask you about one of your customers, a Mr. Medrano."

Mr. Sedonez laughed and pointed at the front of the saloon. "You do not want to talk to him? He's out there now."

"I know." My face flushed. "I followed him here. The problem is, I need to know if he was here the night of December seven. He won't tell me, and that is unfortunate for his sake."

"Was that a Saturday?" Mr. Sedonez asked.

"Yes, it was."

"Then he was here. He's always here every Saturday night." Mr. Sedonez laughed. "He leaves early, too. About seven o'clock. He can't hold his liquor. He comes in at four-thirty, five, has supper, then a couple whiskeys and is quite drunk by that point and leaves. I have heard he goes to his mother's house to sleep it off. I believe it is quite close." Mr. Sedonez closed his eyes. "December seven, you say?"

"Yes. Around five o'clock, perhaps four-thirty."

Mr. Sedonez suddenly rolled his eyes Heavenward. "That was the night he got into a fight with some of the other fellows. I have no idea what it was about. I put them all out into the street. It was just after five. I know because I looked at the clock behind the bar and thought it was going to be a very long night. Thank God, it wasn't."

"Yes. It was quite fortunate, given the turn of events."

Mr. Sedonez' eyes opened wide. "That was the night that poor woman was gunned down in the street, wasn't it?"

"Yes, I am afraid it was."

"I do not think Mr. Medrona did it. If it happened any later than four-thirty, he would not have been able to hold a gun straight."

"Oddly enough, Mr. Sedonez, that is actually a big help."

I left the saloon and headed back to the rancho. From there, I dispatched notes to Angelina and Regina that we could eliminate Mr. Medrona from our search, and received notes back expressing gratitude that we could. Regina also offered congratulations on the sale of my land. I was not surprised that she had heard about it and wondered what, specifically, she had heard.

I looked at the note again. I suppose I should have felt happier and certainly more pleased with myself than I did.

I had achieved a considerable victory, not just for myself, but for the pueblo.

I left my adobe to head for the barracks and dinner. Dark had fallen, and the air was very cold. Wind blew in from the west, bearing with it a faint hint of moisture. But the night sky was clear and strewn with stars. The moon was bright enough, albeit on the wane. It was so different from what I had known in Boston. There would be parties there, visits in sleighs, chilled noses, but lots of warm furs and wool blankets.

And there would be my two sisters, Carrie and Abby, who both loved to hear me tell about my apprenticeship under another lady doctor in Boston. Abby was horrified as I described an amputation, even as she screamed in delight with her horror. Carrie just said that I should not be so indelicate, but then would ask to hear another terrible tale.

I had been away so long that I had not met either of their husbands, nor had I seen their children. Carrie had three that were living at that time. Abby had one and would soon birth her second. I had missed so much by being out west in Los Angeles.

But even as I thought about going back to Boston to visit, my stomach roiled at the thought of having to get on a stagecoach. Twenty-one days just to get to St. Louis, then the train on to Boston. The train wasn't quite so bad in terms of making me ill, and it did occur to me that there was a train from San Francisco that ran all the way to the East Coast. But still, I would have to take a boat to San Francisco, and that was almost worse than the stagecoach.

I went on to the barracks to dinner, only to be pelted with questions from Olivia afterward. As I made my notes in my journal, I looked again at the night sky and sighed deeply.

Chapter Eighteen

I awoke that Saturday morning feeling quite lacking in interest or enthusiasm. But then, I had not slept well that night. Apart from missing my home and my sisters, my neck and shoulders had started aching, and when I did sleep, I had been troubled by frightening dreams of patients long dead and angry because I had not been able to save them.

One of the dark and bitter truths of my profession is that I could not save everybody. I tried, often where others would have given up hope. And back then, in 1872, I had fewer resources than I did even ten years ago before the Great War. If advanced age has blessed me with any insights, it is that there were a great many people that I did save. But those lucky people were not uppermost in my mind that morning.

I again donned my ochre visiting dress, then went to check on Sebastiano, who was significantly improved, but still had a headache. I told him that I agreed most heartily with Elena that he needed to be in bed at least a full week and fully free of pain before he could get up and go about his normal activities.

"You are up and working," he grumbled.

"I did not have an injury to my head," I replied crossly.

He grumbled at me, but remained in the bed. I went to the front parlor, where Marisol had my black gloves ready for me. There was to be a meeting at Mr. Judson's bank, where I would sign the deed for my land so that the transfer could be recorded. Theodora had sent Mr. Ledbetter with her buggy the previous afternoon. I could not help but blink back tears that I would be riding behind one of our mules instead of my lovely roan mare.

However, Rodolfo had a surprise for me when I got outside. In the yard in front of my adobe, under the spreading branches of the large oak tree there, he stood with two horses, both mares. One was a lovely chestnut in color with a white blaze on her face and her front hooves. The other was pure ebony, and her coat gleamed.

"Enrique and I spoke with Mr. Lowman yesterday," Rodolfo said. "He had recently bought several horses."

My eyes shot open. "It wasn't from those horse thieves that I read about in the newspaper, I hope."

Rodolfo laughed. "No. We made sure of that. He bought them from Señor Mariscal earlier this month. Mr. Lowman heard about your accident and offered to sell us one. Enrique and I thought these two would serve you best."

"I only need one," I said, going over to the beasts.

They were quite lovely and very docile.

"Of course," said Rodolfo. "We simply thought that you would like to have the final choice."

The black one snorted and nudged my cheek with her muzzle. I stroked her fine, glossy neck.

"Oh, she is lovely." I whispered, and the mare nickered as if she had understood me.

I stroked the chestnut, as well, and she received my attentions, but there was something about the black one that tugged at my heart.

I stroked her muzzle once again. "My goodness, you are as glossy and beautiful as an ebony table." I looked at Rodolfo. "I will take this one and we will call her Ebony."

Ebony tossed her head and nickered again. Rodolfo had her hitched to Theodora's buggy in short order, then tied the chestnut mare to the back to return her to Mr. Lowman while I was at the bank.

The men from the Southern Pacific were already there, along with Mr. Wills, who carried his ledger. Mr. Wiley and Mr. McKinley arrived shortly after I did. Mr. Judson was, of course, there, and ushered us all into his office. It was a bit over-crowded, but the men insisted that I be seated in front of the desk.

The witnessing, notarizing, and signing all went perfectly smoothly, and the men from the Southern Pacific even had a draft prepared for me in the full amount owed. As the others left, I remained in the office with Mr. Judson that I might deposit the draft immediately, then issue three others.

"You are quite fortunate," Mr. Judson told me, as he entered my deposit into his ledger. "The Southern Pacific had already deposited the funds for the purchase in my colleague's bank, so we will not need to wait until this is cleared with the Southern Pacific's bank in San Franciso."

"Oh." I looked at him. "How long will it take to clear the draft with the other bank?"

"Only a few minutes, I should think." Mr. Judson shifted in his chair. "We can go over there as soon as we are finished here."

"Good. I had hoped to get those drafts for yours and the others' commission written right away."

"You are quite the honorable woman, Mrs. Wilcox." Chuckling ruefully, he handed me the three blank drafts. "I wish others were."

"As do I, Mr. Judson. Which, as I said the other night, is why I wanted you present for the negotiations." I took the pen he handed me and dipped it into his inkwell.

He looked at me sadly. "I know what the other men say about me. What Mr. Hewitt said the night of the party, I have heard it before. Many times."

"I was told that you blamed him for losing the election," I said.

He winced. "Words spoken in anger and the heat of the moment." He shook his head. "Yet, it confounds me, madam. I wish to be as honest and reliable and trustworthy as I can be. I am entrusted with the life savings of entire families. Businesses in the community rely upon me to be circumspect and utterly honest in my dealings with them. If I were not, it would be chaos. Our pueblo cannot grow without an honest and secure bank. How is it that I am despised because I am honest?"

"Perhaps because you insist so vehemently that others be so honest and moral as well?" I smiled at him, although a little surprised by such a confidence from him. "I can certainly understand that insistence when it comes to financial matters."

"I would hope so."

I forced my eyes onto the draft I was writing. "But perhaps if you let others be as they are apart from that." I looked up at him. "In my medical practice, Mr. Judson, I see a great deal of people, many of them at their worst."

I chuckled as he grumbled softly. "Yes, I understand it is unseemly that a lady be exposed to such things. And yet, we women are routinely exposed to those very same things in the course of caring for our families. In any case, I have learned over the years that people are going to act as they will with not the least regard for what I think about it. Indeed, there are those who will be troublesome simply because they know that I will disapprove, and others who feel that they are perfectly justified in their behavior. There are rare occasions when I can convince someone that the path of the upright and decent is the path to take. I assure you that it does not happen very often, though." I chuckled as I thought about Mr. Lowman and his newly pomaded hair. "There are also people who are excluded from the paths of the righteous by no fault of their own, and yet still bear the weight of judgment upon their shoulders. Having come to know some of them and their plight, I have resolved that I should make no judgment myself. We are none of us so pure that we can afford to cast that first stone."

"No." Mr. Judson nodded. "I suppose we are not."

I finished my third draft and looked at him. "And please understand that I am not now casting a stone at you, but I am at a loss here. There is the matter of Mr. Hewitt's and Mrs. Dunbar's murders, and I know you were reasonably close by when Mr. Hewitt was shot and have been told that you were on the street when Mrs. Dunbar was."

"Oh. Well, I suppose you do have to ask." He sniffed. "When I returned to the hall, I stopped near the door and was speaking with Governor Downey when the shots were fired." He thought, then frowned. "I remember being on the street and seeing that poor woman gunned down, but alas, I do not remember what my purpose was in being there. I do believe the horror of that event has driven that recollection from me."

"Quite understandable," I said, then got up. Mr. Judson bounced to his feet as well. Smiling, I handed him his draft. "This is your share of the commission, and it was well-earned, indeed."

"You're very welcome, Mrs. Wilcox, and thank you." Mr. Judson came around his desk to fetch his hat from the hat tree in the corner. "Now, shall we be off to the Farmer's and Merchant's?"

I was not surprised to find that Mr. Judson's counterpart at the other bank was waiting for us. The two men consulted their respective ledgers and otherwise made some notes. Then Mr. Judson smiled at me and said that funds from the Southern Pacific were fully on deposit in his bank. I thought it odd that no money had actually exchanged hands, but Mr. Judson explained that it was a matter of being shipped the actual coinage, as well as comparing the drafts that had been deposited with each bank and working out who owed what based on that. It was all rather confusing, but I got the gist of the concept. Nonetheless, I hurried to Mr. McKinley's and gave him the draft for his share of the commission, then went to Mr. Wiley's office to do the same.

I was just leaving the block where Mr. Wiley's office was when Mr. Wills hailed me.

"Mrs. Wilcox, we are well-met," he said, scurrying up.

I sighed. "And you have gotten a very generous fee today. Surely you do not need to make up to me anymore, do you?"

"No!" He laughed. "It is another matter all together." He made an odd face. "I am given to understand that you are very friendly with Mrs. Hewitt."

"And what of it? I know you seem to be bent on courting her."

"How is she?" he asked rather earnestly. He put up his hand. "I genuinely wish to know about her wellbeing. I know I cannot commence my suit for many months yet."

"She is still very grieved over her loss." I looked at him keenly. "Are you still hewing to the straight and narrow path?"

"Oh, yes." He sighed. "It can be difficult at times. But I do wish to be worthy of her, nor do I wish to burden her with another drunkard, so I have taken the pledge of temperance."

"That is exceedingly admirable of you, Mr. Wills." I paused. "Mr. Wills, you were at the party when Mr. Hewitt was shot."

He gulped nervously. "Actually, I was not there at that time. I had already gone home. I think the clock was striking ten-thirty when I arrived there."

"Why did you leave so early?" I asked. "It was quite a fine party."

"Not for me, it wasn't." His face grew angry. "Mr. Hewitt." Then he suddenly paled. "No, no, Mrs. Wilcox! I would not for the world have hurt him. But it pained me to see him with her." He winced, then gulped nervously. "I could see that the fellow was not long for this world, and I began to hope that I might, at last, have a chance to capture Mrs. Hewitt's heart."

I sighed. "I do wish that there was some encouragement that I could offer you, Mr. Wills, but I am afraid there isn't any. She is quite bereft, and I fear will remain so for some time."

And, I also thought, but did not say so, that having been accustomed to managing the buggy manufactory and her own affairs, Theodora would not likely, nor easily, surrender herself to another husband. Mr. Wills still thanked me for my honesty and sadly moved on down the street toward her house.

For myself, I decided the time was upon me to do what I should have done days before, that is, insist upon speaking to Mrs. Glassell.

I made my way to her home, almost mentally girding my loins, as I did not expect to be admitted. Indeed, I was not, at least, not right away. I saw the curtain in the front window twitch as I approached the white clapboard house, and was not in the least surprised when the maid informed me that Mrs. Glassell was not at home.

"Oh, dear," I said, almost loudly. "I did so wish to speak with her. I know. I shall wait here for her to return."

It took some minutes of waiting outside the front of the house before the maid came out and told me that Mrs. Glassell had returned and would receive me.

I do not know why Mrs. Glassell so frequently wore pink, as the color did not favor her. She was gowned in a pink bombazine walking suit that day, and paced her crowded front parlor.

"I do not wish to be the object of baseless accusations!" she snapped when she saw me.

"And I do not wish to make any." I folded my arms in front of myself. "However, I should think that you would know by now that if I am to avoid doing so, I need you and others to be honest with me."

"I am perfectly honest with you!"

"But you have been avoiding me ever since the party, and that is almost as suspicious as a blatant lie."

She groaned, then sank into the huge chair she kept next to the fireplace.

"I knew it!" she moaned. "I knew you were thinking that I killed poor Mr. Hewitt."

"I have very little reason to think so," I said, trying not to glare at her.

"I didn't! I promise you that I didn't!" She looked up at me, pleading.

"Then why wouldn't you see me?"

She flushed. "It's... It's..." She sighed deeply. "I was too embarrassed. You have no doubt heard that I am planning a temperance revival. Now, Mrs. Wilcox, I do not fault you for your wine business. But I cannot countenance it." She sniffed, then pulled a handkerchief from her sleeve. "Every day, women are forced onto the streets and worse, thanks to drunken men. Why look at poor Mrs. Hewitt! Burdened with that awful man."

"Actually, I agree with you," I said.

She gaped. "You do?"

"I do not think full temperance is possible. But, yes, finding some way to limit the supply of liquor and other such drink would not be a bad thing at all." I sighed. "I do not know how, and considering that I do make and sell wine, I suppose temperance is not in my best interests. But I do care about women, and if one does, one must see that temperance would have some significant benefits in restraining the drunken fools."

"Oh. Oh." Mrs. Glassell paused as she thought that over. Then she gave me a dreadfully guilty look. "But there is also the terrible murder of Mr. Hewitt. And you do know that I not only carry a good, solid gun, but that I can and do use it." She flushed a deep rose. "Furthermore, I was not actually in the hall when the shots were fired."

"Where were you?" I kept my face placid.

She hemmed and hawed, then looked up at me. "At the back of the hall, outside there is a... a..."

"A necessary, and you were there using it."

"I am afraid so." She sighed and waved her hands helplessly. "I am not as young as I used to be, and it can be difficult..."

I tried not to chuckle. "Mrs. Glassell, I am a physician. I am not unfamiliar with that specific problem, either. Sadly, there is not much to be done about it beyond using the necessary when, well, necessary. And, as I said, even with your cause, you had very little reason to kill Mr. Hewitt." I shrugged. "I might not have even thought so, but that you were so occupied with avoiding me, even to the point of hiding when I entered the same shop as you were in."

She gulped. "You knew about that."

"How was I to miss it? Others had seen you in there and as I did not, I realized that you must have hidden yourself. It was simply a dreadfully poor coincidence that minutes later, my horse ran away with the buggy I was in."

"That was dreadful." Mrs. Glassell shuddered. "We all feared for your life."

"I am not entirely unscathed," I said quietly. "But I am well enough. But there was also the matter of your missing carriage robe."

"How did you know it had been missed?"

"Mr. Gluck came to me, hoping that I had found it. Then poor Mrs. Dunbar presented it to me. She had found it near the hall the night of Mr. Hewitt's murder."

"Oh, dear Heavens!" Mrs. Glassell gasped appropriately. "Then we must assume that the horrible man who did the deed used the robe to cover himself, then left it where Mrs. Dunbar found it." She gasped again. "That must have been why the poor creature was killed! Surely, she saw something."

"Alas, no. But she did find the robe, and while I cannot assume the killer used it for cover, it does seem likely." I looked at her one more time. "Very well, then, Mrs. Glassell. I thank you for seeing me today."

The maid showed me out. At a loss for a moment, I realized that I was getting perilously close to being late for lunch. Not wishing to give Olivia any further cause for alarm, I started back through the middle of the pueblo toward the rancho.

I was not far from the Plaza when Rodolfo, still driving Ebony and the buggy, found me.

"I am so sorry!" I gasped. "When I did not see you outside the bank, I completely forgot that you had driven me."

Rodolfo dismounted from the front seat just long enough to help me into the buggy.

"It is no matter," he said, chuckling. "Mr. Judson told me he had taken you on another errand."

"And then I found still more errands," I sighed. "I hope Olivia is not too upset with me."

"She is not even at home," Rodolfo said, getting back up onto the seat. "In fact, I was driving to fetch her as well as you."

A minute later, he pulled up in front of an adobe on the west side of the pueblo. Olivia immediately came out, and Rodolfo helped her into the buggy.

"And what did you find out?" I asked her as we got going again.

"Nothing!" she snapped. "How is it that people all over a street could see a woman being shot, but not the man who shot her? Are they all blind?"

"No. They are simply not looking in the right direction at the right time," I said, trying not to chuckle at her irritation.

I had felt the same so many times before and could not blame her. Besides, I do believe that Olivia had convinced herself that she could find a killer as easily as I could. I did not wish to disabuse her of that particular notion, but she was about to find out just how hard finding a killer could be.

She had prepared a chicken stew for lunch that day, and given the cold weather, it was quite welcome and filling. It being Saturday, I promptly changed to my blue work dress, hoping that the bright color would offer me some cheer. But then I had another thought.

I had already decided that I needed another riding habit even before my beloved dark green one had been all but completely destroyed. I am not a spendthrift by any means. But having put such a goodly sum into my bank account that morning, I was feeling as though I might treat myself, especially since I had some significant need at that moment.

As Marisol helped me into the blue work dress, I told her of my proposal and Marisol told me that she had had another thought and had already spoken with Mrs. Washington, my dressmaker, about the possibility. Delighted by Marisol's good thinking, I thanked her. Alas, not thinking about the risks of riding alone that day, I asked Rodolfo to saddle up Ebony, which he did. Even though I was not wearing a riding habit, I mounted up and soon made my way into the pueblo to the adobe where Mrs. Washington and her granddaughter lived.

They were colored women, both fairly tall. Mrs. Washington was bent over with her years of work, but surprisingly agile and strong. Her hair was gray and her eyes amber. Her granddaughter, Miss Watkins, was darker of skin with hair that was glossy black, but otherwise much the same as her grandmother. The front parlor of their tiny home was crowded with rolls of various fabrics in a rainbow of colors that almost hid the two sewing machines. Books and magazines with colored plates of styles littered the two settees.

It was, perhaps, not the most propitious time for me to be ordering new dresses, given the search I was on. However, on a similar such search at a time of great frustration, I had done just that, and it had proved surprisingly helpful. At the very least, I found visiting Mrs. Washington quite restful and refreshing.

Mrs. Washington was happy to see me and delighted me immediately with her proposal for my ruined riding habit.

"This here bodice is in good shape," she told me, showing me the dress. "And I can take apart the skirt, cut out the torn parts and fashion a new one with some of this wool. It don't match exactly, but it looks nice next to the original fabric, and I have enough for new sleeves, too."

"Oh, it does look lovely." My eyes filled. "Thank you ever so much, Mrs. Washington."

I also spent some time picking out fabrics and plates for two more riding habits and another walking dress. I was not immediately inspired, but I do believe the time spent there helped clear my mind and aided in ratiocination. When we finished, Mrs. Washington brought out tea and regaled me with salty stories about some of her relatives, including one that inspired me in a direction I had not thought about.

Chapter Nineteen

I was glad to find Theodora in her office at the manufactory, although she shrugged sadly when I said so.

"I must say, keeping busy does help," she said softly.
"And since it is Saturday, there are wages to be counted and
distributed. Mr. Ledbetter is seeing to the actual distribu-
tion, but there is accounting to be done, as always."

"As always." I nodded and sat down on the sofa.

Theodora rang for some tea. Then, upon its arrival,
settled herself in the chair next to me.

"What can you tell me about Charles Hewitt?" I asked
gently.

"Him." Theodora shook her head and rolled her eyes.
"There was no love lost between him and my Thomas.
Charles was the older son and the family's darling." She
looked at me. "What do you know of our history?"

"Almost nothing," I confessed. "You were already here
in the pueblo when I arrived."

Theodora nodded. "We are from St. Louis. Father Hewitt was a buggy maker there, and quite a fine one. That's
why Thomas was so good at it. He grew up working for
his father, as did Charles. Thomas cut quite the fine figure
back then and was so very charming. But with Charles
being the apple of their father's eye and another brother in

between the two, Thomas's prospects were not very good. Thomas and I were married in 1856. It was a very bad time to be in Missouri. There was so much anger over the slavery issue. I must confess that both Thomas and I sided with the abolitionists, which one simply did not say out loud where we were at the time. By the time that judge struck down the Missouri compromise... Oh, what was that case?"

"Oh." I had to think about it. "Dread something or other?"

"Dread Scott. That poor fellow. All he wanted was to claim his freedom. But that judge not only denied him, he made it easier for Missourians to keep their slaves." Theodora shuddered, then sipped her tea. "Most of our neighbors were very pleased. But I could see which way the wind was blowing. At the very least, there would be a war. So, I convinced Thomas that we should go to California. It would be better for our children, and, yes, my first was already on the way." She snorted. "I can't imagine what I was thinking of when I decided to travel in that state."

I smiled. "The folly of youth, perhaps."

"To be sure." She chuckled and shook her head. "At least my mother, being widowed, decided to join us. Thomas and Mr. Ledbetter, who was but a lad then, built us a fine wagon and we found three other families to join us. We decided to take the Overland Stage route, as there were stops along the way and fewer Indians. Our original plan was to go to San Francisco. However, when we arrived in Los Angeles, that is when my time came and we had to stop for a few days at the outside, and Jane was born. Thomas said that he liked the place and thought that we could make a life here. So once I was able to, I went about the pueblo and had to agree with him. It was rough, but I could see that it was starting to grow and civilize. And there was plenty of call for buggies." She smiled softly and blinked her tears back. "One of the few good decisions Thomas ever made. He was a very good buggy maker, but he had not the least of a head for business. He always said that he trusted me to make those decisions more than he trusted his own father."

"You do have quite the acumen," I said.

"And some vision, thank God." She sighed. "As you know, I was right about the war coming. Thomas's family was wiped out by it. They'd spent most of their fortune making wagons for the Confederacy, which was never able to pay them back, and they were ruined. Father Hewitt died shortly after, and Charles made his way to us in Los Angeles. He tried to take over our business, insisting that he understood it better than Thomas did and that it was his right to. However, he was already well into his dissolute ways at that point, and whatever money he got, he spent on drink. Thomas asked me to support Charles, but I said no. We had our daughters to think of, since my next oldest had been born by then. Thomas was already starting to be a problem that way as it was."

"So his brother blamed your husband for leaving him destitute?" I watched her.

"Oh, no. He never blamed Thomas. Charles blamed me. Although, I do believe the reason that I prevailed in that argument was that Thomas had no love for his older brother and had often been tormented by the fellow. If he wanted to support Charles, it was only out of a sense of duty to his family." She closed her eyes. "I was so afraid when Charles appeared at the funeral. He is terribly obstreperous, and the most frightening part of him is that it does not seem to matter how drunk he is, he can still shoot straight. In fact, I have been rather frightened that Charles is the one who shot Thomas."

I thought that over. "I suppose it is possible. However, he very probably did not shoot Mrs. Dunbar." I sighed deeply. "It is all still very confusing."

A clock chimed from behind Theodora's desk. It was only three o'clock, which was not all that terribly late, but I did have two other people I wanted to ask questions of and it was not only Saturday, there were only four more days until Christmas and I feared the subsequent celebrations of that reality would result in more work for me than usual.

I bade Theordora a good afternoon and went straight to the livery stable. Mr. Lowman, fortunately, was still taking care about his person, and while he did not have on a good suit, his breath was still breathable and his hair freshly pomaded.

"I want to thank you for selecting such lovely horses for me," I told him. "Ebony is turning out to be the most pleasant of mounts."

"Ah. The black one." Mr. Lowman laughed. "I thought you'd go for the chestnut, and I have to admit I was hoping you would. I liked that black filly."

"Oh. I'm so sorry I took her from your employ."

"That's all right, Mrs. Wilcox."

"Eh, Mr. Lowman, I do have a rather difficult question to ask." I smiled and held up my hand. "I do not believe ill of you, but there are so many rumors floating around regarding the recent murders that I must be certain."

"You mean the Hewitt murder?" He sighed. "It wasn't me. I was at home that night. I did spend some time at the Padrano saloon. But I was home before eleven of the clock. I was getting into bed when I heard the clock strike."

"What about on December seven? Around five o'clock?"

"I was here, taking delivery on the horses I'd bought from Pedro Mariscal. He can vouch for me."

I smiled, even if I did not feel it. "I do not doubt it. Thank you for being so frank with me."

I went next to the jail. As I had hoped, Mr. Lomax was there. He smiled to see me.

"Good to know that you're still alive," he said.

I blew out my breath. "It was near enough, and I do not care to recall that ghastly incident. I am here to find out if you have heard anything about the missing gun."

"I would have sent word, so no." He frowned. "It does seem odd, though. That is one very nice gun, and probably worth a lot of money. Why hasn't somebody been looking for it?"

"Unless that person knows how it was lost." I thought for a second. "Mr. Lomax, what are the chances that gun has a mate? It seems to me that a lot of the men wear pairs of six-shooters, although not all do."

Mr. Lomax's forehead creased. "Most of us only need one. Although, some of the better-heeled fellows like pairs."

"If the gun that you found is one of a pair, then while it would be a loss in terms of its value, it would not be a disaster in terms of being able to defend oneself."

"I suppose so." Mr. Lomax nodded. "But how is that going to help us?"

"I haven't the faintest idea, but it might explain why our malefactor has not been trying to find it. After all, if he has the mate, then searching for the lost one would expose him as the malefactor."

"If he thought we had it."

"You're right." I frowned. "But how would the killer know we had the mate? We haven't said a word about it, and those people I have asked to listen for someone looking for a lost gun are utterly discrete."

"I have not heard anyone mention that we are looking for it." Mr. Lomax thought it over. "The only conclusion I can come to is that the malefactor assumes we have the mate because he knows where he lost it."

"Oh." I groaned. "That is entirely too possible. How utterly frustrating."

"That's usually how it goes when we try to think for others." Mr. Lomax let a small grin creep across his face.

"Hmph!"

After thanking Mr. Lomax, I made my way from the jail into the center of the pueblo and Mr. Handley's office. Fortunately, he chose to receive me.

"Mr. Handley," I said, pacing in front of his desk in the inner office. "I am at odds and do not wish to offend you, and at the same time I do need to verify your whereabouts at certain times in order to eliminate you from the list of persons we have reasons to believe might be behind the two murders."

Mr. Handley's eyes narrowed. "You mean Mr. Hewitt and that other poor woman?"

"Mrs. Dunbar, and yes."

"Well, I was at the party and in the social hall when Mr. Hewitt met his end," he said, blinking behind his glasses.

"I believe I was talking with Mr. Carson and Mr. Caswell at the time."

"I see. And the evening of December seven, when Mrs. Dunbar was killed?"

He blinked again. "I was here, I believe. What time did that occur? If it was after six, then I was at Mr. Mahoney's saloon getting my dinner."

I sighed.

"You have heard differently?" he asked, somewhat anxious.

"Not as such," I said. "Thank you, Mr. Handley. I must be on my way."

I left the block entirely unsettled in mind.

It is imperative to understand that in the time of which I am writing, the art of detection was barely in its most rudimentary form. I have seen the sensational dime novels of our era and must write that I scoff at them heartily. I do know that the Pinkerton people were around, albeit I do not believe they were in Los Angeles. Furthermore, from what I have read, their modus operandi was not actual detection, as in drawing conclusions from evidence, but far more like what we would call espionage today, in that they would pretend to be other than themselves, ingratiate themselves with their targets and find out what they wanted to know that way.

Also, at that point in my life, I had been on the search for enough killers that I was beginning to recognize that there was a point in almost every "case," as I suppose I must call the incidents, when it seemed as though all was confusion and that there would never be a clear answer to what had happened. That did not make that eventuality any more pleasant or easy to reconcile. Indeed, I continued to be utterly aggravated by the happenstance.

I was most certainly at that point that afternoon. I untied Ebony from out front of the block where Mr. Handley's office was and made my way to St. Vincent's hospital in the sourest of moods. Fortunately, Elena was already there and waiting for me with a lovely dinner that Olivia had sent with her. The two of us supped and waited. And waited some more. No one arrived. It was as though peace on earth had finally descended upon Los Angeles.

Elena and I waited until midnight, but it seemed clear that we would not be needed. The good sisters wished us well and sent us home with a full basket of cakes and biscuits, which was exceedingly kind. I made a note to send them several bottles of our best vintages only to find, when Enrique arrived to walk Elena and me home, that I already had.

We left the hospital, walking home, with me leading Ebony, and noted that the clouds had covered the sky and the waning moon was barely more than a bright spot among them. And as we walked, the rain drops finally, finally fell. The smell of freshly moistened earth filled my nose. There is something about that scent that still, to this day, fills me with a sense of peace. I suppose it has something to do with the fact that water in the pueblo was sufficiently scarce that it was a constant source of worry. Or perhaps it reminded me a little of my home in Boston.

Sunday, however, more than made up for the unusual quiet of that Saturday night. No less than four infants demanded delivery, and I thanked God heartily that Elena was more than capable in that regard, despite her young age. There were several pneumonias, and two very old women at the end of their natural years who needed attending as they passed from this life to the next.

Both Elena and I missed our respective church services. Olivia had Armando chase each of us down with a basket of food so that neither of us would miss our lunches, and even later again, our dinners. I waited through the night with Señora Padilla, who was close to ninety years old, her family gathered about her, and hoped that Elena had the chance to go home and rest, which I found out she had. Señora Padilla expired close to midnight.

The next morning, I put on my red work dress at Marisol's insistence. Having worn the blue one two days in a row, it did need some airing, and Marisol wanted to get the mud splatters from the rain the day before off of the skirt. The rainfall had turned out to be fairly light, but it was enough to turn the streets very muddy and sticky with the red adobe soil that abounds in Los Angeles.

I managed to convince my household that I could be far more expeditious in making inquiries if I rode by myself that day. No one was happy, but I suspected Olivia had decided that she could not make much of a fuss because she was intent on doing exactly the same thing, and that kept the others from complaining. I will say that Olivia, Magdalena, Marisol, and Maria all implored me to be careful as I went about my business.

I decided to ride Ebony and soon left the rancho. The day before, I had found a moment to pen a note to Mrs. Downey, and she had invited me to call on her that afternoon. In the meantime, there were several children with fevers and anxious parents to manage.

I do not wish to imply that I took the concerns of the parents lightly. I did not. Fevers can often turn quite serious. But it was also the time of year for such things, and three of the children, all from the same household, had a very mild case of scarlet fever. Most children manage scarlet fever quite well, but it can become very serious. So I told the parents what to watch for and to call me if such transpired. There was naught else to do, anyway.

I was about to head back to the rancho to change for my call on Mrs. Downey, when her new maid caught up with me and begged me to come that instant. I found Mrs. Downey outside her home, huddled behind the carriage house with her cook. I had just dismounted when I heard gunfire and felt myself slammed to the ground. Ebony nickered and stamped, but stayed calm and was unhurt. I was spared broken bones, but felt my aches from the week before. Mr. Navarro rolled off of me, then, pushing me toward the back of the carriage house, helped me up.

"Mrs. Wilcox, you must stop making a habit of getting shot at," Mr. Navarro said, his eyes twinkling. "My wife is sure to be displeased with me for knocking you over so often."

I knew that he was only teasing me, but such was my mood that I dearly wanted to slap him.

"Where is she?" a voice screamed from inside the main house. "Where is my girl? I demand my rights! She's mine."

I swallowed. "That sounds like Mr. Dunbar."

"It is," said Mrs. Downey, looking quite afraid. "I am so glad we were in the kitchen going over dinner when he came. He broke into the house, screaming and shooting. We ran out here and Mr. Navarro saw us."

"How did he come to be here?" I asked.

"I do not know," said Mr. Navarro. "The Ventura County Sheriff wired us to warn us that he was headed here yesterday."

"Mr. Dunbar!" yelled a voice at the front of the house.

"Mr. Wolf," Mr. Navarro said to us. "The new city marshal."

We winced as we heard glass breaking and gun shots.

"I will not be denied my rights. The girl is mine, do you hear? Mine!" More gunfire followed.

"Nobody wants to deny you your rights," Mr. Wolf called. "But you ain't going to get them by shooting at people. Now, put your gun down and come out of there with your hands up."

The only response was more gunfire and glass breaking, then silence. Mr. Navarro poked his head around the carriage house and nothing happened. Another minute later, we could hear Mr. Wolf stomping around the house and cursing. Mr. Dunbar had somehow escaped through a side window and had disappeared into a nearby orchard.

After seeing that Mrs. Downey and her cook were safe, I mounted Ebony and hurried off into the pueblo. It turned out that it was a good thing that I chose not to go directly to Angelina's home, as Mr. Wolf had seen me at the Downey home and surmised that I might know the whereabouts of the child that had so inspired Mr. Dunbar's behavior. As Mr. Lomax later explained in the days after this narrative played itself out, someone had told Mr. Wolf that I nearly always went straight to the funeral parlor to talk with Mrs. Sutton after such events. Another young policeman had been stationed nearby, watching the back entrance of the parlor in the hopes that I would have my conference with Angelina, then lead him to little Shirley.

Yet another policeman found me at the mail office in the United States hotel, gathering my mail as I pondered my next steps. Mr. Resendez had been a member of the force almost since its inception, although our paths had seldom crossed. Why they hadn't, I do not know.

"Mr. Wolf thinks you know where the child is."

I smiled. "I know where several are. Which one are you asking for?"

He glared at me. "You know very well which child I am asking for."

I returned his glare with one of my own. "Perhaps. But if you think that I am going to risk her well-being by saying where she is, then you are quite wrong, sir."

"Why would you deny the poor man his rights to his own flesh and blood?"

"And why would insist upon sealing that poor child's doom by handing her over to that monster?"

Mr. Resendez looked puzzled and held out his hand. "You do not know that he will hurt her."

"I most certainly do know. The man already has on any number of occasions. And did you see what he did to Mrs. Downey's home without even asking whether the child was there first?" I sniffed. "If that man had any rights to that child, he forfeited them a long time ago by beating both her and her mother. No one, Mr. Resendez, has the right to take the life of a human being, including his wife or child."

He sighed. Mr. Navarro came running up just then and pulled his colleague away for a moment and spoke softly with him. Mr. Resendez stalked off, shaking his head.

"You are very lucky." Mr. Navarro turned to me. "The governor has decided that it's best that the child remain in hiding until Mr. Dunbar can be caught."

"Mrs. Downey?" I asked, feeling quite unsettled.

"He holds great affection for her." Mr. Navarro shrugged and looked out at the street. "And just so you know, Mr. Wolf thinks she is being very unreasonable about the child." He held up both of his hands as I drew breath to remonstrate. "Now, don't slap me. I'm only telling you what I heard. As it happens, I agree with you and Mrs. Downey. Men like that, they are a danger to everyone, not least their own."

"Well." I looked down at the letters I held in my hand. They were mostly the usual, except one. "I'd best make my way back to the rancho or I shall miss my lunch and Olivia will be angry."

My sister Carrie and I corresponded quite regularly, and while it would take a month or so for each letter to arrive here, each letter arrived with some regularity, usually on a Wednesday or Thursday. It was a rare event that a letter from Carrie would arrive on a Monday.

I trotted Ebony home, arriving well ahead of lunchtime, and went straight to my adobe. Trembling, I opened the letter from Carrie.

"Is something wrong?" Magdalena asked, coming into the front parlor.

"I'm afraid so," I said, my voice shaking. "My sister Carrie writes that our younger sister has died in childbirth and the baby perished as well."

Chapter Twenty

I spent the afternoon grieving for my sister. I had missed so much by being in Los Angeles. All I wanted was to rush back to Boston, to be near my family. And yet, shortly before supper, I was reminded yet again that I also had a family of sorts right where I was.

Olivia and Anita came into the parlor and brought me warm milk with chocolate and cinnamon, and Magdalena held me as I cried. There was also a note from Angelina, who had apparently been told about my letter, letting me know that she grieved with me, and Regina also sent a note offering her deepest sympathy and her shoulder to cry on, should I need it.

Unfortunately, both notes were quite insistent that, unless I was up to it, any conference together could be put off. Alas, I did not feel that it could be. I sent return notes that I would go to the funeral parlor as soon as dinner was finished, which is exactly what I did, with Rodolfo driving the buggy.

I was the first to arrive, entering through the front of the house. Angelina received me in the family's front parlor, which was upstairs, leaving her young helper, Tai Chin, to wait at the back door for Regina. Rodolfo chose to wait outside with Ebony and warm blankets for both him and the horse, the night being rather cool. Angelina introduced me to Mr. Sutton's sister, Mrs. Albred, or Vina, and her husband, Mr. Albred. Mrs. Albred was almost as stout as her older brother, Mr. Sutton, and in contrast, her husband was quite tall and gaunt. The children were in the back room, which had been turned into a nursery. Mr. Sutton busied himself pouring glasses of angelica for each of us.

"I still say you should turn the child over to her father," Mrs. Albred said as soon as I was settled on the comfortable sofa.

"Have you no care for the child?" I snarled at her.

She sat back, somewhat shocked as we had only just been introduced.

But then the shrieks of an injured child split our ears. Mrs. Albred rushed to the nursery while Angelina slowly rose and sauntered after.

"He is never hurt," she muttered to me as I followed. "He just likes making noise and getting his mother's attention."

"This is the last straw!" Mrs. Albred snapped, her arms protectively around a little tow-headed boy with dark eyes and a face screwed up in rage.

"She pushed me into the stove and held me," he screamed, pointing at Shirley.

I could smell something scorched, but the scent did not come from the direction of the boy.

"Then he must be quite injured," I said. "Mrs. Albred, I am a doctor and can see to his burns."

She gasped in horror and pushed the boy at me. I held him tenderly as I looked him up and down and front to back.

"The good news is that he does not seem to have been burnt at all," I said, still holding onto him. I looked over at Shirley.

The little girl looked terrified and sucked her thumb. Angelina swept her up, then screamed.

"Her clothes are scorched in the back!" Angelina continued her examination. "And her hair is burnt."

"Gently take her clothes off," I said. "Hopefully, they haven't stuck to any burns."

"She bites me," the little boy said.

"Your name is Billy, isn't it?" I asked him. He nodded. "Where does she bite you?" He pointed to his arm. "Let us roll up your sleeve, then, and we'll see."

The arm was unmarked. Shirley's arm and back were anything but.

"These are bite marks!" Angelina snapped at her sister-in-law. "And they are all over her." She looked up at Billy's three older sisters. "Did you see what he was doing? Why didn't you say anything?"

The three girls, the oldest being eleven, simply looked at each other.

"Mama would not believe us when we did," said the oldest lass, her golden curls shifting more in annoyance than fear.

Angelina glared at the nurse. "Did you see him bite her?"

The nurse, a young woman not even seventeen, just shrugged her shoulders.

"You are dismissed," Angelina snapped. "Get your things and leave now!" She turned on Mrs. Albred as the girl scurried out of the room. "You have done nothing but accuse this poor innocent babe of all manner of ills, and look at what your son has done! I do not doubt that boy has bitten your daughters as well."

"You have not seen him actually bite anyone," Mrs. Albred sniffed. "Something else may have marked the child."

"I know full well what a bite mark looks like! I see them often enough in my work." Angelina's eyes blazed.

"He is but a young boy. He can't have done much harm."

"And still you excuse him!" Angelina screamed.

Even more eerie was the way little Shirley cowered silently and hid in Angelina's skirts. I gently pulled Angelina aside and spoke as quietly as I could.

"Dearest, I do believe that given this revelation and the events earlier today at Mrs. Downey's, it would perhaps be safer for the babe to be elsewhere?"

Angelina looked at me. "The rancho?"

"It is well defended."

Angelina gave Mrs. Albred one last glare, then scooped Shirley into her arms, crooning at the child softly.

"Let us go then," Angelina said.

The men did not say anything. Regina was waiting downstairs in Angelina's little study next to the room where she prepared the bodies for burial. She agreed with Angelina and me that the child would be safer on the rancho and offered to follow us there, as she had driven herself in her own buggy, and would bring Angelina home when we were finished.

Angelina took Shirley to the barracks, and when Anita heard what the poor babe had suffered, she held Shirley tightly and told Angelina that she would care for the child as if she were her own. The babe was soon bathed and dressed in fresh clothes and fell asleep next to Sofia, Sebastiano's youngest.

Regina paced in my front parlor, and the three of us settled there. Angelina sighed deeply as I poured out the angelica.

"Edgar had told me last night that we should keep her," she said. "Although that is assuming the father does not prevail with a judge. Or worse, remove her by force."

"It would seem all our hearts are heavy tonight," Regina said, then raised her glass. "However, it is, as they say, always darkest before the dawn, and I am confident that we shall prevail."

I couldn't help chuckling, as did Angelina.

"I suppose it is," I said, softly. "I cannot help but wonder if we have two different killers that we are looking for. Perhaps one person killed Mr. Hewitt and Mr. Dunbar killed his wife."

"Except that he couldn't have," said Angelina. "I wired the Ventura County Sheriff this morning after hearing that Mr. Dunbar was here and found out that he had been in jail since Thanksgiving or so. He was serving a sentence for drunken and disorderly behavior and was released yesterday."

"That's one less person to consider," Regina said, holding out her empty glass. "Which means we are back to one person killing both."

"I am afraid so." I poured for Regina, then smiled as Magdalena brought in a platter of pan dulces. "Thank you, Magdalena. But again, we have too many people to consider, none of whom had that strong a reason to commit cold-blooded murder."

"What about Mr. Wills or Mr. Jessup?" Angelina asked. "They are supposedly both in love with Mrs. Hewitt."

I made a face. "Mr. Wills claims that he left the party early because he found it so difficult to watch Mr. Hewitt. He also said that he saw that Mr. Hewitt was not long for this world."

"So he had even less of a reason to kill the man," Regina said. She took a bite of pan dulce and chewed thoughtfully. "And the other night, I saw that Mr. Jessup had a gun that looked very much like what you described as the one left behind."

"But Mr. Jessup was in San Buenaventura when Mrs. Dunbar was killed," I said. "I saw the passenger list at the stage office myself."

"Now we are back to two killers," Angelina groaned.

Regina stood up. "As much as I would like to continue this all night, it is already quite late and tomorrow I shall be inundated with young women weeping that they have no families to go home to."

"No men?" Angelina asked, her mischief popping out in spite of her worry.

"Most of my clients have families and feel that they should actually be at home." Regina sighed. "Christmas is such a ridiculous custom. And as it happens, I, too, have family in the pueblo and would like to see them."

She meant Mr. Mahoney, who was her brother, and his daughters. I did not ask for details about her visits, though.

Angelina got up and held me close. "I am so sorry you lost your sister. And to be so far away at such a time."

Regina took her turn holding me as well.

"Maddie, dearest," she said, finally holding my hands. "I know you long to go home, and if you feel you must, then go. We will still have the U.S. Mail at our disposal."

"Oh, Regina, that is so utterly kind of you," I said, my eyes filling. I pulled my handkerchief from my sleeve. "I know what that cost you to say, and that you did... It only serves to remind me that I have ties here as well." I looked at both women. "You two are so very dear to me, as is the rest of my household. If I weren't so afraid that the trip would kill me, I might attempt a visit home. But for now, it is most certainly out of the question."

"Then it's all to the better that we are here," Regina said.

She held me once more, as did Angelina, then the two left me.

I must say that what happened the following morning also reminded me of how much I loved Angelina and Regina, and the rest of my household, but, regrettably, not in a pleasant way. Perhaps it was because Mr. Brownlow was so obviously intent on making me a part of his household. He arrived at the rancho shortly after I had broken my fast.

Marisol had convinced me to wear my red poplin work dress again. After all, the weather threatened rain. I must write that Marisol's pronouncements that she did not want to form attachments with the rest of my household because she would eventually leave to marry did worry me a little. She was rapidly becoming indispensable. Already her skills were beginning to outstrip Juanita's, and that truly amazed me.

It being the day before the great feast of Christmas, I was in conference with Magdalena and Olivia about how the festivities would transpire on the rancho when Rodolfo came from the front gate to tell us that Mr. Brownlow was there and hand Olivia a note. I was on the edge of telling Rodolfo that I was not in, in which I would have been well within polite practice and my rights to do so, but thought that it was probably time to make sure he understood that his suit had absolutely no chance for survival.

I met him at the gate and held it open for him to slip inside. Once there, he tried to push a small box decorated with a single rose into my hands.

"Just a small token of my esteem," he said.

"I appreciate your esteem, but you may keep this token and all others," I said, growling rather unbecomingly, and pushed the box back at him.

"Now, now, Mrs. Wilcox." He grinned rather happily. "You do not have to be coy."

"Mr. Brownlow, what do I have to do to dissuade you from this fool's errand you are on?" I snorted. "Have I not made it perfectly clear that I have no possible use for a husband? I do not want a husband, and I will not take a husband!"

He stepped back, rather disconcerted. I suppose I should have had some mercy on the fool. It had probably not occurred to him that a woman, especially a lonely widow, would not be delighted by being courted by a fairly well-heeled fellow of some consequence.

"Why, in Heaven's name, do you continue?" I asked.

"But... You love my daughters. And they love you."

"I am glad of their affection, and they are lovely young girls. But that does not mean that I have any interest in being their mother. And what makes you think that we are, in any way, well suited to each other? Are you willing to support my medical practice, let alone my winery?"

He smiled beatifically. "But of course you will practice medicine. You will be taking care of my girls."

Which, all of a sudden, made the objective of his pursuit perfectly clear.

"You want a doctor for free," I snarled, advancing on him as menacingly as I could.

"No, madam. I want a wife and mother for my daughters."

"But if she also happens to have a great deal of medical skill, that would help as well."

"Eh... No, madam." He tried to smile, but the attempt utterly failed. "I truly have affection for you."

"Of all the men who have tried to win me, for all the ridiculous reasons, yours is possibly the lowest." I stamped my foot in indignation. "Who do you think I am? An utter fool to be taken in by your glorious recognition of me? For Heaven's sakes, Mr. Brownlow. How is it you can admire my masculine brain and still not see that I am not the least bit taken in by your attentions? How is it possible that you did not think that I would see through your attempt to win me?"

He stammered a great deal for a minute or two. Finally, he sighed and his shoulders drooped, defeated.

"My apologies, madam," he said softly.

"Which I will accept on the condition that you end your suit immediately." I shuddered. "I do not understand how it is that you have been so persistent."

"You are charming," he said with a weak smile, and I had to believe that he was genuine in that respect. "But one does not get to be an attorney of my stature without a certain amount of... Shall we say, faith in the righteousness of the mission?" He shrugged.

"If that righteousness means getting the rights of those who are downtrodden, then I say, Godspeed you." I could not help glaring at him once more, especially since I had no reason to believe that he cared about anybody but the men who were paying him. "If your so-called righteous mission is the pursuit of a woman who clearly does not want you, then you had best think again about how righteous that mission might be."

"Yes, madam."

He eventually slunk away, but as he did, Olivia walked up.

"You have sent your suitor away," she said simply.

"Of course. I have no interest in his suit, especially when what he really wanted was a free doctor and someone to mother his daughters."

"Our children are our greatest joy and treasure," Olivia said, quite seriously.

"Perhaps. And his girls are quite charming." I sighed. "Nonetheless, what annoys me is the presumption that I would be in awe and wonder of him."

"What do you expect, Maddie?" Olivia laughed a little. "Even I, who have a wonderfully intelligent daughter, still dote on her brothers. It is what we are taught."

"Elena is a very good doctor, you know."

"I do know. And she will be an even better one some day." Olivia reached over and patted my arm. "But I have news for you. Yesterday I sent a note to Sebastiano's second cousin, Maria Benito. Her daughter is the housekeeper for this Mr. Jessup."

"Why her?"

Olivia shrugged. "Does it matter? He is somebody you are worried about. Maria just sent me a note back. She writes that Mr. Jessup has been here in the pueblo all month and that he has not left at all. Indeed, her daughter was rather annoyed that he hadn't." Olivia smiled. "She has a friend whose visits she enjoys, but he cannot be there when Mr. Jessup is there."

"But Mr. Jessup was on the stage. I saw the passenger list."

"That does not mean he was actually on the stagecoach. He could have bought a ticket, then changed his plans." Olivia shrugged. "It does happen. And it does not mean that the plans changed for nefarious purposes. Plans change."

"That is, indeed, true," I said, thinking it over. "Nonetheless, it creates a most interesting implication."

Olivia smiled, then went on to her adobe.

I was quite nonplussed. Olivia was entirely right that the fact that Mr. Jessup had bought a stage ticket and had not used it did not mean that the inescapable conclusion was something nefarious. At the same time, it was oddly convenient. Mrs. Dunbar had been followed by someone on the few days before her murder. That would most certainly have given Mr. Jessup time to come up with a plan, including purchasing a ticket for a stagecoach ride that he did not intend to take.

I rode Ebony at a steady trot to the funeral parlor in the hopes of speaking with Angelina only to find that she had left earlier with Mr. Sutton who was occupied with seeing his relatives to Wilmington to catch a steamer back to Santa Barbara. It would not be the first time circumstances had made life difficult for us, nor, regrettably, would it be the last.

Left with no other immediate alternative, I mounted Ebony again, and headed to the center of the pueblo.

I am, in fact, trying to reconcile my more rational nature with the concept of the subconscious. Having had several flashes of inspiration that seemed to have come out of nowhere, I must concede that there may, indeed, be something to that particular bit of ratiocination.

I did have some holiday presents that I wished to purchase. My shopping having been interrupted by the buggy incident, there were several items that I had hoped to have ready for various members of my household, not to mention Wang Fu, who did not celebrate Christmas but appreciated the notice. Which is why, I thought, I had gone to Mr. Carson's stationery store to find what I wanted to buy.

Mr. Carson stocked some lovely toys, including a porcelain doll that I bought for Shirley. I also purchased a journal for Fu. We'd had several disagreements over the need for taking notes, me being quite strongly in favor of the practice, Fu believing that since he fashioned each of his treatments specifically for each patient and circumstance, notes were of little use. I picked out another journal for Elena as well.

As the clerk wrapped my purchases, I heard both Mrs. Carson and Mrs. Glassell coming into the main part of the shop from the back.

"I honestly do not know why you are worrying, my dear," Mrs. Carson snapped, still in the corridor to the back of the business.

"But Mrs. Wilcox came asking about it," Mrs. Glassell sighed.

"You have a perfectly good reason for being where you were that night," Mrs. Carson said. "Indeed, if you have recounted the episode accurately, then she not only understood that, she proposed that there was no remedy. More's the pity, in my opinion."

"That may be, but it is still humiliating."

"Darling, you have no reason to be humili—" Mrs. Carson arrived in the shop proper and smiled at me with no warmth whatsoever. "Mrs. Wilcox. What a pleasure to see you here."

"What a pleasure to see you," I replied, not because I believed it to be, but because it was the polite thing to say.

"Pray forgive us," Mrs. Carson continued. "Dear Mrs. Glassell is worried that she might come under suspicion of killing Mr. Hewitt."

"She has already shared that concern with me," I said, a very false smile pasted across my lips. I looked at Mrs. Glassell. "I did try to reassure her."

"You did," Mrs. Glassell squeaked.

"Nonetheless," Mrs. Carson continued. "You are forgetting that there was someone else who entered the hall well after the shots were fired. Besides Mrs. Glassell."

"And who would that be?" I asked.

Mrs. Carson simpered. "That would be Mr. Jessup."

Chapter Twenty-One

I must concede that the only happy part of that exchange was that I finally had some confirmation regarding what had happened to Mr. Hewitt. The problem I had was what to do about it. I rode past the buggy manufactory and was happy to see that while the street in front was relatively busy with people visiting each other or hurrying home to prepare for Christmas Eve, none of Theodora's suitors were in evidence.

I returned to the center of the pueblo just in time to see Angelina and Mr. Sutton pull up next to the funeral parlor in their buggy. I trotted Ebony over.

"I thought you'd gone to Wilmington," I said as I dismounted.

"No." Mr. Sutton grunted a little as he lifted Angelina off the buggy's seat. "Just to the train station."

"I left early to do some shopping," Angelina said. "Edgar met me in town."

"We must conference quickly." I tied Ebony to the hitching post outside and followed Angelina through the parlor to the back room. "I finally know who killed both Mr. Hewitt and Mrs. Dunbar."

I told her what Olivia had said, as well as what Mrs. Carson had seen the night of the party.

Angelina gaped. "So, he was here all along?"

"He was, indeed. He has also been loitering outside the buggy manufactory every so often. Alas, so have Mr. Wills and even Mr. Lowman."

"We knew he had feelings for Mrs. Hewitt." Angelina folded her arms across her chest. "We must tell Regina."

"At this hour?"

Given that Regina's business usually went on until quite late at night, she was seldom awake before the noon hour. Angelina looked at the clock ticking pleasantly in the corner.

"You have a point," she said.

"We should probably warn Theodora," I said. "Then we can pay a call on Regina and formulate a plan to capture Mr. Jessup."

Angelina nodded, and we were soon on our way to the buggy manufactory, although we went by foot. I could not ride as Angelina was not a horsewoman, nor would I be able to keep her on Ebony with me. Mr. Sutton had already left for the stable where they kept their horse and the buggy.

We walked quickly, but even as we went, I began to get the odd feeling that all was not as it should be.

"I do believe someone is following us," I said softly to Angelina.

She looked behind us. "So do I. I saw a man dart into that alley we just passed."

"What do we do?"

"Hurry on to warn Mrs. Hewitt."

So, we did.

As we approached, I gasped and pointed. "He's there."

Mr. Jessup was, indeed, standing across the street from the manufactory and house, leaning against the wall of an adobe and gazing at the two buildings and ignoring the passersby going back and forth.

"Should we go in with him there?" Angelina asked.

"Why not?" I said. "There is no reason I should not be talking to Theodora." I looked up at the second floor of the manufactory and saw a curtain twitch. "She's in her office and I am certain has seen Mr. Jessup as well."

We started along the street and were almost directly in front of the manufactory when the loud roar of an infuriated man hit our ears. I slid my hand into my leather satchel and turned toward Mr. Jessup, only to hear Angelina scream behind me.

I turned. A man with dirty brown hair and beard and wearing a ragged, dirty suit had grabbed Angelina about the waist and lifted her into the air.

"Where is she? I demand my rights!" The man shook Angelina for good measure.

"Let go of me!" Angelina screamed, kicking and scratching at her captor.

"She's my girl. You got no right to keep her!"

Fortunately, his rage was so complete that he did not see me withdraw my gun and approach. Still screaming, he turned away from me and I saw my chance. I slid up behind and stuck the muzzle of the gun into his ribcage.

"Let the lady down," I said firmly, but loudly enough to rise over his screaming.

He stopped his cries and slowly set Angelina on her feet. Sadly, I was not sure of what to do next, but did not get long to consider it. Mr. Dunbar suddenly whipped around and grabbed my gun. Laughing, he pointed it at me and I backed up.

"You're going to tell me where you got my girl," he demanded. "I won't have it. I'll shoot you if you don't!"

"I cannot say," I said as calmly as possible.

"You surely can."

"No, sir."

He cocked the hammer on the pistol and laughed. But then a shot came from across the street, and Mr. Dunbar crumpled. The shot had hit straight in the heart, and I do believe that Mr. Dunbar was dead before his head hit the ground.

Mr. Jessup trotted up and shook his head. "Are you ladies all right?"

"We are, sir," I said brightly, then swallowed. "No little thanks to your quick action."

That is when I saw the gun in Mr. Jessup's hand. It was a large six-shooter with a well-polished silver barrel covered by scrollwork and a dark mother-of-pearl handle. Angelina's eyes widened as she saw me. Then Mr. Jessup saw that I had recognized the gun as well.

"Well," I said rather breathlessly and nodded toward the house. "We'd best be getting inside. Mrs. Hewitt is no doubt waiting for us."

"You're not going anywhere, Mrs. Wilcox," Mr. Jessup growled, lifting the gun. "Your little friend here neither."

I swallowed. "And what are you going to do, Mr. Jessup? Shoot us out here with all these people present to witness it?"

A crowd was in the process of gathering, although given the gun in Mr. Jessup's hand, they kept something of a distance.

He gestured with the gun. "Into the manufactory. Now."

I would have preferred to stay on the street, where the presence of others might dissuade Mr. Jessup or even subdue him. But there would be men working inside the manufactory who might also be able to subdue him. Angelina and I both slid backward into the building as Mr. Jessup pushed forward, stopping only to stoop down and pick up my gun that Mr. Dunbar had dropped.

However, as we slid inside the building, it was oddly silent. The workers were gone. Mr. Jessup laughed.

"Mrs. Hewitt gave her men the afternoon off," he said. "Tonight is Christmas Eve."

Indeed, a half-built wagon lay on its side in the middle of the room. Tools had been neatly put away over the bench table and on the other walls. Bars of iron stood on end next to the forge anvil, and the fire was out. The back door was firmly closed and bolted.

My heart pounded as I struggled to keep calm.

"Alas, you will still be a wanted man," I said.

"Not if I had to defend myself," he said, grinning. "And that's what I'll say happened."

"Against two defenseless, unarmed women?" Angelina asked.

"You're not defenseless and we all know it." Mr. Jessup looked around the shop. "Besides, I'm not staying here. I've got business interests all over this state and all the way up to the Washington Territory. They'll have a time and a half trying to find us."

"We're not going anywhere with you," I said.

Mr. Jessup glared at me. "You two are not going anywhere."

"Mr. Jessup, what is going on here?" Theodora slowly came down the stairs.

"We're leaving, Mrs. Hewitt. You and me." Mr. Jessup gestured at Angelina and me. "I've just got to figure out how to get these two taken care of, and then we'll go."

"I don't understand," Theodora said.

"He killed your husband," I said, backing up to get closer to the side of the wagon.

Angelina inched her way closer to the bench tables.

"What?" Rage filled Theodora, and she rushed at Mr. Jessup.

He swallowed and backed up. "I had to! I couldn't bear seeing that drunk embarrass you and embarrass you again. You didn't deserve that."

"Nor did I deserve to have the man I loved ripped from my arms that way!" Theodora's tears ran down her cheeks and she grabbed an iron bar and hefted it.

Mr. Jessup pointed both guns at her and she backed away.

"He also killed Mrs. Dunbar," I said.

"I had to. She saw me." Mr. Jessup glanced back at me, then turned his attention to Theodora, who had advanced again. "I saved you from that lout! He had humiliated you in front of the entire pueblo!"

Theodora stayed silent.

I slid behind the wagon bed to find a table with a mallet and several iron bits on it. I picked one up.

"Jessup!" called Mr. Wolf's voice. "We know you're in there. Drop your gun and come out with your hands up, or we're coming in firing."

"I don't have to!" Mr. Jessup yelled back. "I've got three ladies in here with me, and if you want to see them alive again, you're going to do what I say."

Theodora caught my eyes and blinked, followed by a quick glance toward the benches. I guessed that Angelina also had armed herself.

"What do you want, Jessup?" Mr. Wolf called.

"I want a wagon and a team of horses and five thousand dollars from my bank account."

"I don't see as we can do that," Mr. Wolf called back.

"No!" screamed a third voice, Mr. Ledbetter's. "Jessup, you harm one hair on that dear woman's head, and I swear to God that I will hunt you down until I find you and kill you!"

"She'll be the last to go," Mr. Jessup called. "But if you don't agree to my terms, I am going to start with the little Mexican one."

I peeked through a hole that had been drilled into the wagon bed next to me. Mr. Jessup looked around, suddenly realizing that Angelina and I had found cover. His two hands, each carrying a gun, spread wide, with one aimed in Angelina's direction, the other at Theodora. His back was to the street door, and he knew that I had to be close by.

I sent a bit of metal skittering toward the back door. Mr. Jessup quickly shot through the bottom of the wagon, albeit away from the side where I was hiding. Looking through the hole, I saw another projectile fly his way from the bench tables. He turned in that direction, but the small hammer hit him hard in the shoulder and he dropped the gun he'd aimed at Theodora. She started toward him, but he whipped the other gun in her direction and advanced on her, sliding to the side of the wagon behind which I was hidden. I slid around to the other side, fully expecting Mr. Jessup to continue around to the side where I'd hidden.

But he did not. I peeked around the front, and he advanced on Theodora.

"You had better not try anything," he growled, his gun aimed. "Not if you want to see your friend keep living."

"Jessup!" Mr. Wolf called. "We're losing patience out here."

"I already got one dead." Mr. Jessup returned. "Want another one?"

A rumble of alarm rose up on the street outside. Mr. Jessup breathed heavily and took another step toward Theodora.

"You drop that bar real gentle now," he told her. She hesitated, and he cocked the hammer on the gun. "I mean it. Drop it!"

She bent and tossed the bar of metal in my direction. As slowly as I dared and as silently as I could, I picked the bar up.

"Now, you're going to come over here," Mr. Jessup told her.

"No," Theodora whispered and backed up.

"I mean it." He stepped toward her. "You'll learn to love me."

I did not wait. I ran at him with the bar in my hands. Theodora dove for cover behind the anvil. Mr. Jessup turned toward me just in time to receive a crushing blow to his upper arm from the iron bar. I brought it down again onto his shoulder and he sank to his knees, howling in agony. The gun, my gun, as it turned out, dropped from his hand. I knocked it away, then pushed him onto his face, firmly pushing the end of the bar onto the back of his neck.

"I would not move, if I were you," I said, increasing the pressure on the bar I held. "I am a doctor and I know exactly where to put this bar to end your life."

Angelina rushed to the door and threw it open. "We're alive and he has been captured!"

I wish that I could write that effecting the capture of Mr. Jessup put me in Mr. Wolf's admiring and good graces. Regrettably, it had the exact opposite effect. Both Mr. Lomax and Mr. Navarro were on hand that day as well, and were quite amused when their superior continued to insist that we three women had simply gotten lucky.

We were restored to our loved ones en masse, out in front of the manufactory. Mrs. Hewitt's mother and daughters rushed out, embraced her then pushed her into their house. Mr. Sutton quickly swept Angelina back to the funeral parlor after we'd all told our tale. Olivia and Sebastiano grabbed me and hurried me back to the rancho. We sent little Shirley to the Suttons' with Armando and Anita. After they gave Shirley to Angelina, Armando took Ebony, who had remained tied up at the Suttons' house.

I was still shaken, but decided to attend the solemn midnight mass at the plaza church with my household. The Suttons were there also, Angelina happily holding the sleeping little girl. It was a lovely ceremony filled with the old Latin hymns, and even as I sneezed at the incense wafting through the church, I finally began to feel at peace.

At the rancho the next morning, after a truly magnificent breakfast, presents were given all around. Then the visiting began. The Lomax family stopped for a while. Mr. Navarro and my dear Juanita came by as well. The Suttons spent most of the afternoon and well into the evening there. Regina finally showed up, quite out of temper that she had missed the excitement the day before, yet happy that she had spent the time with her brother and nieces.

We spent the next day visiting other friends, then those among the sons and daughters on the rancho who were older than fourteen went to the masquerade party at the skating rink, and Ramon won a prize for his bear costume.

By that spring, Mr. Brownlow found his second wife on a trip to San Diego and promptly married her. She was nice enough, but not in the least bit sensible. I continued to care for his children for many years, and even cared for their children when they had them.

Angelina was made little Shirley's guardian and eventually she and Mr. Sutton adopted the child. Letters to San Buenaventura turned up that Shirley had not been baptized, so Angelina arranged for that and invited me to the ceremony. It would be some years before the child lost her timid mien, but otherwise, she was quite a happy little girl and both Angelina and Mr. Sutton doted on her.

My sister Carrie and I wrote more letters than usual that winter, hoping to assuage our mutual grief. My father was also very grieved by Abby's loss, and Abby's husband even more so to the point that their young son went to live with Carrie and was essentially raised by her.

Mr. Ledbetter continued to work for the buggy manufactory, but eventually lost interest in Theodora. A rather pretty young woman named Caroline Walsh arrived in the pueblo that spring with her parents. Mr. Ledbetter was hardly the only man whose eyes she'd caught, but she decided that she liked him best and the two would marry a year or so later.

Mr. Jessup was eventually tried and found guilty of murder. The hanging, I was told, was well-attended. I did not go, nor did Theodora.

"I should be happy that justice was done," she said the day after the hanging. She was still in full mourning and would stay that way for another two years. "But I am not."

"How do you mean, dearest?" I asked.

We sat in her living room sipping tea. She dabbed at her eyes with her handkerchief.

"Several well-meaning souls have said that I should feel relieved that Mr. Jessup was caught and hung. But all I really feel is pity for the poor wretch and for Mrs. Dunbar, and still the terrible sadness of my loss." She looked blankly at the opposite wall where a photograph of her dear Thomas still hung. "I was going to lose Thomas, anyway. I thought I had steeled myself to it. But I can't help feeling angry that I did lose him, and the more I think about it, it doesn't really matter how I lost him. I still did. As for Mr. Jessup, I heard about the speech he made yesterday, that he did it out of love for me. It is as though he never understood that his love for me would never be requited, even if he'd had the patience for Thomas' disease to progress to its inevitable end."

"That is the frustration of it," I said, and frowned. "And there is the irony that poor Mrs. Dunbar hadn't seen him and posed him not the least bit of danger. One likes to think that justice was served in Mr. Jessup's execution, but in a way, that, too, seems rather needless." I sighed. "I have no answer for it."

And I still do not, alas. Yes, murder is the most grievous of all crimes, not only because taking a human life is so terrible but also because it so seldom gets the killer what he wants.

Coming Soon

Death of a Boston Brahmin

Maddie Franklin Wilcox finally gets to go home to her beloved Boston. She's bringing Elena Ortiz to the New England Female Medical College, and it's also a chance for Maddie to visit her father and sister.

But at a dinner with the family of Maddie's late and very much unlamented (on her part) husband, events are more than a little reminiscent of the violence of Los Angeles. One of the guests, distant cousin John Wilcox, is shot during his talk on natural history, then the next morning, the elder Mr. Wilcox is found dead, also of a bullet wound. Maddie quickly concludes that the attack on the oh, so very charming natural historian was merely a diversion to cover the murder of her former father-in-law.

The Boston police are on the job, and Maddie's father is up in arms at their ineptness. The last thing Maddie wants is to be dragged into the investigation. She'd rather be fending off John Wilcox, a rascal with possibly more than one reason to want the old man dead.

Other Books by Anne Louise Bannon

I'm so glad you liked this book! Check out my other novels, available in print or ebook at your favorite retailer:

Old Los Angeles Series:

Death of the Zanjero

Death of the City Marshal

Death of the Chinese Field Hands

Death of an Heiress

Death of the Drunkard

Operation Quickline Series:

That Old Cloak and Dagger Routine

Stopleak

Deceptive Appearances

Fugue in a Minor Key

Sad Lisa

These Hallowed Halls

My Sweet Lisa

A Little Family Business

Just Because You're Paranoid

From This Day Forward

Freddie and Kathy Series:

Fascinating Rhythm

Bring Into Bondage

The Last Witnesses

Blood Red

Daria Barnes:

Rage Issues

Mrs. Sperling:

A Nose for a Niedeman

Brenda Finnegan:

Tyger, Tyger

Romantic Fiction:

White House Rhapsody, Book One and Two

Fantasy and Science Fiction:

A Ring for a Second Chance

But World Enough and Time

Time Enough
And I would be honored if you left a review for this and
any of my books on the below sites. It really helps.

bookbub.com/profile/anne-louise-bannon

goodreads.com/author/show/513383.Anne_Louise
_Bannon

facebook.com/RobinGoodfellowEnt/

amazon.com/stores/author/B00JCRXST2?ingress
=0&visitId=bfadb491-d1ac-4575-84da-bb4f7d325a
d9&store_ref=ap_rdr&ref_=ap_rdr

 pinterest.com/AnneLouiseBannon

Connect with Anne Louise Bannon

Thank you for sticking it out this long! Please join my newsletter. It's the best way to stay up-to-date on my upcoming projects, blog posts and even the occasional game and giveaway.

You can sign up for the Robin Goodfellow Newsletter here: http://eepurl.com/zH0Ab or by visiting my website, annelouisebannon.com

And don't forget to connect with me on your favorite social media platforms:

bookbub.com/profile/anne-louise-bannon

goodreads.com/author/show/513383.Anne_Louise _Bannon

facebook.com/RobinGoodfellowEnt/

amazon.com/stores/author/B00JCRXST2?ingress =0&visitId=bfadb491-d1ac-4575-84da-bb4f7d325a d9&store_ref=ap_rdr&ref_=ap_rdr

pinterest.com/AnneLouiseBannon

About Anne Louise Bannon

Anne Louise Bannon is an author and journalist who wrote her first novel at age 15. Her journalistic work has appeared in Ladies' Home Journal, the Los Angeles Times, Wines and Vines, and in newspapers across the country. She was a TV critic for over 10 years, founded the YourFamilyViewer blog, and created the OddBallGrape.com wine education blog with her husband, Michael Holland. She is the co-author of Howdunit: Book of Poisons, with Serita Stevens, as well as author of the Freddie and Kathy mystery series, set in the 1920s, the Old Los Angeles series, set in 1870, and the Operation Quickline series, plus several stand alones. She and her husband live in Southern California with an assortment of critters.